THE FINE ART OF MURDER

Only one painting hung in this smaller room—an almost life-size portrait, its colors so vivid they seemed to reach out and grab me, yet at the same time draw me toward them gently. The painting had a life, a moving energy. I wanted to touch it. To sit and look at it for hours. There were no words to use, and I stood there mutely staring.

The subject was a woman. But diaphanous, like a cloud. Ephemeral. She was there one moment, and the next she was gone. Trick lighting? I wondered. But it seemed to be the same track lighting as on the stairs.

I walked closer, leaving Iverson behind. And then I saw it. A chill ran through me. The name on the brass plate at the bottom of the frame. *Anna.*

"Your brother named the subject *Anna*," I said hoarsely. "Do you know why?"

I felt Iverson behind me, and could smell his subtle cologne. "No . . . I've always assumed she was someone he'd read about, or possibly even known."

"When did he die?"

"In 1950," Iverson said.

The same year Anna Biernej-Browne was murdered. "*How?*"

"He committed suicide."

Before I could ask more, we were interrupted by pounding feet. "Mr. Iverson!" It was the butler who'd taken our wraps at the door. "Mr. Iverson, come quickly. Something terrible has happened. One of the guests . . . I think he's been murdered, sir."

HARE TODAY, GONE TOMORROW

MEG O'BRIEN

A Jessica James Mystery

(Book 3)

BANTAM BOOKS
NEW YORK • TORONTO • LONDON • SYDNEY • AUCKLAND

HARE TODAY, GONE TOMORROW
A Bantam Crime Line Book / May 1991

*CRIME LINE and the portrayal of a boxed "cl" are trademarks of
Bantam Books, a division of Bantam Doubleday Dell Publishing Group, Inc.*

ISBN 0-553-28978-0

Published simultaneously in the United States and Canada

Bantam Books are published by Bantam Books, a division of Bantam Doubleday
Dell Publishing Group, Inc. Its trademark, consisting of the words "Bantam Books"
and the portrayal of a rooster, is Registered in U.S. Patent and Trademark Office
and in other countries. Marca Registrada. Bantam Books, 666 Fifth Avenue, New
York, New York 10103.

PRINTED IN THE UNITED STATES OF AMERICA

RAD 0 9 8 7 6 5 4 3 2 1

In memory of my mother,
Margaret Anne O'Brien—
who forgave me my "serpent's tooth."

CHAPTER 1

It was early October, nine-thirty P.M., when it happened. I was coming home from a trip to NYC, where I'd been interviewing a crooked senator—although why that should be news, I don't know—for *Newsweek*. Mrs. Binty, my landlady, was visiting her sister in Cleveland, and Bastard, the dastardly dog, was traveling through New England with the Flynns from next door—who had practically adopted him, thank God.

I crawled out of my car, so tired my eyeballs felt like they had fallen out somewhere back on the Thruway and rolled the rest of the way home. I stretched and breathed in fresh air from a recent rain, lifting my hair off my neck and shaking it. I rolled my shoulders, too, to work out the kinks from the trip. The air was crisp and sweet, with a scent of firewood, of apples and pumpkins and cinnamon doughnuts, of cider and—

Well, maybe it didn't really smell of pumpkins and cider, but a body can dream. I love fall. Not, maybe, as much as spring and lilacs, but God—summers in Rochester, New York, are hell, and just when you think you can't stand sweat under your armpits another day, it's here, it's arrived, it's glorious and cool and . . . FALL!

I pulled my tote out of the old Dodge Dart that a chop shop had stuck me with (long story), and glanced around automatically as I locked the car. The houses on either side of Mrs. Binty's were dark. There were no signs of life in Mr. Garson's Victorian across the street; the TV didn't flicker, and his porch light was off. Genesee Park Boulevard seemed quiet enough —although that can be deceiving, since we're only a few blocks from the inner city. Once I was mugged just a block down the street, and my apartment has been broken into three times in the past three years. True, twice it's been "friends" who did the dirty deed—but we won't go into that.

1

It was dark, but a movement of light caught my eye. I looked up at the double windows of my apartment, which takes up the entire second floor of Mrs. Binty's sprawling house. The windows open onto a wide roof that is sheltered by trees, but the leaves had turned and begun to fall, so I could see fairly well.

What I saw made my stomach lurch. A flashlight bobbed and weaved inside my dark apartment, reflecting against the windows and out onto the dry brown leaves of the trees. My heart began to pound.

Not again.

I made a quick decision. I could go to Mr. Garson's to phone the police, but by the time I woke him up, explained what was going on, and made a complaint to the cops, whoever it was could be gone.

So I didn't follow the prescribed procedure for such matters. I have sometimes been described as reckless, and I suppose it might seem that way if you're the type of person who believes in doing everything by the book. If, on the other hand, your life's work is as an investigative reporter and you spend your major hours hobnobbing with the mob and assorted criminal elements, it can seem *pro forma* after a while to handle things yourself.

I unlocked the car again, quietly, popped the trunk, and raised the lid, wincing at the tiny screech. I reached in and grabbed the tire iron. Lowered the lid but didn't shut it tight. Headed up the sidewalk to the house, the iron close to my side. Up the three wooden stairs to the porch. A creak. I stiffened, then began again. Crossed the L-shaped porch to the door that led to my stairs. My Nikes felt heavy as lead, and my heart was doing flip-flops. I opened the downstairs door cautiously, wishing I'd had the sense at some time to arm myself, as various friends had urged me, because of my work, to do. But the iron felt solid and efficient against my palm. If my stomach didn't strangle from the knots in it, I might be okay.

I crept silently up the soft, gray-carpeted stairs, which muffled my steps. I walked on the outside of the tread, and no boards creaked. At the top of the stairs I paused, my hand on the knob of my apartment door. I listened. Soft footsteps inside, a rustle of paper. The opening and shutting of drawers.

Was it a neighborhood tough, looking for cash? He could be high. Or somebody connected with the story I was working on now? Either way, if the intruder were armed, I'd be at a disadvantage if I snapped on the lights. Better to make my approach in the dark. My palm felt wet and slippery on the brass knob. My legs were weak, and I almost turned and ran. I didn't, because I couldn't. I felt as if I were in a dream, the kind of nightmare you have over and over, where you're being chased and finally, one night, it's just plain easier to stand your ground and fight your pursuer than to flee.

The door was unlocked and I opened it quietly, inch by quarter inch. A dim figure moved from my bookcase, which held drawers of cassette tapes, mostly interviews. I saw it cross the front windows, vaguely outlined by light from a full moon. It stopped at my desk in the side bay. Drawers were opened again and closed. The figure straightened and headed toward the kitchen, the flashlight pointing away from me. Holding my breath, I slipped through the door and moved into place several paces behind the intruder. I hefted my weapon.

Halfway to the kitchen, I blew it. My toe hit against something on the floor that shouldn't have been there, something heavy and thick. I tripped, stumbled, and fell forward on my hands, touching the thing, and it felt like leather, like skin . . . *Jesus, God, don't let it be a body, please.*

The intruder drew in a harsh breath, and I could feel displaced air as he whirled in my direction. The flashlight fell with a thud to the floor and went out. I pushed myself to my feet fast, but not before an eerie "*Aaiiiii*" split the air and a cement wall connected with my chest, knocking me down. I was on my back, flashes of light pulsing through my head, and for precious moments I couldn't breathe or move. I heard the sound again, "*Aaiiiii!*" and struggled to squirm out of the way of the next blow.

In that instant there was an explosion of noise and light, a blare of rock music and singing. My apartment lights came on. The television had come on, too, and there was something else, something strange, a whirring, grinding sound I couldn't place. I blinked, struggled halfway to a sitting position, then fell back on my elbows and froze.

There stood before me a woman, not tall, in her late fifties. She had a hard, angular face and short, brownish curls held in place by a black headband. She wore those loose white pants you see in Bruce Lee movies, topped by a matching loose shirt. Her hand was raised in a karate-like chopping motion, poised to strike. Every muscle in my body went weak.

It wasn't the woman's position, so much as the eyes, that filled me with fear. They had that look the ancients called the "evil eye." Their light was fierce, and they fixed on me with a dreadful glare.

Those eyes frightened the shit out of me—almost as much as they had when I was ten and threw a baseball through our dining room window, breaking a soup tureen.

I couldn't move, so I did the only thing I could think of, the same thing I'd done back then. I smiled as winningly as possible and said in a shaky voice, "Hi, Mom."

CHAPTER 2

Mom had changed in the last few years, there was no doubt about it. Living in California any length of time does something strange to people, as almost anyone from New York knows. And Mom had been living in Mill Valley with Aunt Edna. *Marin County*, for heaven's sake! There's some kind of weird energy there, something to do with this huge mountain shaped like an Indian woman that stands above everything and reportedly emits signals from another sphere.

The advantage to all this metaphysical input—as far as I was concerned—was that Mom was no longer as unyielding or unforgiving toward me as she had been when Pop died.

The disadvantage was that you never knew what the shit she might do.

"Hi, Mom," I said again. "Okay if I get up now?" I looked warily at the deadly weapon, her still upraised hand.

"Jesse!" Her face crumpled into an apologetic, worried frown, and she dropped her militant pose. She knelt to touch my collarbone, then my chin, looking for damage. The way it felt, there was plenty. Coshed by me own ma.

"Oh, baby, I'm so sorry! But why did you sneak in like that, why didn't you say it was you? I thought you were a burglar, you frightened me out of my wits coming up behind me like that!"

"Mom, what were you doing creeping around in my apartment in the dark? What are you even *doing* here? And how did you get in?"

"You told me once in a letter that you kept a key under the lilac bush in the front yard, don't you remember? You said if I ever came to town unexpectedly . . ."

I said *that*? I must have been drinking still.

"And I was in the dark because the lights had gone out from the storm, and I was looking for candles—"

"What storm?"

"The storm this afternoon, I guess, I mean they didn't go out right then, but a few minutes ago, and I was looking for candles—"

"Mom, what are you doing here? And since when did you learn karate?" Last year it was windsurfing, and the year before that, Tibet. I let her help me up and massaged my collarbone as she fussed, picking at lint on my sweater the way mothers do. I looked around the room. The leathery thing I'd fallen over was a long, soft suitcase, and probably wouldn't feel a thing like a body now that the lights were on. Against my desk leaned an oil painting, about thirty by thirty, of a rabbit. A gray rabbit on a darker gray background, with yellow roses at his feet.

Other than that, things looked pretty much the way they should. Mom hadn't gotten around to moving the furniture yet. She was probably too busy watching MTV, which accounted for the rock music that had blared forth when the electricity was restored.

"Why do you watch this stuff?" I groused, turning it off.

"I was exercising, dear. You know how much better it is with a good beat . . ."

She was still explaining as I limped to the kitchen for aspirin—and only then did I realize that the whirring, grinding sound was still going on. I knew what it was, too, as I was struck in the face, on the arms, and on my white *FREE ITHACA!* tee. The splatters were red and gooey and smelled like a fucking fruit farm. I groaned.

My blender.

Mom must have been making one of her California health drinks when the electricity died. Now that it was back on, the untended blender had discovered a life of its own, like a kid when its mom is on the phone. The cover had tumbled off, there was strawberry puree on the cupboards, on two white walls, and on my brand-new microwave. And now there was strawberry puree all over me. I glared at my mom, standing there in her karate lounging pajamas, a black sweatband over her short, curly, gray-brown hair. She looked at the strawberry glop on my face, tossed back her head, and laughed.

This was not going to be an easy night.

"I told you about Charlie," Mom said after we had cleaned up the mess. We were sitting on my long sofa, she at one end, me at the other, legs up and toes almost touching. Mom was sipping her health drink, and I was eating Häagen-Dazs—double fudge ripple. "We met at one of those dating things in Mill Valley. Not computers, but an actual matchmaker, like in the old days, Jesse, it's so *neat*! She puts together people who're hard to match—like older people, or fat people, and women who're rich."

"Mom—you aren't any of those things." The truth is, Mom is dancing near sixty—but she has the spirit and verve of a fifteen-year-old. And she certainly isn't rich.

"Thanks," she said, smiling and touching her hair. "But face it, Jesse—I'm not that young. On the other hand, I didn't want to make age my entree to this matchmaking program . . . after all, no point in drumming one's years into the ground. So . . . I said I had money. As with a capital M."

"You *what*? Mom, I can't believe it! You *lied*?"

"Jesse," she said, her tone only a little embarrassed, "when a woman is my age and she wants to meet a man, she uses whatever she's got. I've got a well-developed talent for lying. So I used it."

"But you *don't* lie!" Whatever else you might say about Katherine Marie James, nee O'Donnell, she was one of the most honest people I knew.

Mom lifted an eyebrow. "No? How do you think I managed to keep my chin up all those years with your father? I wasn't exactly a tower of strength, you know."

"You *weren't*?"

"Jessica," she said patiently to the child who still lived in me, "all the times we were evicted . . . the times we had no food—"

"And you went out and did waitress work—"

"I was scared to death," she said.

I looked at my mom and saw somebody I had never known.

She had always seemed like a rock. Intimidating, even, in her power. "I'm sorry, Mom. I didn't know. I guess I thought . . . you didn't seem to really mind." How stupid could an adolescent be?

"Never mind that now, dear. Now I have Charlie, and I'm happy as a clam . . . except that he's in trouble, Jesse. We need your help."

"Wait a minute. What's this *we* business? I don't see Charlie here."

"He wanted to come, but I told him I wanted to talk to you first. He'll meet us tomorrow at the Armistead Gallery."

"What kind of trouble is Charlie in?"

"*We*, dear. I keep telling you, *we*."

"What kind of trouble are *we* in, Mom?"

"We've stolen a painting." She lowered her voice. "A *very valuable* painting."

My glance flicked nervously to the hare, leaning against my desk.

Mom nodded. "We stole the *Hare*," she said.

Okay, I've been known at times (a lot of times) to be at the wrong end of the law myself. But my mom? I had to think about this one. I got up and went over and looked at the rabbit—*Hare Amongst the Roses*, a brass plate on the lower edge of the frame proclaimed in elaborate script. I didn't know a lot about art, but I'd done a series of articles once on art theft, and my appreciation had been raised to such a level that I knew this was good. Not a masterpiece, I didn't think, but excellent work. There was no artist's signature, so far as I could see.

"Where did you get this, Mom?"

"I can't tell you that. Not yet." She flushed at my expression. "Charlie asked me to wait, to let him explain."

"Right." I didn't know about this Charlie. Even when Mom first wrote about him, I'd wondered. He had seemed too good to be true . . . wealthy, good-looking, a world traveler. . . .

His last name was *Browne*, for God's sake. Charlie Browne.

What had this jerk gotten Mom into? I walked back to the sofa and sat down. "Are the police after you?"

Mom's glance flicked away. "Not yet."

"But they will be?"

"Well . . ." She gave me a defiant look, her green eyes glistening.

"Mom, this'll be the first place they look, after Aunt Edna's. And you know her; she can't keep quiet about anything. Does she know you're here?"

"Of course not. No one knows but you, dear."

"You can't be sure."

Mom smiled. "Charlie handled everything. He's wonderful that way. You know, Jesse, I always did love a man who takes charge."

"Like Pop?" Pop had taken charge, all right. Of every beer and Jack Daniel's bottle in town, for twenty-odd years.

"Charlie isn't at all like that. Wait until you meet him, Jesse. You'll love him, just the way I do." There was a faint note of anger in her voice, and I had to admit, she had a right to it. I am sometimes a snot.

"It's that serious? You love this guy?"

"More than anything," Mom said. More than life and freedom, her tone implied.

Well. I cajoled and wheedled, but I couldn't get her to tell me any more about what was going on. "Charlie can explain it so much better." Being so tired, I wasn't very sharp—while Mom was clearly sharper than she'd been in years. It was pretty much a dead heat when we ended it around eleven P.M.

I got her a blanket and pillow, and I wanted to give her my bed, but Mom insisted she didn't want to put me to any trouble.

Trouble? It looked like we were all in deep shit, no matter how you shoveled it.

I sat on the window ledge in my room until after midnight, looking out at the leaves blowing from the trees, listening to their rustle, and thinking. I watched the moon, which had been a harvest blob when I came in on the Thruway, hanging low over Rochester like that big white ball that used to chase Patrick McGoohan around in *The Prisoner*. It was high now and pale, half-obscured by the dark clouds that scudded through the sky.

I thought about the way my mom had approached me, just before she turned in, about staying here with me for a while.

"Jesse, we always got along all right, didn't we? Before the trouble?"

Mom used the word "trouble" in the way of the old Irish when talking about the Rebellion. But I knew what she meant: the way Pop had died—my fault in it—and the way she had rejected me afterward.

And I knew what she wanted to hear.

"Yeah, Mom, we were just like sisters. It was fun."

It wasn't fun. At least, not that often. It was hell growing up with a drunk for a father. And if Mom had once—just *once*—had the guts to leave him—

Our relationship was too tenuous still, I thought, to risk it with close proximity now. We were too newly healed after five years of *trouble*, of resentment and blame.

It couldn't possibly work. Mom and me together, under the same roof, for God knows how long?

May the saints preserve and protect us, as Aunt Edna used to say.

CHAPTER 3

When I woke there was the smell of fresh coffee, the sound of dishes clattering in the kitchen, and Kate James's happy little hum. Mom always did hum around food.

I love living alone. Yet, there's something to be said for lying in bed and listening to the clink of silver or glass in the kitchen. It takes you back to when you were a kid, and even though things were sometimes bad, you felt cared for. Somebody was out there looking after things. Taking care.

I stretched, and felt good suddenly. I jumped out of bed, dashed into the shower that I'd hooked up inside my old claw-foot tub, and scrubbed my hair and skin. I put moisturizer on my hair, which was curly and brown like Mom's, but long. Climbing out of the shower, I wiped the sweat off the mirror and looked at the fine lines around my thirty-one-year-old green eyes. Yeah. I was an adult, wasn't I? I could handle whatever came along with my mom.

I went back in the bedroom and pulled on jeans and a thick brown sweater, then boots. I found Mom in the kitchen still.

"I heard you come out of the shower. I fixed your coffee, Jesse. Just the way you like it."

It wasn't. But Mom couldn't know I'd stopped using cream and sugar months ago. The last time I was in California visiting her, last spring, there was nothing but herbal tea in the house she shared with Aunt Edna. Being a New Yorker, and only a few months sober at the time, it almost drove me nuts. There were few enough pleasures when I stopped drinking, and coffee was one I could not do without.

So I had trotted down the hill into the little village of Mill Valley at seven-thirty A.M., to an espresso bar I'd seen. It was closed. The sign said: WE OPEN AT EIGHT. I came close to committing my first major crime in years. There were all those

11

tall glass jars of beans inside on a counter, and I could read the exotic names: Kenya, Mocha Java, Amaretto . . . I imagined I could smell them right through the window. I jiggled the doorknob, just in case; if I could only get in, I'd eat the damn things as is.

No luck. Locked up tight.

People passed by, looking at me curiously. Local broccoloids, no doubt, who didn't understand about being a New Yorker and needing a fix.

There was a restaurant across the street, but it didn't open until ten. I paced nervously outside the espresso shop and nearly attacked the clerk when she arrived at eight. She gave me a few beans to chew on while the water heated. When the copper pots were hot, I ordered three espressos at once and topped them with a cup of mocha cappuccino.

Bliss.

I went back to Aunt Edna's buzzing, my pupils dilated like blackened quarters. They must have thought I was doing drugs—which, of course, I was. The best around.

I took the cup from Mom now, with its cream and sugar, and drank it down. It wasn't all that bad—real coffee, too, not the instant stuff I'd been having a lot of since I got the microwave. There was also bacon frying, and the kitchen window was open to the scent of burning leaves from Mr. Garson's yard. Mr. Garson is over eighty, and doesn't buy into the law that says you can't burn anymore. Somehow, he never gets caught—a state of affairs I heartily approve.

God, everything smelled good!

It reminded me of a trip we'd taken once when I was a kid—to the amusement park across from Niagara Falls, in Canada. We left before dawn and stopped along the road for breakfast. Not at a McDonald's, or even one of those manicured rest stops they have now. Just a grassy area under trees, probably the edge of somebody's farm. We took out a charcoal camp stove, and when the coals were ready we cooked coffee, bacon, and eggs on it. It was the most fantastic time I'd ever had in my life—for a few hours, anyway. We were nearly to Niagara when Pop pulled over to a country store and said casually, "Anybody want anything?" like he was going in for bread and salami. He came out with three six-packs of beer. When we got to the amusement park, Mom and I went in alone. Pop sat in the car and drank. "Too damn hot out there for me."

When we came back there was a big argument and Mom wouldn't get in the car until he turned over the keys. It ended with him yelling and her crying, and me crying too.

Some fun. And Christ, the memories that were already being stirred up, just having Mom here. This was only my third month of sobriety this time, and I didn't know if I could handle the stress.

"Have you talked to Charlie yet?" I said.

"He's meeting us at the gallery at noon. I told him you wanted to talk to him."

Hell, I wouldn't say "want" was the right word. But I felt I had to look out for Mom's welfare, see what this guy was like. Wealthy, she had said. She'd had enough of counting pennies, and a rich man was as easy to fall in love with as a poor. Easier, in Charlie's case.

But if Charlie was so all-fired rich, what was he doing stealing a painting that was worth, according to Mom last night, $70,000? Why not just buy it? There was something about all this I didn't like. If he was working over my mom—

We had breakfast at my round table in the dining area bay, and I cleaned up afterward. Mom dressed in her Lunch in the Upscale Suburbs outfit, silky pants and a long peachy top with shoulder pads. Charlie had bought it for her, she said . . . and Charlie was the one who'd taught her martial arts, too. . . .

Charlie, Charlie, Charlie. . . .

"The Hare," Mom said hesitantly as we prepared to go. She stood before my desk. "I don't think we should just leave it out like that, Jesse."

"Why leave it here at all? Why don't we take it to good old Charlie, let him worry about it?"

"It's our job to keep it safe," she said.

Oh. Well, then.

I picked up the phone and called the pool hall down on Genesee Street. Abe was hanging around, as he often does, mornings, and I asked him if he or one of the Genesee Three would keep an eye out on my place for a while.

"Something going down?" he said.

"Not much. Or at least, nothing I can go into right now. I just don't need any problems."

The point being, *nothing*'s safe here. Anybody can get into this place.

So now the Genesee Three (Abe, Percy, and Rack—the best second-story men in town) would look after things. They were always reconnoitering the neighborhood anyway, seeing who they could rip off or save, depending on said person's standing with them on any given day.

Before we left, Mom and I settled for sliding the painting under the bed.

"Nobody could possibly find it here," Mom said.

A certain naiveté runs in the genes.

CHAPTER 4

The Armistead Gallery and Museum was in Pittsford, an eclectic little hamlet southeast of the city where the lords and landowners live. My shrink is there, too, at the Center for Natural Healing. Pittsford is kind of a haven for the New Agers, of which Samved is one. Mom hooked me up with him, and I've never been sure whether to thank or throttle her for that one.

In the gallery were hushed halls, polished wood, the patina of old money. It was sexy and powerful, yet at the same time induced a feeling of reverence and awe. The early-morning sun filtered through high-arched windows. Not even a trace of dust motes was visible in the filtered air. Soft classical music played. There was apparently an important show going on and we'd arrived when the matrons from Pittsford were out and about. Dressed in preseason furs and wafting floral perfumes, they drifted silently from room to room, subtle as only well-bred monied women can be.

Mom pointed Charlie out. He was talking with a tall, distinguished man. The man looked like he was connected to the gallery. A director, perhaps. Certainly not an artist. Someone of monetary importance.

Charlie, on the other hand, looked like The Man From Glad. He had crinkly silver hair, beautiful blue eyes, and a California tan. Easy to see why Mom had been charmed. When he saw us Charlie broke away, shaking the hand of the distinguished man, whose parting words carried across the tomblike room. "In the gardens, then. Twenty minutes."

Charlie was a charmer to the nth degree. He strode across the marble floor and gripped my hand, pumping it vigorously. At Mom's introduction he looked me straight in the eye and said, "I'm very pleased to meet you, Jesse. Your mother talks about you all the time."

I didn't even say thanks.

He ignored my ungraciousness and gave me a twinkle. His mouth widened into a grin. My impression changed. He wasn't The Man From Glad. He was Paul Newman as the aging pool shark in *The Color of Money*.

He put his arm around Mom and gave her a little hug. She dimpled and kissed him on the cheek.

Dimpled. Katherine O'Donnell James. My mom.

"I missed you," she said.

"Me too."

I cleared my throat so they'd quit all the cute stuff and look at me.

"Oh, I'm sorry," Mom said. "I promised Jesse we'd talk, dear."

"Of course. Why don't we go outside." Charlie put his arm around me too. All folksy-like, as if we'd known each other for years and had just gotten together after a long separation. Well, I'd had my share of charmers, and he wasn't winning me over that way. I shrugged him off and stomped ahead.

There were twenty acres, all told, surrounding the gallery. Most of it had been landscaped with gardens. Beyond that was a thick ring of trees. I had been here once or twice, and I led the way, taking a path to a far end of the gardens. A fountain with modernistic sculpture dominated several rose beds. I stood looking into the water, hands in the pockets of my jeans. Mom and Charlie arrived at last, having hugged and nuzzled along the way, so it took them a while. Mom sat on the fountain's low stone wall and dangled her fingers in the water like Audrey Hepburn in *Roman Holiday*.

(She likes to tell me I see things in terms of old movies, the way some people speak in clichés. It's not true. I hate clichés. Old movies, on the other hand, are art. Not like some of the stuff I see in galleries these days.)

Charlie had worn a blue blazer and knitted dark blue tie, but he opened his jacket now and removed the tie, folding it and putting it in his pocket. He perched sideways on the wall, legs bent, hands linked around his knees, looking for all the world like a middle-aged Pan. The seat of his pants was probably getting dirty, but he had a rich man's disdain for that sort of thing. What the hell, he probably had forty-three more suits just like this one in a 9 × 12 closet at home.

On his feet, Charlie wore L.A. Gears. He was younger than Mom, I decided, in his late forties or early fifties. It was hard to tell. Charlie had that sort of hell-bent-for-leather quality I'd always thought of in conjunction with the older movie stars like John Wayne and Gregory Peck. *The Zero's at twelve o'clock high, men . . . man your stations! . . . we're going in!*

"You want to know about the painting, of course," he said, smiling with too much assurance.

"I want to know why you've involved my mother in the theft of it. I don't give a shit about the painting, otherwise."

He blinked, as if noticing for the first time that he didn't exactly have a friend in court with me. For a moment, I thought I saw something hard in those gorgeous blue eyes. Then it was gone.

"Fair enough." He glanced at Mom. *I told you Jesse could be difficult,* her look said.

"The reason your mother helped me is that she trusts me," Charlie said reasonably. "That doesn't mean that you should. I understand that."

"It doesn't even mean that *she* should."

"Jesse!"

"It's all right, Kate." He addressed her, then me, in a voice like a fur-lined razor. "Your mother and I have known each other several months. I hope to get to know you too."

"You plan to be here that long?"

"I'm not sure of my plans yet," he said. "When I am, I'll be sure to let you know."

"Fine. Now that we have that settled, let's stop beating about the damned bush. Why did you involve my mom in this theft?"

"Jesse, I insisted!" Mom replied. "He didn't want me to—and anyway, that part is not your business." Her lower lip stuck out.

"It is when you show up at my door with stolen property." I turned back to Charlie, whose expression had not changed. "Are you here to move that pricey little piece of art? Is that what your talk with the man inside was about?"

"No, I am not trying to sell the painting, Jesse. And I won't. I was talking to Iverson about other things."

"Iverson. This is the tall man, with the mustache?"

"Yes."

"You were talking about what?"

"He'll join us in a few minutes, you can see for yourself. Everett Iverson is the chairman of the board of directors here, an honest man with an excellent reputation. He's helping me with the provenance of the painting."

"The provenance. Meaning, its history."

"Yes."

"And once you have that, it'll be worth all that much more to you."

"That isn't what this is about." The edge was back.

"Jesse," Mom interrupted. "Enough! I don't want you questioning Charlie as if he were some kind of criminal or something."

I gave her a look of wonderment. "You think he's not?"

"You don't know anything about it!"

I folded my arms. "Then tell me something so I will."

"I can't tell you the full story yet, since I don't know it myself," Charlie said. "But the painting was in a small gallery in Sausalito. Your mother and I saw it on a walk one day, and—" He didn't finish.

"Did you buy it?"

A slight hesitation. "No."

"So you did steal it."

"Not in the sense you mean."

"Oh, there are two senses here, then—the sense I mean, and the sense you mean. Why don't you tell me the sense the cops will mean when they catch up with you. *And* with my mother."

He flushed.

I glowered at Mom. "I want some answers. Why am I hiding that goddamned painting under my bed?"

Charlie said angrily, "Don't speak to your mother that way."

I almost socked him in the jaw. I actually doubled up my fists to do it. I think I would have.

But Iverson, the man Charlie had been talking to inside,

was coming across the lawn. Charlie stood to greet him, brushing off the seat of his pants.

"I've told him only that I want to locate the owner of the painting," Charlie warned in a low voice. "I'd appreciate it if you wouldn't say anything."

Like I was in the mood to do him favors.

But Iverson, now. *Everett Iverson.* He was another whole story.

Within moments my anger was swept away. I fell in love.

Well, let me qualify that. I fell in love for my mom. This, I decided, was the sort of man Kate O'Donnell James needed. Everett Iverson was around seventy, I guessed . . . tall and soft-spoken . . . distinguished, with a tiny gray mustache over a warm smile. His hairline was receding, a salt-and-pepper gray, and he had the best manners of anyone I'd ever met.

He kissed my mother's hand!

I slid mine back into my pocket just in time. Iverson noticed. He gave me a wry smile and a little bow.

"Hi," I said. "I'm Jess. Jessica James."

"Hello. Let me think now. James. I've read your work. *Excellent* material. The piece you wrote for *Newsweek* about the Switzer Gallery's involvement with hearing-impaired art students . . . brilliantly researched and written."

I grinned. "Thanks."

"I'd like to talk with you sometime about the grants I've arranged, in conjunction with Switzer, for the hearing-impaired. I don't want praise, you understand . . . simply for word to get around about the availability of funds. I know you would handle it beautifully."

Wow. A glutton for praise, myself, I wanted to hear more.

But Charlie was clearly impatient with the whole thing, running fingers through his crisp silver hair. Mom made as if to sit on the concrete wall again, but Iverson stopped her, pulling a neatly folded red silk handkerchief from his pocket. He spread it out, then waved a gallant hand for her to sit. "I wouldn't want you to get that lovely frock smudged, my dear."

Mom blushed. I glanced at Charlie to see how he was taking all this, but he was still distracted.

"Look, Iverson," he said, "I don't mean to rush you, but—"

"Of course." Iverson gave him his full attention. "However, I'm afraid the news isn't good. I've had my clerks go through all the appropriate catalogs, using the Polaroid you left with me earlier this morning. They've just now finished, and I'm sorry to have to tell you that we can't find a record of that painting ever having been bought or sold."

"Damn!"

"Further, since it's unsigned and you don't know the artist's name, I don't see how we can locate the owner for you."

"What about the gallery in California, the one I told you about?"

"The gallery denies knowledge of the painting. I'm sorry. I take it this work is important to you. You'd like to purchase it if we do locate the owner?"

Mom started to answer. "Oh, no. We have—"

I stomped on her foot. She looked startled, but fell silent.

Iverson's sharp glance told me he had caught the slip. He would probably assume now that Charlie had bought the painting and was having second thoughts, thinking perhaps it had been stolen.

"My curiosity is piqued," Iverson said. "There are a few more contacts I could make. One or two on the continent, several in South America. Tell you what. I'm having a little gathering at my house on Friday evening. Why don't you come"—his glance took in all three of us—"and by then, I may know more. At any rate, there will be people there you may wish to meet. They could be of some value in your search."

"I don't know . . ." Charlie began. His demeanor was suddenly aloof.

But Iverson was smiling winningly at Mom, who was blushing again. I rushed in. "We'd love to," I replied.

And gave a shrug at Charlie's irritated stare. "What time would you like us there?" I said.

CHAPTER 5

We left Charlie in the city making calls on other galleries, and got back to my apartment mid-afternoon. By my downstairs door, on Mrs. Binty's porch, was a large brown parcel that had been delivered by UPS. We lugged it up the inside stairs, balancing the light but awkward package precariously. I finally got my key out and opened the door, and we dropped the bundle on the living room floor.

It was addressed to Mom, who looked puzzled and intrigued. "I wonder what it could be."

She ripped the strapping tape open while I was halfway to the kitchen looking for a knife. Inside the box were men's shoes. Seven pairs of men's shoes had been delivered by UPS, in a plain brown box. They were all new, but not in store boxes. Each pair was wrapped in newspaper. It was weird.

"Oh, these are Charlie's," Mom said with a laugh. "He gets them all the time."

"Charlie gets shoes mailed to him like this?"

She nodded. She was unwrapping and looking at them: black, brown, crocodile—

"But why would he have them sent here? And where are they from?"

"Well, I'm sure I don't know, dear."

"You never asked?"

"Of course not."

"Mom—"

There was a knock at the door. Toni Langella stuck her head in.

"Anybody home?"

"You know darn well we're home," I said. "You were looking out your bedroom window when we drove up, like you always do. I saw you."

21

"I just thought I'd be polite," she said with a pout.

"Since when?"

"Jesse!"

Mom's objection to my bitchy attitude didn't take into account what I knew about my twelve-year-old neighbor. Toni Langella is a martinet. The little bully monitors my eating habits, my exercise time, my social life. When she's around I can't eat sugar, drink booze, or watch television, and it's only because of her I bought the exercise bike that now sits in a corner of my bedroom gathering dust.

Toni is a gymnast, Olympic material. She has a coach, a sour little woman with pasty white skin and black Reeboks, who lives on bamboo, like a panda bear, which she sort of resembles.

"Don't mind her," Mom said to Toni. "She always was moody."

"I was not."

"You were, and you are. I'm Jesse's mother," she said.

Toni smiled enthusiastically. "Hi. I'm Toni Langella. I live next door."

"I was just about to get dinner," Mom told her, closing up the box of shoes. "Why don't you come out to the kitchen and help?"

Toni, who loves the motherly types, followed her like a happy puppy. I just stood there glaring, not quite sure why I was irritated. When I was a kid, Mom never would let me in her kitchen. Other kids watched their moms bake cookies and licked the bowl and all that crap. Not me.

I listened to my messages, one from *Newsweek*, another from a small but award-winning paper on the West Coast that I'd done a story about drug running for. I wrote the numbers down, then picked up the phone and called Marcus Andrelli. Alfred, his new assistant, answered.

"Andrelli Enterprises."

"Let me talk to Marcus," I said.

"He's not here," Alfred cooed.

"Don't give me that, Alf. I know Marcus is there. He's in the shower or he's talking to London or buying real estate on Baja or Mars, but he's there, and I'm warning you, if you don't put him on the line right now—"

"I'm hanging up."

"No! DO NOT HANG UP! Listen to me, Alfred, and listen well. If you hang up on me this time, I will slice you and dice you and feed you to the pigeons in Dwight Square, so just be a nice little boy and put Marcus on the phone and don't give me any crap."

He clicked off. Alfred's a snit, but he speaks seven languages, including Japanese, so Marcus keeps him around to impress his business cohorts over there. Alfred, however, doesn't impress me. He almost never lets me talk to Marcus, and for that, I will one day have his head on a tray, and a few other appendages as well.

The phone rang. I picked it up on the first beat.

"What kept you?"

Marcus laughed. "Must you give Alfred trouble every time you call?"

"He lives for it. And he never lets me talk to you. He's like a little kid who wants his daddy all to himself and won't let him talk on the phone."

"I'm afraid you're right. And I'd speak to him about it, but it'd spoil all your fun."

"Listen, can I come over?"

"Well . . . I've got meetings here until eight or so."

Marcus always had meetings. I'd gone into this relationship for danger and excitement; instead, I'd gotten Donald Trump.

"Would it help if I had an accent, and something to sell?" I asked testily. "How about a small Middle Eastern country or two?"

There was a silence long enough to count to five. "Why don't I pick you up around eight?" Marcus said. "We'll go to dinner."

"I can't. I, uh . . . I've sort of got company."

"Oh. Someone special?"

"My mom," I mumbled. Then, gathering volume with strength, "My mom's here."

"Your mother? She came to see you?"

"You don't have to sound so surprised. Parents do that sort of thing all the time."

"Of course they do."

A small silence.

"You could invite me over," he said.

"For *dinner*? With my *mom*?" He had to be kidding.

"Why not?"

"Marcus, you aren't exactly the kind of catch a girl brings home to dinner."

"Try me," he said.

"No way. How would I explain about you—"

"Jesse," Mom called from the kitchen, "if that's your mobster friend you're talking to, tell him we're having seafood casserole and there's plenty to go around."

Amongst the many attributes I may have forgotten to mention, my mom has ears like Dumbo. She never misses a thing.

Marcus had worn an unstructured gray suit with pleated slacks, and a black crewneck sweater. His black hair was damp from a sprinkle of rain that had begun around seven o'clock. He arrived bearing yellow football-sized mums for my mom. Her favorite flower.

As we sat over a steaming seafood casserole, Marcus couldn't have been more at home. I forget sometimes that he was once part of a warm Italian family. They must have gathered around the dinner table drinking wine and dunking *biscòtti*, teasing each other and telling stories of what had happened that day.

That, of course, was before Marcus became part of Jimmy Lucetta's organization at the age of seventeen, and more recently—at forty-two—the head of an upscale new branch of the mob in Western New York. Lucetta had sent Marcus to Harvard Business School; he paid his expenses and took care of his family while Marcus was there. His mom was going through bad times because Marcus's father had died, and she never even knew that Lucetta was helping her at the time. When the truth came out later, it caused a rift that has never quite healed. When Marcus graduated at the top of his class, he became Lucetta's financial advisor. Now he deals in high finance, in buying and selling real estate and corporations. No drugs, prostitution, or everyday street crime. Nevertheless, every OCB cop in the state is after Marcus Andrelli for one infraction or another. When I'm being honest about these things I'm more than willing to admit that this is at least half of his fascination for me.

What I couldn't figure out at the moment was why my

mom—who wouldn't even let me date Jimmy Deaver in eighth grade after he got home from juvie—had welcomed Marcus to our table like he was the goddamned parish priest.

"Have another piece of garlic bread?" She beamed.

"Thank you," Marcus enthused. "It's excellent bread. Did you buy it here in the neighborhood?"

"From DiAngelo's, down on the corner."

"I grew up with Connie DiAngelo," Marcus reminisced. "A wonderful family."

"Lovely people," Mom agreed.

I felt like I was at the Mad Hatter's tea party.

Toni, who had refused to go home, sat watching the whole thing with a kind of evil glee. Her brown eyes darted from Marcus to Mom, and now and then she'd look at me and mouth, "Cool." I pretended not to understand what she meant. Until now, I'd managed to keep Marcus from the stares of most of my neighbors. The fact that he occasionally picked me up in his limo, however, and that I often didn't return until early the following morning, escaped no one. Toni was going nuts. I'd never hear the end of this.

In the middle of dessert, Charlie arrived. My door was unlocked and he just let himself in, all hale and hearty, tugging off his tie. He introduced himself to Marcus and Toni and wasted no time bussing Mom on the cheek and plunking himself down in the chair next to hers. Mom cut him a piece of pumpkin pie and laughingly fed it to him, like a bride feeding cake to her groom.

Marcus sat back throughout all this, a slight smile on his face, his chair tilted back. He toyed with a piece of silver, and you'd have thought he was still relaxed if you didn't know better. Ordinarily, Marcus will dominate a room or conversation. He doesn't mean to. But in size alone he's an imposing figure—taller than Charlie at six feet or so, and solidly built from working out every day.

He was deliberately taking a backseat now—the better to watch Charlie from, I knew. Telltale lines had appeared around his eyes . . . a sign of heightened cautiousness when anyone new and questionable arrives on the scene. Marcus generally travels with a bodyguard, but he hadn't gotten around to trusting anyone with the job since Tark left for Italy in July.

Charlie pretended to eat his pie, but he obviously was put off by Marcus's watchful air. Finally, he laughed and put the pie down, then made a production of feeding Mom the piece she'd cut for herself. She giggled and blushed, and I couldn't stand it anymore.

"Excuse me. I need some air."

I shoved myself back from the round glass table, ignoring Toni's look (the kid thinks she knows so much about me, and she's all wrong). Grabbing my leather jacket, I clomped down the inside stairs and out onto Mrs. Binty's porch.

The rain had stopped, and the air was laced with a woodsy scent from neighborhood fireplaces. People had piled leaves up in their yards, and a yellow moon was just visible through the trees. It was the kind of autumn night I remembered loving as a kid, before I realized that life wasn't going to be fun the way I'd thought it would be when I was eight years old.

I was halfway down the street when Marcus caught up with me. We walked in silence a while.

"Remember how kids used to play in the leaves on autumn nights?" he said as we turned the corner.

"I was just thinking about that."

"I wonder where all the kids are now."

"Inside playing video games. Doing drugs. Just as well— it's not safe out here anymore."

"I suppose. Is that how you're feeling with Charlie and your mom here? Unsafe?"

"Look, if we're going to psychoanalyze things here, why pick on me? Where's *your* kid? You know what *he's* doing right now?"

"I'd rather not—"

"Discuss that. I didn't think so."

"Jess—" He made one of those Italian gestures of exasperation. The kind reserved for fishmongers and nagging wives. "It's complicated, you know that."

"Little boy needs a father. Seems pretty simple to me."

We kept on walking. Past Mrs. Rosetti's Victorian, Mr. Garson's, and Mr. Flynn's . . . people who had lived in this neighborhood for over thirty years. Their dining room lights cast yellow patches on tidy front yards. A glance inside showed varying scenes: traditional families, Donna Reed style, grouped around dining room tables . . . and old men or women alone, left behind by spouses who had worked themselves to death raising large Catholic families or working in the vats at Kodak.

Pop had worked at Kodak.

"Have you noticed," I said abruptly, "how she's just taking over? Christ, she's turned my whole apartment into a scene from *Little Women*."

"Is that so bad?"

"And Charlie. Him and his painting . . . and his goddamned shoes!"

"*Shoes?*"

"We got home today, and there were all these shoes. Seven pairs of them. In one big brown box, delivered by UPS."

"Most definitely damning," Marcus said.

"Not funny."

He took my hand as we walked. "Jess, you didn't have an exactly normal childhood. I think sometimes you're afraid of anything that smacks of normal."

"Afraid?" I snorted and kicked at leaves. "Try bored. I mean, here she is all of a sudden, playing the mom she never was when I was little and needed her—"

"She worked as a waitress to support you, didn't she? You said she never had much time."

"I know, and I'm not griping about that, that's all done and past. It's just that, well, here she is in the middle of my life all of a sudden, just when I'm starting to get it together, and she's got this jerk, Charlie—and dammit, Marcus, what *about* that painting?" I had told him about the *Hare* on the phone. "The man's a crook, a con man. And she thinks he's Mr. Clean."

"He gave no explanation at all?"

"Just what I told you. He saw it in a gallery in California, and next thing I know—*poof*—it's under my bed."

"I suppose there could be a reasonable explanation."

"Like what?"

"I don't know. But if your mother likes him—"

"My mother is bonkers about the man. She'd believe him if he said the sky was cerise and the moon a lavender green."

"Hmmm. Would you like me to do a background check on him?"

Marcus has a computer system that rivals even New York

State's. It can track down anyone, anywhere, unless he's never attended school, driven a car, been in the service, or filed his nails. It helps if a person's been fingerprinted, but even that's not necessary anymore. We're all in it. So are our likes and dislikes, the kinds of television we subscribe to, where we shop, work, and pray. Big Brother is here, as promised.

Might as well invite him in to play. "Please," I told him. "Find out anything you can."

"And if I discover that Charlie's a crook? Will you tell your mom?"

"Probably. But first, I'll break his bones," I said.

Marcus called around seven the next morning. I grabbed the phone by my bed so it wouldn't wake Mom. Charlie had made a call to someone after dinner and gone off to his hotel, looking distracted again.

"I'm afraid you were right to be concerned," Marcus began.

I woke up. "You got something on Charlie? He's got a record?"

"No record."

"Oh." I was almost disappointed. "Then, what?"

"The usual childhood stuff—grade school in San Francisco, then high school in Seattle. After that, the Carlisle Foundation for the Arts, a private school in San Francisco, for two years. Graduated in 1964. In 1965 he was in West Germany, in a branch of the Army assigned to track down paintings that were stolen in France and Italy by the German government during World War II. Whatever hadn't been found in the late forties, early fifties, that is. Browne was in West Germany until 1969."

"And then?"

"Then, nothing. The record stops right there."

"That can't be."

"No, it can't. But it is."

"But he'd have to have *worked* somewhere—" Although, Mom had said Charlie was rich, so maybe not. "Surely he's driven a car."

"A lot of Charlie Brownes have driven a car. Not this one. I had three people on it all night, weeding the wrong ones out."

"What about family?"

"Both parents dead. His mother was an artist. That's the other odd note in all this. She died under mysterious circumstances in 1950. The police records are a bit sparse on the subject. Browne was eight years old at the time."

"What about his father?"

"Justin Phillips Browne, according to the birth certificate. Apparently disappeared sometime after Charlie was born. When the mother died, Charlie went to live with an uncle in Seattle. He's dead now, too."

"Did the computer turn up any property?"

"Nothing."

"Arrests—"

"Not a one."

"A *voting* registration, then!"

"No."

"Dammit, this just isn't possible, Marcus."

"Not under ordinary circumstances, no."

"What do you think?"

A small silence. Then, "I think your mother's friend, for whatever reason, Jess, has taken great pains to have the past twenty years of his life wiped clean."

CHAPTER 6

I didn't tell Mom what Marcus had found. I just couldn't. She woke up singing, and even I could see she was the happiest she'd been in years.

I wasn't about to just let the whole thing drop, though. Mom would have said, "You never can let things be, Jesse, you're always poking and prying."

She was right. And while I didn't have the heart to drop this bomb about Charlie on her over morning coffee, I couldn't sit by and not do anything at all.

Marcus and I had agreed that the best place to begin was in San Francisco, where Charlie had grown up, and where his mother had died. Mysteriously, the report had said. And she had been a painter. Marcus had told me he had a contact there in the art world, a dealer named Laurence Higgham.

"What kind of business do you have with this guy?"

"Oh, this and that," he said.

This and that. What's that old saying? *To catch a thief you hire a thief?*

I called American Airlines and booked a round-trip ticket on the noon flight to San Francisco. Shoving some things in a carry-on, I told Mom I had business in New York.

"I have to talk to my editor at *Newsweek*," I lied. "We're working out a feature story, so it may take a couple of days. You'll be all right, won't you?"

"Of course I will, dear."

"Mom . . ." I didn't know how to say it. "I'd rather Charlie didn't stay here with you while I'm gone."

"Well, all right, of course, if that's what you want. But why?"

How could I tell her that the man she loved had no background, that he wasn't what he seemed to be? That he might, in fact, be a Bluebeard? A double agent? A Russian mole?

"Let's just say I don't believe in unmarried couples sleeping together under my roof."

"Jesse, sometimes I worry about you," Mom said.

I got into San Francisco around three. It was a gorgeous day, no fog, the sun streaming off the blue waters of the Pacific and the white buildings of what certain journalists have romantically called the Emerald City. It fairly glistened. I felt excited, the adrenaline pumping. San Francisco! *Baghdad by the Bay!* What excitement, what verve!

Start thinking that way, and watch out.

A shuttle took me to Union Square, where I found a room at a hotel described by the driver as "moderately priced." Checking in, I found it was moderate for San Francisco; one night was a third of my rent at home.

So much for Oz.

I washed up, changed into navy slacks and a white silk blouse with flats, and grabbed a corned beef sandwich at Lefty O'Doul's. Then I headed out.

I had been in the Bay Area twice since helping Mom move to Marin a few years ago. I'd stayed at Aunt Edna's before, but I kind of knew my way around the City. San Francisco isn't that hard. Up is away from the Bay—down is in it. West is the ocean—east is Oakland, and Hell.

I headed up—to Nob Hill—thinking I'd go over to Sausalito later, check out the gallery where Charlie had "found" the *Hare*. Mom, with only a little casual persuasion, had let slip the gallery name.

Marcus's dealer, Higgham, reigned over a hushed, private establishment on Nob Hill with not even a sign out front. A plum-colored awning proclaimed the address: *Seven-Nine-Seven.*

I had to show my I.D. at the door to a security guard in maroon uniform with gold tassels. Satisfied that I was who I said I was—the person Marcus had called ahead about—the guard ushered me into a large room lined with soft gray velvet. Only one painting was displayed, a subdued abstract in blacks and grays that looked like marshmallows on a campfire. Farther along, small niches held sculptures and tiny little oils with presumably frightening prices. There were no tags visible, of course, but in these places less always means more.

Laurence Higgham rose from his seat behind a cherrywood desk to greet me. A slender, dapper man. Reserved. He had a habit, I soon learned, of leaving his sentences dangling.

After the introductions and the obligatory questions like "How is Marcus . . . (fine) . . . And is this your first trip to San Francisco . . . (no, my mother lives in Marin) . . . (Ah, Marin)" . . . we were able to get down to business.

"Charlie Browne," Higgham said in answer to my question. "Now that's a name I haven't heard for a while . . ."

"You know him, then?"

"I know *of* him. I remember his mother well. Anna Biernej-Browne. A beautiful, talented artist, cut down in her prime. . . ." Higgham shook his head sadly.

"How did she die?"

"It was all most mysterious. And with someone like Anna, of course, one never knows—" He shrugged.

"Meaning?"

"Well . . . Anna was a world unto herself. Perfect for San Francisco in the forties. She and the City were a couple of bawdy girls together, as Herb Caen might say . . . shining their wares for all to see."

Uh-oh. "Wares?"

"Oh, I didn't mean that. Their personality, their sheer love of life. I remember once . . ."

"Yes?" I prompted, when it seemed he was planning to remember in silence.

"Anna had us all dancing in the street. She and Charlie started it—I believe he must have been six or seven then, and they seemed more like friends than mother and son . . . giggling together, thinking up schemes. I and perhaps a hundred others were at one of her parties, and San Francisco was having one of those terrible hot spells that come only once or twice a year. So many people were in Anna's house—which was small—and Anna decided to move the party outside. I remember her standing at the head of the stairs, calling . . . 'Charlie, come along, dear, we need to set the pace.' Or something like that. She grabbed his hand and the two of them simply dashed down the stairs, laughing, and next thing I knew we were all in the street. Anna had somehow persuaded someone to open a fire hydrant. There was water everywhere, and even the most conservative matrons were splashing each other—their jewels glimmering beneath the streetlights, silk chiffon dresses clinging to their portly frames—and of course, the reporters loved it. It was all over the papers the next day."

"There were reporters at the party?"

"Oh, indeed, Anna's parties were always big social events . . . even though, as I remember, she wasn't in the social register, so to speak. Anna simply drew people, gathered them in through sheer force of spirit."

His smile was warmly reminiscent. "I miss that San Francisco. *And* people like Anna. No one seems to have fun anymore."

"And you don't remember what happened to Anna?"

"I'm not sure I ever knew. One day, she was gone. Just like that. I think, at the time, I assumed it was some devastating accident. Then the rumors began."

"Rumors?"

"Well, the police were asking questions of her friends. Taking down names. Nothing ever came of it, so far as I know. I suppose they have to check out any kind of suspicious death . . ."

"Suspicious? In what way?"

"I'm afraid I don't know." He held his small white hands palm up. "I simply assumed, what with the police and so on . . ." He squinted, as if looking into the distance. "A funny thing, though. Looking back, I tend to remember Anna's light. Yet there always seemed to be something dark around her. As if you saw her light because of that . . . as in contrast. Do you know what I mean?"

"I'm not sure." But it was a thought worth storing away. "What about Charlie? You didn't really know him?"

"Only as Anna's son. A little boy, hanging around at her parties. One minute, as I've said, the life of the party along with her . . . the next, off in his own world."

That sounded like Charlie, all right.

"You don't know what happened to him after Anna died?"

"I remember hearing that he'd gone to live with a relative . . . an uncle? . . . I believe that was it."

"I understand he attended schools here in San Francisco."

Higgham appeared to be thinking. He nodded now and then as if confirming the thoughts as they flitted through his mind. "Yes . . . I do believe you're right. His name was mentioned in connection with something . . . Oh, of course. The Carlisle Foundation."

For once he sounded definite.

"This foundation. It has something to do with art?"

His smile stopped just short of patronizing. "The Carlisle Foundation is a major contributor . . . yes . . . yes, indeed, I'd say it has something to do with art."

"Where is this place?"

"I'll write down the address for you. I daresay you'll need some kind of *in*, however. They don't see just anyone."

He printed something neatly on gold-embossed notepaper and handed it to me. "It's in Pacific Heights. High-rent. Gates, most likely. Guard dogs." He smiled slightly.

Had my reputation preceded me?

"I appreciate your time, Mr. Higgham." I stood and held out my hand. His was wispy soft, like a moist little leaf.

"My pleasure, Ms. James. If I can be of further service, either to you or Mr. Andrelli . . ."

"Thanks."

I whispered my way out of there, past the guard and through the brass-plated doors.

I tried to call Marcus from a phone booth, to see if he had an *in* with the Carlisle Foundation. He wasn't home—or Alfred wouldn't let him speak to me, whichever. Someday I'm going to bring Alf to San Francisco and dump him off the Golden Gate Bridge.

Meanwhile, my cabbie knew how to find the Carlisle Foundation—which was a miracle, since he didn't know how to drive. As an alternative, he had obviously seen movies of driving. We whomped up and down the hills of San Francisco like Steve McQueen in *Bullitt*, and when we finally arrived my rear end was beaten senseless from thumping along on the springless seat of his rusted old Chevrolet.

As we idled outside the gates of the Carlisle Foundation, I tried to come up with an approach. I could pretend to be a

feature writer from an elite arts magazine. Or *Time*. I could
say I had an appointment, and some secretary had messed up
by not writing it down.

Or, I could do the unthinkable, and tell the truth.

Given the jet lag I was beginning to feel, the latter, most
effortless, way seemed best.

I paid the cabbie and crossed the street to the gates. A
speaker was set into one Spanish-style pillar attached to a high
fence—white, with red tile along its top. I punched a talk
button. Said, "Hello?"

"Carlisle Foundation. May I help you?"

"Yes. I'd like to see someone in charge."

"Of what department, ma'am?" The voice was pleasant and
male.

"I'm not sure. I don't even know exactly what you do."

"Can you tell me what this is about?"

"I'm trying to locate someone who used to study with the
Carlisle Foundation, or who was involved in it somehow."

"We don't have a registrar's office on these grounds," the
voice said. "Perhaps if you tell me the name of the person
you're looking for."

"I know him as Charlie Browne. With an 'e'."

There was a silence at the other end of the line.

"Hello?"

"Yes, I'm here. One moment, please."

Another silence as the speaker crackled off at his end. I
tapped a foot and looked off down the hill to the Bay. You
could just see an edge of Alcatraz sparkling out there. It could
be any island in any country; Monaco, for instance, with its
glistening gambling casino. Hard to tell from here—

"Ma'am?"

"I'm here."

"Push the red button below the talk button, please. The
pedestrian gate will open for thirty seconds only, at which time
you may pass through."

Wow. So the mention of Charlie's name opened doors? I
didn't know whether to be impressed or nervous. I pushed
the designated button. The small wrought-iron gate next to
the driveway swung open. I passed through.

And found I was in Oz after all.

I must say, right up front, that I love the many gardens that grace the Flower City of Rochester, New York. The lilacs and roses, the green, green grass and trees. But this was something else. Tropical flowers everywhere. Orchids and birds of paradise—others I didn't even recognize. There were palm trees lining the drive, and lush green ferns. As a kid who grew up on Eastern city streets, I didn't recognize the flora by any authentic terms. I just knew I was in Paradise. The scents were out of this world. Fountains glittered in the sunlight. Birds chattered. I passed a goldfish pond, with foot-long orange and white specimens. I was so stunned by all the beauty, I almost got lost.

I paused to admire the vast complex of buildings, all done in white Spanish architecture with red tile roofs, and surrounded by palms. A soft voice spoke behind me.

"We believe that if art mirrors life, then life must be made as splendid as possible."

I turned. The man who faced me was perhaps in his mid-sixties. He wore blue work clothes and work boots that were muddy. He carried a gardening tool, the little spade-like thing that people use for digging into pots. He was barely more than five feet tall.

"Would you like to see the greenhouses?"

"I . . . I don't know. I'm here to talk to someone—"

"About Charlie." He nodded gently. "I know."

He spoke like a monk who hadn't used his voice in several years. Tentatively, yet with utmost calm. His hair was thinning and looked soft, a mere suggestion of white filament over a sun-pinkened scalp. His eyes were a startling blue.

"Yes—Charlie. How did you know?"

"Forgive me. I'm Avery Carlisle." His look encompassed the posh surroundings, and he smiled shyly. "I'm the keeper of all this, I'm delighted to say."

"The gardener—?"

I bit my tongue. Carlisle. As in the Carlisle Foundation.

"I'm sorry. I'm Jessica James," I said.

He smiled again. "I'd offer to shake hands, but as you can see, mine are quite muddy from all the potting."

I grinned. "Shaking hands is a tiresome custom, anyway. It

used to mean fellowship. Now it's a way to win over customers."

"Today's society is an effort on many levels," Avery Carlisle agreed.

I felt, in that instant, the kind of chemistry that tells you you've found a friend. All the tension, even the jet lag, evaporated. My spine relaxed, and my nerves stopped zinging.

"Why don't we sit down over there," my host said, pointing to a lacy white gazebo fifty feet away. "There's a thermos of juice, and a small box of sandwiches I bring along when I'm working in the gardens."

I followed him . . . slowly, for that's the way he walked. Not like an old man, but as if every step had some deep significance . . . as if by hurrying even one moment, by spending it too quickly, something of vast importance would be lost.

We sat in the coolness of the gazebo, a welcome relief from the sun. Autumn, Mom had told me when she first moved out here, is one of the warmest seasons in San Francisco. The fog backs off and Indian summer sets in. It had been hot ever since I'd stepped off the plane. I sipped at a glass of juice, something pink and tropical, and kicked back for the first time since Mom had arrived on my doorstep, packing a wallop, three days before. Long moments passed. An occasional plane passed over, so high it was barely there. The soft whoosh of sprinklers was the only other sound. That and the birds. Avery Carlisle sat across the little table from me, his feet not touching the floor, he was that short, and seemed content to wait for me to begin. I was no longer in so much of an all-fired hurry to solve the mystery of Charlie Browne.

A young Oriental woman passed by on the path and waved. She carried a sketch pad and what looked like a plastic bag of pencils. Her dress was a flash of white against the greenery, then it was gone.

"One of our most promising artists," Carlisle said.

I roused myself. "This is a school, then?"

"In part. We also have a conference center. Our guests often spend weeks in residence here."

"I can see why."

"They learn," Carlisle said, "to look for the creative wellsprings within themselves. For this reason, they value their privacy. We try to protect that for them."

Thus the gates and walls. Yet, at the mention of Charlie Browne's name, I had been let in—no further questions asked.

"Was Charlie Browne a student here?"

A soft, gentle smile played on Carlisle's lips. "How is Charlie? Where is he now?"

"Charlie's . . . back home in New York State. With my mom."

"Ah."

He was leaving me an opening, and I took it. "She thinks she's in love," I said.

"I see. And you are not happy about this, I think."

"I just . . ."

"You wonder if Charlie is too good to be true?"

"Well, I personally don't buy his charm . . . but yes, I guess it'd be safe to say my mom thinks he's Mr. Wonderful. And that worries me."

Carlisle chuckled softly. "That would be Charlie. Yes."

"Will you tell me about him?"

He set his glass down and leaned back in his chair, folding his hands in his lap. Then he nodded. "I'll tell you what I can."

Charlie had been a student at the Foundation after high school. Then, after his discharge from the Army in 1969, he had been hired by Carlisle. His experience with tracing lost works of art was just what Carlisle needed. Charlie's job was to track down stolen art around the world and return it to its rightful owner.

"Often," Carlisle said, "when masterpieces are stolen, they're kept in cellars or attics, out of the public eye, for years. An outrageous loss to society."

There was no profit involved for Carlisle in turning up these works. He was born with money, and this is what he'd decided, somewhere along the way, to do with it.

"Charlie finished his schooling while he worked for me. A bright young man, but with a mission. Every moment of his spare time was spent in the search—"

He broke off and shrugged, smiling apologetically. "I'm

sorry. It's much too nice a day to go into this. Wouldn't you rather see the greenhouses?"

"No, please go on. What did you start to say?"

"Charlie was searching . . . almost obsessively, I'd say . . . for his mother's killer."

I felt a chill, despite the day's warmth. "Charlie's mother was murdered?"

"Yes." Carlisle's voice was barely a whisper. I had to lean forward to hear. "A terrible tragedy. Anna Biernej-Browne was one of the bright lights of the artistic establishment here on the West Coast. A beautiful woman, full of life and spirit. In the forties, she held salons, with all the best literary and art figures from around the world attending at one time or another, as well as promising young students. I remember . . ."

He drifted off.

"You knew her?" I prompted.

He roused himself. "Oh, yes. Everyone in the art world knew Anna. She was a legend. And great fun. She would take everyone from her parties, without a moment's notice, and drive off to the beach in the middle of the night. There we would be forced to scamper and splash in the light of the moon, even the most staid among us . . ." His bright blue eyes were warm with the memory Anna evoked. "She taught us to play. That was Anna's special charm."

His smile faded. "One morning, after a party, Charlie came home from a friend's house . . . and there was Anna, on the floor. Dead. Charlie was eight years old."

"Good God. He didn't see the murder?"

"No . . . no, he was spared that. But even later, as a young man, his primary agenda, always, was to find the person responsible for his mother's death. An unhealthy obsession, I believe, in many ways."

"I understand the police investigated. What did they find?"

Carlisle was silent a moment. "Death by person or persons unknown."

I wondered why Higgham hadn't known that. Maybe he just wasn't close enough to the situation. Or maybe Anna's murder had been hushed up for some reason.

"Is Charlie wealthy?" I asked.

"Wealthy? I don't know if I'd use that word. I pay him well, but certainly not enough to make him—"

"Charlie works for you still?"

"You sound surprised."

"It's just . . . Charlie doesn't seem to have a record of jobs these past twenty years or so. Do you know why?"

He shook his head. "I can't help you out there. Oh, now and then Charlie will show up looking for a job to do. But he's never been one to work long hours or worry about that sort of thing. He prefers time to travel and learn about life."

Right. Time to meet rich widows—or pretend ones, like my mom.

We sat a little longer, talking about nothing of importance while I tried to rearrange my original picture of Charlie to fit all the new facts I'd learned. It wasn't easy. There were too many holes, too many questions unanswered.

I finally had to stir myself to push on. "I have to go," I said. "But thank you for your hospitality." Something about this gentle little man reminded me of my manners. I was acting almost sedate.

Avery Carlisle walked me to the gate. There, he snipped a dusty-pink rose from along the wall and held it a moment by my cheek. Nodding. "An old-fashioned woman at heart, I think." He handed me the rose. "For you. In the hope that you will remember this old man with a bit of goodwill."

My knees melted. I took the flower and held it to my nose.

As I was walking through the gate, I remembered something else I'd wanted to ask.

"What kind of paintings did Anna do?"

"Oh, they were very unique. Not unlike Galanin's, which I also very much admire—but different in texture and shape."

"Galanin?"

"Rabbits. Anna loved rabbits. It's all she ever painted," he said.

CHAPTER 7

I took the ferry to Sausalito, mulling over rabbits along the way.

Anna Biernej-Browne, Charlie's mother, painted rabbits. Charlie had taken (stolen?) an unsigned painting of a rabbit from a gallery in Sausalito, and that painting now resided beneath my bed. What did it mean?

Was the *Hare* his mother's painting? If so, why hadn't Charlie just claimed it—or for that matter, bought it? Why take it illegally, as it seemed he'd done? And why bother to hide it now?

The other question, and one I didn't have enough information to ponder intelligently, was: Did any of this have to do with Anna Biernej-Browne's murder? Charlie had apparently chosen to work in the art field in order to give himself an avenue into the mystery of her death . . . but had it done him any good? Had he learned anything over the years?

And more importantly—why had the past twenty years of his life been erased? So far, his connection to Avery Carlisle was the only thing I knew about those two decades. But Charlie had only worked for him "now and then." The rest of the time, Charlie "traveled."

There were too many things I didn't know. I finally stopped chewing on all the questions and let myself be seduced by the ferry ride. The sky was clear, the water blue, and gulls chased us across the Bay. The air turned brisk as we passed through the Golden Gate Strait, then settled down as we neared land again. I thought of Avery Carlisle and his gardens . . . the peace he'd surrounded himself with. For that brief hour I'd been with him, I'd felt as if my soul had been massaged.

Which sounds hokey and stupid, I know, but there was something about Avery Carlisle. Just being in his presence had

41

brought out something astonishing in me: a softness I hadn't even known was there.

I had turned down one of Carlisle's proffered sandwiches, and was hungry now. There was a little hamburger joint in Sausalito, no more than a hole in the wall but with the greatest grilled-on-the-spot burgers in the world. I thought maybe I'd stop there and get one, then feed the pigeons in the park. Mellow out some more. (If anything feels good, my addictive personality always craves more.)

But once off the ferry, my mood changed. A hundred other tourists piled off with me, jamming the parking lot. There were a thousand people at the burger hut; the line curved way out onto the sidewalk. And there were bikers all over the place. Not motorcycle bikers—those, I can take. These were those horrid little aliens in skintight black shorts and helmets that make them look like Bugs from Space. They were worse than a swarm of gnats. You could hardly walk, and drivers were angry, too, honking their horns and cussing.

The first time I'd been to Sausalito was when I'd helped Mom move out here to live with Aunt Edna, right after Pop died. The last time was just last spring. I'd loved the town on sight: an old fishing village that had grown by piling houses Mediterranean-style up a hill. Shops and restaurants rimmed a main street along the Bay.

It was being spoiled, now, more and more every year, by . . . well, by people.

Thinking about that, my mood darkened even more.

There was a dim little bar—the no name—that I'd spent a few hazy evenings in when I was here before. I considered stopping in to see if anyone I remembered was around. Saying hello. But now that I wasn't drinking, it probably wouldn't be the same.

Nothing was the same, I thought, frowning. Ever. Just when you thought you had things down cold, they drifted away, like smoke.

Okay. So maybe I'd drop in and have a beer. One beer, what the hell?

I stood looking in the window of the no name. Other people sat inside drinking—presumably without guilt. I saw my reflection, looking tired and defeated. How had I come to this, so soon after that serene hour with Avery Carlisle? What kind of psychological twist had taken place? For a moment, I had it—but then that drifted off too.

I veered away, looking for the art gallery, which wasn't hard to find. There were only three on this block. It was the second one I came to. *S. J. Timmons*, Mom had said.

CHAPTER 8

The clerk—a young blond guy—was alone. The great horde of tourists was outside lapping ice-cream cones with screaming kids in strollers, or poking around in the T-shirt shops. Art is dead: Long live I GOT CRABS IN SAUSALITO.

I ambled around a little, stopping now and then at a painting to stand back appropriately for perspective, but repressing the urge to sight through my thumb.

"Help you with something?" the clerk finally said. In the art world—I've learned through doing feature articles—sales-clerks have a unique approach. Rather than the hard sell, they pretend to have something precious to gift you with, should you prove yourself suitable for such generosity on their part. That way, when you end up back home trying to figure out where to stick the blob of oranges and reds that you knew you *should* like, but *didn't*, and that don't go *at all* with your purples and greens, you have no one to blame but yourself.

"I saw a painting in here a couple of weeks ago." I smiled. "I was wondering if you still had it."

He ambled over, but hadn't yet acquired the necessary pol-ish for the job. His eyes held a glint of greed. "It's possible. Everything we have is out here. What was the subject?"

"A rabbit," I said. "A rabbit with roses at his feet."

It wasn't my imagination that he paled.

He cleared his throat. "I, uh, I don't think we have anything like that." He ran a hand through his Dutch-boy cut.

"Oh, you sold it already?" I sounded dismayed.

"No . . . I, uh, I don't think we ever did have anything like that." His voice rose. "I'm sure we didn't."

I looked around curiously. "But I thought sure this was the right place. S. J. Timmons?"

"Yeah, but we never had a painting like that. I'd remember,

44

and we didn't. Not since I've been here. I've been here three months, and I've never seen anything like that at all."

He was talking too much, and he realized it and switched to a more businesslike patter. "How about something else? We have a great still life over here, and this seascape is nice . . ."

He went on like that, from painting to painting, no one of them having anything in common with the other. He was clearly giving himself time to think, with no concern for his customer's tastes.

I followed, pretending to look where he pointed, but my own thoughts were on the rest of the store. Sometimes galleries on a main street like Bridgeway, with tourist traffic, have discreet electronic metal detectors affixed to frames. That might be the case here.

I wondered what they did for security at night, however. Assuming the *Hare* was in this store until a few days ago (which I had no reason to doubt, since Mom had confirmed it), and assuming Charlie didn't *buy* the *Hare* (another thing I didn't doubt, since he himself had admitted to it), it seemed likely that somehow Charlie had ripped the painting off.

There was a back room, a kind of storage and work area that I could see through an open door. Beyond that, I figured, would be another door leading into an alley for deliveries. For someone like Charlie, with a disappearing past and eyes like a pool shark, gaining access to the gallery probably wouldn't have been too hard. Hell, *I* can pick almost any lock around, and I haven't had any hands-on experience with crime since eighth grade.

(Well, not really. There *was* Daphne Malcross's Jag, and then there was the chop shop in Syracuse, and a few assorted break-ins to get a story—but that's all done and past. I'm clean now. Sober. Upright.)

But even while I was thinking that, a little voice said: *Jesse, the real problem is that at thirty-one, you're too damned old.*

" . . . a wonderful watercolor by a local artist, Chris Hammond . . ." the clerk was saying, " . . . worth a lot more, one day soon . . ."

"May I use your rest room?" I said.

"Uh . . . gee, I don't know. It's not really for customers . . ."

"I promise not to steal the graffiti."

He smiled. God, he was cute. Tall . . . broad-shouldered. And young. And it was true—at thirty-one, I was too damned old.

"Okay," he said at last. "This way." He led me through the gallery into the back room and showed me to the bathroom, against a side wall. I noted in passing that the back door, while heavy with security locks and a wire alarm, wasn't as up-to-date as it might be. The Genesee Three, back home, could have handled it in no time flat. Charlie had probably had no trouble with it at all.

I washed my hands and face, and cleaned a juice stain from my blouse. That reminded me of Avery Carlisle, and I had to smile, feeling the effects of those gentle blue eyes long after the fact. But when I looked up into the mirror, my own green eyes were strained. They looked tired. Drawn. Nothing unusual; I get that way when I'm not drinking. Worn and dry. It's almost as if the booze brings me to life, like a parchment sack that fills up and smooths out when you wet it down.

Oh, well. I could survive another day, another week, another month, without a drink. I'd learned that about myself by now. The only question, as always, was: Did I want to?

Samved says—(Samved's my New Age shrink, the one I mentioned, and how I got into that is a whole other story and one that Mom's to blame for)—anyway, Samved says we create our own reality. That what we want, on some level that we aren't always aware of, is precisely what we get.

So now and then I ask myself what my reality is—and did I really create it for myself?

I have my job, which I'm more or less happy with. I'm free-lancing at last, and making enough to pay the bills, although I'll never be rich. I have my apartment, which—despite the growing incidence of crime on Genesee Park Boulevard—I love. I have a great landlady, Mrs. Binty, and a dog, Bastard, whom I hate (but Samved would say that on some level I wanted and created him too), and I have—

Marcus. Who is not what every woman's mother wants for her child.

So why was my Mom so all-fired hot to like him now?

Marcus had come into my life a year and a half ago almost by accident (okay, Samved, I hear you, there are no accidents), and we'd been together ever since. Grady North, a friend for years and a cop on Homicide, is the one I should have ended up with—or at least you'd think so, given all the signs. But Grady is too damned nice.

Marcus would never, by most people's standards, be called nice. He's tough. Cautious. Watchful. Cynical. Illegal.

In many ways, a lot like me. And I've loved him for all those things.

Now, however, and not for the first time, I found myself questioning the status quo. The dark mood I'd felt after the ferry came back, then flitted away. I wondered how much all this questioning had to do with Avery Carlisle?

I kept seeing that idyllic world of his—the gardens and the serenity, so removed from the stresses I knew in Rochester and the kinds of relationships I had there. A crack opened in reality and revealed another world of possibilities—a world where people don't dabble in the darker side of things, where you might be able to drift along without all the troubles I took as everyday necessity. It was a whole new "field of dreams."

Shit.

I shook myself free of all that, dried my hands, and thanking the clerk for his help, I got the hell out of there.

Too much introspection is bad for the soul.

CHAPTER 9

It had been clear I wouldn't get anything more out of the clerk at S. J. Timmons. But I had another source in Sausalito. When I was here before, hanging out at the no name bar, I'd become friends with a guy who lives on the houseboats. His name is Ben Jericho, and he was once a San Francisco cop, but he'd quit the force when his wife died. He was running charters now while raising his little girl. I'd learned through our conversations that he kept an ex-cop kind of watch on what went on around town.

Ben didn't have a listed phone, and I wasn't sure I'd catch him in. But there he was, down at the Schoonmaker Marina, scrubbing down the deck and battening the hatches, or whatever it is you do with a sailboat. My experience extends to helping Marcus build a replica of a wooden Nova Scotia Whaler, and to sunning myself on the deck of his yacht. Of modern sailboats, I know zip—except that Ben Jericho's was one of the largest, sleekest and most powerful sailboats in the marina. He'd sunk his entire life savings into it when he quit the force five years ago. Powered with a Lambert-Carlson engine, it had maroon sails, teak decks and—always—fresh white paint.

"Ben Jericho?" I called out from the dock, shading my eyes.

"Yeah?" He straightened and looked around, squinting from under a Giants cap. "Sonova bitch. Jesse James?"

"You got it."

"Hey!" He was beside me in one smooth leap that shook the dock and left it quivering. "What're you doing out here?"

"Poking around," I said, smiling.

Ben was the kind of guy you felt easy with right away—old Marin County, rather than upscale new. No Rolex watch, no gold chains or BMW . . . nothing to intimidate a woman who

48

isn't all that secure to begin with. So it was a while into the friendship before I'd even thought about how good-looking he was. Tall—about six-two—with a solid build and curly, sun-streaked brown hair. A deep tan, and a jaw like Tom Selleck's. I'd have fallen in love with him on looks alone, if it hadn't been for the kid. Missy. His little girl.

There's always something, isn't there?

And the irony is, Missy's a great little kid. I just can't stand kids. Or dogs.

I picked a flake of paint off Ben's chin. "I can see you're busy. Do you have any time to talk?"

"I was just about to break for a beer. Join me?"

"Thanks. I'll take a Coke if you've got one."

He went ahead and turned to help me board. I took his hand, clambered up, and was just coming down off the rail when he caught me, lifting me to the deck. As he did, he gave me a closer look. The kind people give to people they used to know as drunks, but who have (to everyone's surprise) sobered up.

"Diet Pepsi okay?"

"Perfect."

He grinned.

I sat on a padded bench along the prow. Ben went below for drinks. Since he charters, there's always food and beverages aboard, although according to local code, he isn't supposed to live here. He and Missy have a houseboat at Issaquah Landing, with pots of flowers and stained-glass windows all around. They seem pretty happy there, the two of them.

He came back, handing me an opened Pepsi, and I said, "Where's Missy today?"

"At home, cooking dinner."

"Cooking dinner? Isn't she a little young for that?" Missy was nine—maybe ten.

"She wanted to do it. The baby sitter's helping. Tacos and salad, I hear, is the fare. With Häagen-Dazs for dessert. Wanna come?"

It sounded real homey. And depressing—all that family crap. Like Mom, Charlie, Toni, me, and for God's sake, even Marcus Andrelli—King of Corporate Crime—sitting around over Seafood Surprise.

"I think I've got to get back to the City."

He gave me a teasing look. "Gotta eat somewhere, though. Sometime."

"Maybe room service."

He grinned.

I'd never told Ben Jericho how I felt about kids. I never had to.

"What's up, Jess? You on a story?"

"Sort of. I've just come from the Timmons Gallery. You know anything about it?"

His eyes narrowed beneath the Giants cap. "Back up. What kind of business have you got at Timmons?"

"Then you do know it."

"I know a few things. It'd take a while. Why don't you tell me first what you're looking for, then I'll tell you if you've found it."

"Okay. First, I want to know if a robbery's been reported by them in the past week or so."

"You mean a B&E?" He shook his head. "Not that I've heard. Did you check down at the station?"

"I don't know anybody there. Ordinarily, I'd just ask as a reporter to see the record of complaints, but this is a small town. I don't want word to get around that I'm asking questions."

"Well," he said, "I can find out for you, but I really don't think there's been anything like that. Besides—"

He was silent, rubbing the moisture on the can of beer with his thumb. Ben had rough workman's hands, and they squeezed the aluminum can, leaving a dent. "The Timmons Gallery," he said, "isn't a place you want to be hanging around right now."

"Oh? Why not?"

"You could get hurt, that's all."

A shadow passed his face. It wasn't a cloud; it was the memory of Janet, his wife, I suspected . . . and how she had died.

Janet was a police officer, too, and she had become involved in a case that Ben was on. She was shot in the line of duty while Ben was questioning other witnesses. He wasn't there to help. She lay with a bullet in her chest for a long time before she was found, and no amount of advice from anyone—"she should have waited for backup, shouldn't have gone in alone"—could clear that horror from his mind. It was why he'd quit the force, to make a more peaceable life for his child.

"It doesn't get any easier, does it?" I said.

"Not much. Pops up at the damnedest times."

"Why don't you tell me about the gallery, then." I'm not good at offering comfort. Changing the subject is generally the best I can do.

He stretched out his legs and pushed back his cap. "The problem is tracking down the owner. He's hiding in back of so many corporate names, he's damned invisible. But the gallery is under suspicion for trafficking in stolen art."

"Ah." The scene becomes clear, as old Samved would say. Or maybe just clear-er. Unfortunately, improved vision almost always leads the mind into further query.

Such as: Did Charlie work for this gallery, moving stolen art? Avery Carlisle had said that he didn't get wealthy working for him. Charlie had to be getting his money somewhere—if indeed he had any.

And: If this was the case, had Charlie found the *Hare* while moving stolen art for Timmons—and recognized it as a painting of his mother's?

Was the *Hare* in fact painted by Anna Biernej-Browne? And if so, what was it worth? And why wasn't it signed? What, again, did any of it mean?

I sighed. Too many questions—and all of them leading back to Mom. What would I tell her if I came up with all the wrong answers?

Bright sunlight sparkled on the water. A seaplane buzzed overhead. Somewhere on the boats a jazz aficionado was playing a mellow sax. Between all that, the water lapping against the hulls, and a certain laissez-faire that had been returning at regular intervals all afternoon, I felt my brain begin to turn off. Yep, there it went . . . *click*. Just like that. I didn't even try to find the switch that would hoist it back on.

I leaned back, let the sun do its job, and gave a deep, contented sigh.

Ben Jericho laughed softly. "Come home with me," he said.

I smiled. Shook my head.

But finally, I said, "Okay."

* * *

"Do you miss being a cop?"

"No way. I like being my own boss."

"You don't miss the action?"

"There's more good clean action in sailing a boat or catching a fish. The only action in police work has to do with violence. Who needs that?"

We were on the houseboat at Issaquah, relaxing on the deck while Missy and her baby sitter, in the kitchen, hung fried tortillas over the wooden handle of a spoon to make tacos. The air was pungent with the fishy scent of bay water, cilantro, and taco mix.

Ben sipped at a frosty beer. He said, "Sometimes, Jess, it really hits me—how much I have to be grateful for. I've got Melissa, our place here, and I've got my boat. Seven out of eleven small businesses go bankrupt in the first year of start-up, but I've made it. And I'm doing something that's more like play than work. What more could anyone ask?"

What, indeed? Ben Jericho had created the perfect reality for himself, if that was the way it actually worked. And no one deserved it more.

Missy called from the kitchen, "It's ready, come and get it!" and we went inside, loading up pastel plates and taking them back out onto the deck. The sun was going down, and the sky had ruby streaks that were reflected in blue water. The sax player from the marina was a memory now, but blues music drifted from another houseboat. Someone had a ballgame on —(was it really almost time for the Series? It seemed like mid-summer here)—and people were grilling steaks or burgers on their decks. Lights winked on along the hills, and I had a feeling I'd never want to go home.

At one point, Ben went back to the kitchen for more drinks. Missy sat on the railing facing me. She wore tennis shoes, white shorts, and a pink-and-white camp shirt. Pushing her long blond hair from her face, she said, "Are you and Daddy going out after dinner?" She swung her legs, bumping the railing with the heels of her shoes.

"Not that I know of, " I said.

"You used to, when you were here before."

"You remember that?"

She took a bite, chewed, and swallowed. Wiping taco sauce from her chin, she said, "Sure. I thought maybe you were gonna marry my dad."

I had to wipe my own chin after that one. "Really? What made you think a thing like that?"

She shrugged. "I don't know."

I poured some more Coke into her glass, and dumped the remains into mine. "Did it bother you, thinking that?" I asked curiously.

"No." She pushed her hair away from her face. "It bothered me more when you went home and never came back or were heard from again."

Christ. Talk about a punch in the gut.

I looked—really looked—at Melissa Jericho, age nine going on forty-one—and for the first time realized what a shit I'd been. The evenings with Ben last time never went anywhere; they were mild flirtations that turned, by some quirk of fate, into friendship. But how could Missy have known that? Children live in fantasy worlds, and because for them anything is possible, they're too damned vulnerable. You can hurt them without even trying. That scares the hell out of me.

"I'm sorry, Melissa. I didn't think. God, that was stupid of me."

She shrugged again. "No big deal." She slid off the rail and headed for the kitchen. "Daddy, bring the ice cream! I'll get the spoons."

Sometimes things happen that you don't foresee. All of a sudden you're ready for a relationship—and bam, it happens —a friend becomes a lover, and your whole life is changed.

Things didn't happen for me and Ben Jericho that night.

I went back to the hotel and circled the emotional campfire with the wagons. I lay on the bed and stared at the ceiling. Finally, around the time the sun was coming up, I fell asleep. Two hours later the alarm went off, and I dressed, shuttled to the airport, and slogged on home.

CHAPTER 10

Home.

Home is where the heart is.

A (wo)man's home is (her)his castle.

There's no place like home. . . .

None of those clichés fit what I found when I walked through my apartment door.

First of all, there was Mom, sprawled on the couch, an ice bag on her head—not to mention a lump beneath it the size of Kansas. And there was Toni, playing Florence Nightingale with tea and toast on a little tray that held a chrysanthemum from Mrs. Binty's garden in a crystal bud vase. And there—(the worst aggravation of all, for reasons having to do with none of the above)—were the last seven days' worth of *Rochester Heralds* on the coffee table.

I dropped my carry-on to the floor. "What the hell happened?"

"Jesse, you're home early! How nice."

"What *happened?*"

"Now, don't get excited. I'm sure it was just a burglar, dear."

Just a burglar. "*Just a burglar?* Christ, Mother, what happened to you? What's wrong with your head?"

"There's really no reason to get so upset . . . and don't touch it like that, it hurts."

I drew my hand away, thinking it must hurt like hell. I looked at Toni. "What is all this about a burglar?"

"Everything's okay now," she said. "Your mom just had a little run-in with somebody coming up the stairs last night. The doctor says she'll be fine."

"The doctor."

"We took her to Strong Emergency. Me and Charlie. It's just a bruise—"

54

"I knew it! That damned painting!"

"I doubt it had anything to do with the *Hare*," Mom said. "You've had break-ins here before, haven't you?"

"Those were done by friends."

She looked at me strangely. "You have friends who break into your home? What kind of friends would break into your home?"

"It's a long story, Mom." I sat on the coffee table, beside her. "Are you all right? What can I do for you?"

"I'm fine, dear, and don't worry. Toni's taking wonderful care of me. She's made this nice tea, and she brought all those newspapers in from the yard the way I asked her to. I don't know why you never pick those things up—"

"Mom," I sighed, "I didn't want them brought in. I've been leaving them out there on purpose."

Mom removed the ice bag and stared at me. "Why ever on earth would you do that?"

"Because," I said patiently, "the boy doesn't deliver them right. He throws them in Mrs. Binty's hedges, and I've refused to accept the paper until he learns to do it right."

"Well, you could at least pick them up; they were all over the place."

"It doesn't work that way," I argued, my irritation growing. "If I pick them up, then they think I'm taking them inside and reading them, and then they charge me—oh, forget it!" I stood, hands on my hips. "Did you report the break-in to the police?"

"Good heavens, no. I didn't want the police here, they ask too many questions."

"That's what I thought." I crossed to the telephone on my desk and dialed Grady North down at Homicide. A bit of an overkill, but as a friend, he might help out without making it official.

"Could you come over?" I said when Grady answered. "My mom is here, and she's knocking herself out to say hello."

Grady arrived a couple of hours later. By then I'd called Marcus and asked him to unearth the corporately hidden owner of the Timmons Gallery for me, and I'd ascertained that Charlie was "somewhere out there"—(another cliché I find truly tiresome these days)—still trying to trace the provenance of the *Hare*.

Grady knew Mom from way before she moved to California. He always liked her and was sure we'd patch things up someday. Grady is sort of Brady Bunch that way. He likes to think the best of people, although he's generally cross with me about my attitude toward life.

"That's a pretty nasty-looking bruise," he said with a frown. He gave Mom a hug and a kiss on the cheek. "What happened?" He tugged at his tie, loosened the top two buttons of his white shirt, ran a hand through his sandy hair, and made himself comfortable on the floor. Grady does that. Sort of folds himself up, like a yogi, and plops down anywhere at all.

"Grady Aloysius North, you are more handsome than ever," my mother observed, ignoring his question. "If I were Jesse, I'd see to it you didn't get away—"

"Mom!"

"Your daughter and I have enough trouble just remaining friends," Grady said. Underneath the attempt at a light tone, there lay a sour note. "Tell me how you are. I didn't realize, when Jess called—Where did you get that lump on your head?"

"It's nothing at all," Mom said airily. "I was bending over the kitchen cupboard, and when I stood up I struck my head on an open door—"

"She did nothing of the sort. She was attacked on the stairs last night."

Grady looked at me sharply, then at her. "A mugger? Was he after money?"

"That's it," Mom answered quickly. "He wanted money, but I wouldn't give it to him, so he knocked me down—"

"Hold it." I glared at her. "He was opening the door to my apartment," I informed Grady, "when Mom caught him at it. He did not take her purse."

"I see. Jess, what do *you* think he was after?"

I stopped short of telling him about the painting; I wasn't sure why. "I don't know. But I think it's likely this has something to do with Mom's new friend." Mom gave me the old evil eye. "His name," I continued, "is Charlie Browne. With an 'e'."

Grady lifted a sandy brow.

"And?"

"And I think you should just . . . see what you can find out about Charlie Browne."

"Kate? You agree with this?"

"Certainly not! Charlie is a wonderful man. We've known each other nearly a year, and nothing like this has ever happened before." For the first time, however, she sounded unsure.

"Where did you meet this man?"

Mom flushed. "Well . . ."

I answered for her. "Through a dating service. In California."

"A dating service." Grady's suspicious tone was nearly overridden by the surprise in his eyes.

"It was an impulse," Mom explained, her face a peony pink. "But it worked. I met a wonderful man—"

"A man who seems to have no past," I announced, sick of all the tiptoeing around.

Mom's green eyes flashed my way. "Jessica, that is ridiculous—"

Jessica. I was in deep shit now. But I'd said it, and I couldn't take it back. "Charlie has no past," I repeated. "Marcus did a computer check. Charlie has no background at all, starting with 1969 and his discharge from the Army in West Germany."

I tried not to flinch at Mom's indrawn breath.

"What do you mean, no background?" Grady's cop voice clicked on.

"I mean there is absolutely nothing, in one of the most sophisticated computer systems in the country, on this Charlie Browne." I ticked the offenses off on my fingers. "No driver's license—"

"A lot of people don't drive!" Mom said.

"No voting registration—"

"That's hardly a crime, or you'd be in jail right now, Jessica Rosemary James!"

"Rosemary?" Grady said with another upraised brow.

It was my turn to flush. "Never mind. Charlie's never owned property—"

"He lives in hotels. Dear God, Jesse, what's wrong with that?"

"No work record at all—"

"He's *rich!*"

"*And*"—my final thrust—"his mother was murdered. In 1950, by person or persons unknown. She was a well-known artist for her time. She painted *rabbits*," I said, looking pointedly at Mom. "And her son Charlie found the body. He was eight years old at the time."

Mom paled. This clearly was something she hadn't known. "That doesn't mean . . ." Her voice trailed off uncertainly.

"We don't know *what* it means, and that's the point. Charlie is one big question mark."

"I guess you'd know all about questionable friends," Grady said to me.

I didn't even bother to respond. Defending Marcus Andrelli to Grady North is like defending a shark to a minnow.

"I just think you should look into Charlie. You've got some contacts on the San Francisco P.D. Maybe they'll be more forthcoming with you than they would be with me. Unofficially, of course."

"I can't promise to keep this unofficial if I turn up something illegal—"

"I know, I know. Christ, I've heard that often enough before."

Grady unwound himself and stood, bending to kiss Mom again. He said sympathetically, "I'll do what I can, Kate. This could all prove to be just one more erroneous by-product of your daughter's overly suspicious mind."

"Thank you, dear." Mom's chin went up. "I knew you'd understand."

After Grady left, Toni, who had been listening quietly with folded arms, lit into me. "I think you're mean!" She plopped down next to Mom, putting a consoling hand on her shoulder. "You're just trying to spoil things for your mom and Charlie because you're never happy yourself!"

"Hush, Toni," Mom said.

But Toni flew to her feet, her long black ponytail swinging. "I don't care! She obviously doesn't like mothers any more than she likes children or dogs!"

Shit. Another kid who had me down cold.

I jammed my hands in my pockets and scowled at both of them, issuing one last petulant but winning thrust.

"Oh, yeah? Well, just so you know . . . Charlie isn't rich!"

I stormed out of the apartment and down the hallway stairs, my muffled steps on the gray wool carpet like the sound of one hand clapping.

CHAPTER 11

"I think it was those rotten newspapers that did it," I said apologetically the next evening. "I'm sorry, Mom."

"No, you had every right to be upset, Jesse. This is your home, after all, and I've just been butting in. Picking up your papers, for heaven's sake, like a visiting mother-in-law looking for dust balls under the bed!"

I'd spent the night with Marcus, and the next morning at his penthouse using the phone—calling magazines I had deadlines with and putting them off. Now I was standing with Mom in front of my bathroom mirror, feeling guilty and having second thoughts about trying to nail Charlie. We were squeezed into the tiny bathroom, vying for space, but agreeably. Mom was leaning over the sink, putting on eye makeup and looking fresh and pretty like Betty White on *The Golden Girls*, while I was simply doing my best to cover up a zit. It will always be thus with Mom and me.

"I'm turning into a bitch," I said. "A thirty-one-year-old curmudgeon."

"You are no such thing!" Mom exclaimed. "You just worry about people, that's all. You've always been that way."

"Toni was right, though." I sat on the closed toilet seat and watched her add blush to her cheeks. "I thought about it all night, and I guess I'm jealous. It used to be you and me against *them*, Mom. You were the one I could run to, to protect me from Pop when he was yelling and drunk, and now, even though I know that all men aren't like that, there's something in my gut that says they're going to start yelling again, and you won't be there—because you've gone over to *them*."

She dropped her blush as her mascara started to run. "Damn!" She blinked and blotted the corners of her eyes with

60

a tissue. "Jesse, why must you pull these things out of a hat that way?"

I didn't remind her that I'd learned to do that long ago; that if I didn't say something right out when I had the chance, she'd be gone, and it would never get said.

I stood and gave her a hug. "I just wanted you to know. I want you to be happy, I really do. I'm having a hard time dealing with the changes, that's all." Her powder smelled the way it used to when I was a little kid, kissing her good-bye when she went off to work nights. I had a confused reaction to that memory. Mom's tips may have paid the rent when Pop was drunk, but there were long periods when I'd hardly see her, between my school and her job.

"Look," I said. "I've got to admit defeat. In three days of really working at it, I haven't managed to turn up anything actually bad on Charlie. Grady hasn't done any better. So if it's what you want, I'll drop the whole thing. I'll make it up to Charlie when he gets here, okay?"

She gave me a return squeeze. "Oh, thank you, Jesse. I so much want for you two to like each other."

Charlie was due to pick us up in an hour, for Everett Iverson's party. I remembered that my original thought had been to sway Mom away from Charlie and toward Iverson, who had shown an obvious interest.

Oh, well. There's another thing they say about home: Home is where you go and, no matter what you've done, they have to take you in. I'd taken Mom in, and now, despite any remaining qualms, I figured that in the absence of genuine damning evidence against Charlie Browne, I might as well be a good sport.

Charlie arrived in a god-awful powder-blue stretch limousine that put Marcus Andrelli's ordinary black one to shame. The uniformed driver played his part to the hilt, jumping out and holding the door and then standing there at attention while Charlie fetched Mom and me. Dressed in a black tux, he escorted us gallantly down the stairs, out onto the front porch, down the walk, and to the limo. There, the driver snapped to and bowed smartly, holding the door while we passed through into Paradise—if Paradise is cold champagne and Perrier in crystal, fresh orchids in a silver vase, and a smooth, silent ride all the way to Pittsford.

Mom was appropriately impressed. As for me, it was bad enough having Toni and her mom, Mr. Garson and Mrs. Donatello, and even Old Lady Pickens staring through their front windows as we ventured forth. Once out of the neighborhood and rolling past Genesee Street, it was worse. I hunkered down in my seat, praying that none of my many street friends could see me through the opaque glass—see how far I'd come down in the world.

"You look great tonight, Jesse," Charlie said. He'd already complimented Mom on her pale blue silk; now he was being charming with me.

I smoothed my short black dress, wondering what was wrong with it, the way I always do when people give me compliments. "So do you," I said, charming him back with an admiring glance that took in his elegant attire, crisp silver hair, and vivid blue eyes. Mom smiled happily.

Charlie put a tape on—the forties music I'd grown up hearing Mom sing around the house in the sixties, those few times when things were good. Pretty soon she was humming along to "Smoke Gets in Your Eyes," and Charlie was too. I gathered this was something they did often. By the time we reached the outskirts of Pittsford they had broken out in full song, and even I had pitched in on a chorus of *"That Old* (finger-snappin') *Black Magic."*

I was only mildly relieved, and embarrassed, when the limo pulled to a silky stop at Iverson's front door.

The estate was on several acres. The lawns were manicured and vast, with graceful lampposts lining the drive. The house looked as if it had been transported, stone by stone, from the French countryside. Dusk was upon us, and light spilled onto the velvety lawn through several rows of French doors. Classical music spilled along with it. I tried to imagine myself as a kid, doing cartwheels down that wide green lawn, getting grass strains on my best Sunday dress as it tumbled over and over my head. But all I could remember was running through open fire hydrants on Genesee Street, trying to keep cool in the summer's oppressive heat.

Which is not to say that I stick my nose up at this kind of

luxury today. Give me a few drinks (please) and I might even now do cartwheels on Iverson's lawn, park my shoes under his bed, and generally prostitute myself for a taste of this kind of honey. Why my mom couldn't be just as happy with somebody like Iverson as with Charlie Browne—

I quit my ruminations as Iverson met us at the door. He had left his guests; I could hear the tinkle of glasses and soft laughter from a room adjacent to the flagstone entryway. A butler took our wraps.

"What a wonderful house!" Mom exclaimed as Iverson kissed her hand. "Charlie and I saw one similar, but not nearly so exquisite, in the Alsace this summer."

"This has been in my family since the early 1900s." Iverson smiled proudly. "I've added on a gallery upstairs, and a wing to the south for guests." He ushered us into a large but cozy living room with yellow silk drapes, the heady scent of greenhouse roses, and perfume from elegantly dressed women who were accompanied by men in just as elegant evening dress. I thought that if there was ever a home I wished I'd grown up in, this was it. Like an old movie with Greer Garson and Walter Pidgeon . . . although they were English, weren't they, so I guess the architecture doesn't quite fit.

Introductions were made, champagne and other beverages passed, and Charlie and Mom went off to mingle. Mom blended into this crowd like good chiaroscuro. (I'd spent some time brushing up on my knowledge of art on the plane.) Being with Charlie had given her self-confidence, I'll say that. No one in this crowd would have guessed my mom had been a waitress in greasy cafes half her life, or married twenty-odd years to a man who drank up the rent money so often that I kept forgetting where we lived. I'd start home from school, then remember that the house ahead was last month's house: Oh, yeah, we'd been evicted, and now we lived somewhere down the street.

But I'd acquired a certain amount of polish, too, what with being a reporter and hanging out with the upscale likes of Marcus Andrelli. I'd been to plenty of yuppie parties in the eighties, and although I couldn't generally be bothered using the conversational skills I'd developed at them, they were up there in the gray cells, lurking. As I mingled, murmuring blasé responses like "indeed," "ah well," "too bad," I found myself rubbing elbows and short black dresses with the Pittsford Country Club crowd.

". . . You're absolutely right. The cost of real estate . . . why, just look at Corn Hollow. Anyone who bought land along the Genesee River twenty years ago is in hog heaven, darling, today."

". . . And Pittsford, good lord . . . a two-bedroom condo now is twice the price this entire estate would have gone for in the sixties . . ."

I mingled in another direction.

". . . market shares doubled, as you know . . . the thrust is perpendicular financing . . . money funds . . ."

". . . did you see that Monet . . . in her *bedroom*, no less? She thinks it's one of his best, but personally, I prefer his earlier work . . ."

I was bored, and longed for Marcus beside me, who never talked business on a date but listened, taking all the information in, while still managing to be attentive. Mom was talking animatedly with a distinguished-looking woman with short, perfectly waved gray hair, and Charlie was engaged in deep discussion with an eclectic-looking man of approximately his own age, who sported an orange ascot with purple polka dots. An actual artist in the midst of all these potential patrons?

I gave the living room a better once-over and realized that it was fashioned like a breezeway. Longer than it was wide, it had a fireplace at one end and rows of French doors down either side. The back row opened onto a terrace, and I wandered out there, looking for air.

The moon was on the wane, but the night was clear, the stars bright. Something hooted, an owl, I supposed, although I've never known much about birds. I had a cageful of finches foisted upon me once by a boyfriend who turned tail and left them behind. I gave away the finches, but never did have the heart to get rid of Pav's dog. His name was Gypsy, but I renamed him Bastard, and he's been with me ever since.

I cannot stand that dog. He is a miserable, rotten mutt, and why the neighbors even bother to take pity on him—carting him off on camping trips or to visit relatives—I don't know.

Movement at the far end of the lawn caught my eye. There

was a complex of buildings there in the same design as the main house. I took them to be garages, or stables . . . possibly an old converted carriage house. I squinted, trying to catch what it was that had moved, but decided finally that it must have been a dog or other animal. What kind of dog would Iverson have? A collie, perhaps. Or a big red Irish setter. Something masculine, appropriate for a country squire.

Unlike Bastard, who's part terrier and part city rat.

Samved tries to tell me I just don't want to get close to a dog since my puppy was killed when I was five. I keep telling him I actually throw balls into the street for Bastard to chase when the traffic's at its heaviest. He doesn't believe me.

I ask you, what good is a shrink if he doesn't believe you when you tell him the God's honest truth?

I had been sitting there on the terrace wall for possibly ten minutes when Iverson broke my reverie. He stood beside me with a glass of champagne, which I didn't accept, but thanked him for anyway. "It's a lovely night, isn't it?" he said, setting the glass on the terrace wall. His tiny mustache glistened, as did his steel-gray hair. He was a trim man, in all ways. Nattily attired and groomed. Straight to the point in his conversation. Maybe a little like David Niven.

"I often think how silent it is here at night," he said. "I enjoy it, after the hustle and bustle of the day. And yet, what if it were this way all the time? Silent, as it is every moment for the deaf."

That was the second time he'd mentioned the deaf. "I'm curious," I said. "How did you become involved in sponsoring hearing-impaired artists?"

He answered with some hesitation. "My younger brother . . . Robert . . . lost his hearing at a young age. No possibility of improvement. Our parents were devastated, but I always believed that if you have something special, some skill or talent—as my brother Robert did, with his painting—what may at first be seen as a handicap can be turned into a blessing. Robert learned to listen through his fingers. A great talent came through them, appearing on his canvases as if by magic, and almost overnight."

"I don't think I've heard of your brother," I said apologetically. "Is he famous?"

"No . . . I'm afraid he died. At a very young age."
"I'm sorry."
Iverson sighed. "It's been many years, my dear. And as
I'm sure you know, the Switzer Gallery has been featuring
the work of hearing-impaired students for quite some time.
They were the forerunners. I simply decided, a few years
back, to work with them in setting up grants for talented
students—in my brother's name. It seemed appropriate.
Would you like to see Robert's paintings? They're in the gallery
upstairs."
"I'd love to."
We went back through the living room, and I noted that
Mom was talking now to a short, kind of nerdy-looking man
with glasses. Charlie was nowhere in sight, but other lighted
rooms opened off the living room, and the crowd seemed to
be dispersing into them.
Iverson led me up a winding stair with a gleaming mahogany
bannister. The wall, all the way up, was lined with landscapes
"Durbars," Iverson told me proudly, "I have all but one." Recessed track lighting cast a gentle glow, perfectly illuminating the
works of art without glaring on the stairs themselves. We walked
along a pale yellow-carpeted hall, then through a door. Iverson
closed the door behind us, shutting out the noise from below.
We were in a gallery approximately 100 feet long. His brother's paintings covered both sides of the gallery. Strangely (I
thought, although I know little about these things, as I've said),
they were all of one size, and all in simple, modern, white
frames. I had never seen anything like them. I loved them on
sight. There were rainbows and crystal palaces, snow maidens,
turrets and gleaming rivers of silver—fantasy worlds, like children's books, but without the wolves, witches, and gnomes. I
remembered an antique book I once had as a child—Aunt
Edna had given it to me for Christmas, saying I needed a little
fantasy in my life. The book had castles and spires in the clouds
like this, but only when you lifted up the orange cellophane
on each page could you see them. It was magic to me then,
the way Robert Iverson's paintings were magic to me now.
I walked slowly from painting to painting, while Iverson
stood back patiently, giving me time. When I reached the last

one, having come full circle, he said softly, "Amazing, aren't they?"

I nodded, thinking how sad it was that his brother hadn't lived to do more.

Iverson nodded, seeming to read my thoughts. "Well." He said it with a slight, sad smile. "Perhaps we should go back down now."

"Yes." I took another glance around the gallery, caught up in something beyond logical thought.

So I wasn't fully conscious of what I was doing when my hand reached to open the door. I was ahead of Iverson, but still looking back, and it was an automatic reach behind me . . . a gesture like stepping into Wonderland. The hole is there, and you just fall right into it.

Iverson said loudly, "No, my dear, that room isn't—"

But I had already turned the knob—of the wrong door, a door next to the one into the corridor—and stepped across its threshold. A light clicked on automatically when the door opened. I turned, looked, and gasped.

Only one painting hung in this smaller room—an almost life-size portrait, its colors so vivid they seemed to reach out and grab me, yet at the same time draw me toward them gently. I don't know how to put these things in "art-ese." The painting simply had a life, a moving energy. I wanted to touch it. To sit and look at it for hours. There were no words to use, and I stood there mutely staring.

The subject was a woman. But diaphanous, like a cloud. Ephemeral. She was there one moment, and the next she was gone. Trick lighting? I wondered. But it seemed to be the same track lighting as on the stairs.

I walked closer, leaving Iverson behind.

"Who is she?" I said.

It was several seconds before he answered. "I don't know. Perhaps only someone in my brother's mind." A silence again. Then, "Incredible how he's captured her so completely. Almost frightening." He laughed uneasily.

"Yes."

I drew closer. And then I saw it. A chill ran through me. The name on the brass plate at the bottom of the frame. *Anna.*

I looked back up at the woman's face. It seemed that she had faded a little. I shivered again.

"Your brother named the subject *Anna*," I said hoarsely. "Do you know why?"

I felt Iverson beside me, and could smell his subtle cologne. "No . . . I've always assumed she was someone he'd read about, or possibly even known."

"You said your brother died at an early age?"

"Yes."

"When? When did he die?"

"In 1950," Iverson said.

The same year Anna Biernej-Browne was murdered. "*How?*"

"He . . . he committed suicide. Sometimes I think . . ." He glanced around fretfully. "I don't really like to come to this room."

Before I could ask more, we were interrupted by the sound of pounding feet. "Mr. Iverson!"

It was the butler who'd taken our wraps at the front door. "Mr. Iverson, come quickly. Something terrible has happened."

Iverson ushered me from the small private gallery and pulled the door closed. "What is it?"

"One of the guests . . . I think he's been murdered, sir."

I don't know why the butler's words sent me racing out of there. He didn't say *who* had been murdered. But I took the stairs two at a time, looking about the living room frantically, only to find that Mom was nowhere in sight. Nor was anyone else. Everyone, the butler said as he followed, had gone down to the "car barn." I ran along with Iverson and him to the buildings I'd seen at the end of the lawn. Several classic cars stood in what used to be stalls. The party guests had crowded around a scene at the far end. I raced down there, pushing through.

Next to a silver Lamborghini was the man with the orange polka dot ascot. His head had been bashed in with something heavy; one side was a mass of blood, bone, and tissue. Beside him was Charlie, sprawled facedown on the cement floor. Mom was weeping and kneeling close to him, touching his hair. I knelt next to her and felt his neck for a pulse. It was erratic, but definitely there.

"He's okay, he's not dead," I reassured her.

"Stand back." I looked up to see two uniformed police officers. One had jittery young eyes, like a rookie who'd never seen a murder before. The other spoke again, taking my arm. "Stand back. Don't touch anything."

I pulled Mom to her feet. "Do as he says," I whispered. "And for God's sake, don't say anything. Not until we find out what's happened."

The cop examined Charlie, and then the guy with the orange ascot. I heard him murmur to his young partner, "This one's dead. The other one's still breathing. Call for backup, and make sure nobody leaves."

I wondered how they had arrived on the scene so quickly. But then, it was Pittsford. They'd have an efficient police department here, I supposed.

"Anybody know this guy?" the older cop asked, indicating Charlie. He looked at Mom, who was crying quietly. She nodded.

"You come with him?"

She wiped at her eyes. "He's my fiancé," she said.

"Anybody know the victim?" He was pointing to the orange ascot.

Iverson answered. "He's . . . he was my assistant," he said.

The cop—who was thin, lined, and looked weary, like a veteran of a city force who had semiretired here—said, "All right. Let's clear this end of the place out, then. All you people"—he indicated the crowd of stunned onlookers—"wait down there, by the door. Mr. Iverson, have the butler, there, check to see if everybody's here who was at the house. I don't want anyone to leave."

Iverson nodded and issued quiet instructions to the butler, who went off to take a head count. Iverson put an arm around my mom. "Katherine, my dear, I am so sorry. I'm sure Charlie will be all right."

The cop was examining Charlie more closely, and he nodded agreement. Mom buried her head in Iverson's shoulder. "I couldn't bear it," she said, "if anything happened to him."

"Shhh . . . I'm sure he'll be fine."

A siren could be heard in the distance.

"There, you see? Help will be here soon."

Charlie stirred. "Kate? Kate, where are you?"

"I'm here, darling, I'm here!"

Mom knelt beside him once more, hugging him as best she could. Charlie struggled to a sitting position, shaking his head and wincing.

"Oh, thank God, you're all right," Mom said.

The cop moved in. "*Are* you all right?"

Charlie nodded. He got to his feet, swaying and rubbing the back of his head.

The cop took out a pencil and pad. "What happened here?"

"I . . . I don't know. I was struck from behind."

"What were you doing here?"

"Just . . . looking at the cars," Charlie answered. "I have an interest in antique cars."

"You know the victim?"

"Burton? No . . . I never saw him before."

The cop stopped writing. His tired eyes narrowed. "That's his name, Burton?"

Charlie looked confused. He seemed to realize then that he hadn't yet glanced around, hadn't actually seen that the man in the orange ascot was dead.

"The victim," the cop repeated. "How did you know his name?"

"I . . . I talked with him, up at the house."

"Uh-huh. But you knew, did you, that he was dead, before you came to just now?"

"Yes. I saw him lying there, just before I was struck."

"And you knew, just from seeing him there, that he was dead?"

"No . . . I don't know."

"You had business with this man? You came down here to talk to him?"

Charlie shook his head. Winced again. "I don't think I want to answer any more questions," he said.

Another officer, a new arrival, came to stand beside the first. He was younger, yet was deferred to, and seemed in command. He looked at Charlie, said, "Identification, please," checked the I.D. Charlie pulled from his wallet, then nodded briskly.

"Come with me," he said. He reached for Charlie's arm.

"Wait! No, you can't do this!" Mom cried. "He hasn't done anything!"

The man in command stared at Mom.

"That remains to be seen," he said.

We watched Charlie leave without protest, a cop on either side. Mom looked after him, aghast. Everett Iverson put an arm around my shoulders, and then around Mom's. "Don't worry about a thing," he said. "I'm here."

CHAPTER 12

The police wouldn't let us go. They herded all of us—I counted fourteen guests, plus Iverson and the butler—into one end of the car barn for questioning. Other cops had arrived on the scene and had been dispatched to the house to look for strays.

Charlie was up at the main house now. The paramedics, Iverson learned, had checked him out and declared him fit for questioning. Charlie's state when he was found, including the lump on his head, should have indicated innocence. But there were too many questions Charlie couldn't, or wouldn't, answer. And the police were maintaining that the injury was small enough for him to have done it himself by knocking up against a wooden post and then faking unconsciousness.

It seemed a stretch. But Charlie was the only one found at the murder scene—and the handiest one to blame. In Pittsford these matters are apparently dispatched quickly, giving the residents little time to have their sleep disturbed by thoughts of madmen on the loose.

I opened the door of a creamy antique Rolls and sat Mom down on the brown leather seat to rest. She was dazed, and complaining that she wanted to be with Charlie. She didn't want him to "go through this alone." Iverson was being questioned by the new cop on the scene.

"The dead man was my assistant," Iverson explained. "Rather a secretive fellow . . . I hired him a few weeks ago to catalog paintings that had just come in from France."

"Do you know why he'd be meeting with this . . ."—the cop checked his notes— ". . . this Charlie Browne?"

"I've no idea. But I'm sure Browne had nothing to do with this tragedy. Surely he came upon it and was struck down to give the villain time to escape."

"The victim," the cop said. "Any family? Relatives? Where did he work before you?"

"He had an excellent resume," Iverson said. "Experience on the West Coast principally, but his references checked out. About his personal life, I know nothing. As I've said, Burton was with me only a few weeks. He never talked about family or friends."

"The two of you worked together, cataloging these paintings?"

"Actually, I was out of town a good deal of the time. Burton worked alone."

"Here, on the grounds?"

"Yes."

"You trusted him to be here while you were gone?"

"I never had any reason not to."

"How many people are there on your household staff?"

"Ordinarily, just Stewart, the butler, one maid, and a cook. The maid and cook come in days. Stewart lives in. Tonight, of course, there are caterers and serving people."

The cop turned to another, who had just come up and was listening. "We'll question the staff next," he said. "See if anybody noticed Browne with the victim before this."

The second cop nodded. "I think we can let the rest of these people go home. Everyone's I.D. has been checked, and they've all agreed to come in for questioning in the morning."

The first one addressed Iverson. "I'd like to go up to the house now. Talk to the caterers, the rest of the staff."

"Certainly." Iverson turned to Mom, who was still in the Rolls, listening intently. "Katherine, my dear . . . come with me. We'll see how poor Charlie is doing."

Mom nodded. Iverson took her hand, and they walked together to the house. I walked behind them, thinking Mom looked smaller than usual, and much too tired.

Charlie wasn't doing so hot. We arrived at the house just in time to see him being packed into a police car, his wrists cuffed. He turned to Mom and flashed her a strained, apologetic look. She made a sound like a whimper, a fist going to her mouth.

Iverson took aside the cop who was with us and whispered something. The cop shook his head at first, but then he nodded and said wearily, "Okay. But make sure all three of you are at the station when I get there. I've still got questions for those women."

Iverson agreed, and spoke to Mom and me. "We can follow Charlie to the station. We simply have to remain there for questioning."

The cop disappeared through the front door with Stewart. Iverson led us to a late-model black Lincoln off by itself at the side of the drive. He helped Mom in, while I took the backseat. Iverson drove.

"Don't worry, Katherine," he said. "We'll sort it all out."

Mom murmured something, then was silent for the fifteen minutes or so it took to arrive at the police station. I sat quietly, thinking about things.

At the station, we were shown to a nondescript room, where we waited for Charlie to be booked. He was being held in another area, pending the arrival of an attorney: someone he himself had called, we learned. I couldn't help thinking that it was handy, having an attorney available, just like that, in a strange town.

Mom sat across a long table from me, her face pale. Her silky blue dress was crushed. There were black marks, like grease stains, on one sleeve. Iverson went out to find coffee, and came back with three foam cups filled with a black, sludgy brew. Mom shook her head, so I drank mine, then hers, straight down.

We waited. A clock ticked, driving me nuts. 11:45. I ran a fingernail along scars in the wooden tabletop. I wished I had jeans on instead of the black dress. Nikes instead of stockings and heels. I felt incompetent this way.

Mom covered her face with her hands, and sat there with her head bowed.

I couldn't stand it any longer.

I went out into the corridor and found a pay phone. Dug into my purse for a quarter. Dialed Grady North at home.

"Do you have any idea what time it is?" he growled, once he was awake enough to know it was me.

"Time to call in old debts," I snarled back.

"Huh?"

"You remember how I helped you nail Paulie Gandolo a few months ago? How I risked my very life, in fact, to do so?"

"I remember how you were trying to clear your pal Andrelli," he countered sourly. "I don't remember it starting out as any favor to me."

"Nevertheless."

He sighed. "Why don't you just tell me what you want, so I can say no and get back to sleep?"

"Mom's friend, Charlie Browne. He's being questioned by the Pittsford police. Regarding a homicide. I want you to haul ass and get over here and help us out. And Grady . . ."

"It's almost midnight," he complained.

". . . if you don't do this for me, I'm going to tell every damn paper in the state how you twisted evidence in that case to get yourself promoted."

"You know damn well that's not why—"

I hung up.

Grady was livid. He stomped around the little room I'd found to talk with him in alone. He'd pulled a green T-shirt over jeans, and it was half stuck in, half out. His eyes were bleary, and his sandy hair stuck up in tufts. A beard was showing on his chin.

"The least you could do, if you're going to be in trouble all the time, is remain in my jurisdiction!"

"We were at a party, dammit!"

"I don't care. How can I help you, if you're halfway to hell in Pittsford?"

"Well, maybe you can't. I just thought—"

"That's just it. You always come looking for me when it's too damned late—"

"All *right!*"

Shit. Charlie was in jail, Mom was weeping copious tears once more, and Grady was playing Father Knows Best.

"Just because my mom is alone and defenseless here," I said more quietly, "just because she doesn't know anybody here anymore, unlike *your* mom and dad, who have all those bridge-club friends and neighbors, that doesn't mean—"

"Oh, put a sock in it!" Grady ran a hand through his hair.

"I'll help her, okay? I'll even help Charlie. But I'd just as soon *you* were out of my life, once and for all."

"Oh." I tried not to feel hurt, but the truth is, I did. "Well, if you feel that way . . . I guess I could go away somewhere."

"Try North Dakota. Or Guam. Anyplace, so long as it's out of yelling distance."

"*Okay.*"

Crimin*ee.*

I stomped out of the office, wanting to kill somebody. *Charlie.* I am going to kill Charlie, I thought—while the calculating half of my brain said: Why not? Might as well strike while he's down.

Charlie was down, and so was his handsome face. It was long enough and morose enough to scrape the floor.

"Charlie, you've got to level with me," I said.

"I already have. I wouldn't hurt your mother for anything in the world."

"Right. That's why she's been out there in the waiting room three hours, crying."

He winced. And okay, it was a low blow. I knew he couldn't do anything for Mom. His lawyer hadn't yet arrived to get him out.

"God, I'm sorry about Kate," he said. "Look, Jesse, I'm stuck here. You've got to talk to someone for me."

"Sure, I'm dying to do you favors."

"He's a friend. Carlisle is his name. Avery Carlisle. He's in San Francisco—"

"I've already talked to him," I said with some satisfaction. "He agrees you're a con."

"No!" Charlie blanched. "No, he can't think that—Jesse, help me, *please.*"

"I'll help you on one condition," I said.

"Anything."

"Once this is over . . . once your name is cleared, if it ever is, and you're free . . . you'll go away and leave my mother alone. You won't ever see her again."

"I can't do that."

"See you sometime," I said. I pressed my palms against the table and stood up to leave.

"No, wait—"

I waited.

Charlie ran a hand through his crinkly silver hair. "You don't leave me much choice."

"That's right."

"Okay," Charlie said. "Okay." He smiled engagingly. "God, you drive a hard bargain."

I didn't respond.

He studied me a moment, then sighed. "Sit down," he said shortly. "I'll tell you everything I know."

Everett Iverson's assistant—Arnold Burton—had approached Charlie at the party, and told him he had information about the provenance of the *Hare.* The assistant said he had learned through Iverson about Charlie's search. He seemed nervous about being seen with Charlie. The two had arranged to meet in the car barn.

"When I got there, he was already dead. I was bending over him, searching for a pulse, when somebody knocked me out. When I woke up, you and your mother and the cop and Iverson were there. That's all I know, Jesse, I swear it." He frowned. "But I'd sure like to know where Everett Iverson was at the time."

"Iverson? Forget it. He was with me."

"Oh?"

"We were upstairs in the house, in a private gallery. Looking at a painting, as a matter of fact . . . of a woman named Anna."

Charlie stared. "What did she look like?"

"Dark-haired . . . beautiful, but ephemeral, as if the artist couldn't quite catch her spirit." I shrugged. "I don't know. It was one of those vague kinds of paintings, not abstract, but—"

"Impressionist?"

"I guess."

He rubbed a hand over his face. "This is crazy."

"Do you know something about Iverson? Did he know your mother, and is that why you came here?"

"No. He was recommended as an authority, that's all. I really have just been trying to find the former owners of the *Hare.*"

"The woman in the painting may not be your mother." I didn't tell him that the woman had vivid blue eyes, just like his.

"Who was the artist?" he said.

"Iverson's brother. His name was Robert. He's dead."

Charlie shook his head. The name clearly meant nothing to him.

"Jesse, look. I don't know what the hell's going on. But I need you to go to my hotel room. I'll have my lawyer get a key to you. In my suitcase there—the small black canvas one, it looks like an oversized briefcase—you'll find a sketch of a man. I need you to find that man."

"Who is he?"

"I don't know. But he's the answer to all this. He killed my mother . . . and I've been looking for him all my life."

"If you've been looking for him all your life," I said with irritation, "what makes you think I'll have any better luck?"

"Because something is happening now—I've struck a chord in someone, someone who didn't want Iverson's assistant talking to me. I knew it would happen one day, if I just made enough contacts, went to enough auctions, shows, and parties, talked about it—" He closed his eyes and rubbed his face. "Christ, I am sick of this."

"The person in the sketch. What makes you so sure he killed your mother?"

"The sketch was beneath her hand when I found her—half-finished, and scrawled, as if she'd done it as she was dying. A piece of charcoal was clutched in her fist. It was a message, like the drawings she used to put in my lunch box for school rather than just tell me things. She did it all the time."

I had a vivid image of the little boy, opening his lunch box in the school cafeteria and finding . . . what? A sketch of a kid with a happy face, picking up his room? Finishing all his sandwich? It was an image I found appealing—Anna Biernej-Browne, the renowned artist, finding time in her busy, creative day to communicate with her son.

Charlie was remembering, too. There was moisture in his eyes.

"How did she die?" I said.

"A head injury. The police . . . they never did say, exactly, how it happened. My uncle wouldn't talk about it, and I never asked before he died—"

"But you've tried to find out, as an adult."

"There are no records of the investigation. That's the hell of it. Only the findings: death by person or persons unknown. Jesse, will you help me with this? You know your way around—"

"I'm a reporter, not a cop. What you need is to tell the police about this, let them look into it."

"I can't do that—" He fell silent a moment. I could see the wheels turning. "Jesse, you'd do it right—you'd care, if only because clearing me would be helping your mother. And you'd have a fresh eye. Sometimes I think I'm too close, that there's something staring me in the face that I'm not seeing."

I got up and walked around the bare, depressing room . . . brown metal chairs, brown table . . . even brown lights, from all the cigarette smoke coating the bulbs. None of it helped the feeling that I was about to be buried—under the cold, pitiless ground. What if I didn't help Charlie? Would my mother ever forgive me? What if I ended up freeing him? Would I ever forgive myself? Christ, what a dilemma.

"First, tell me about the *Hare*," I said.

He stared, then shrugged, turning up his palms. *Fair enough.*

"My mother painted it for me," Charlie said, "for my sixth birthday. She left it unsigned so it wouldn't be worth much if anything happened to her. That way, she hoped, the creditors wouldn't try to sell it." He gave a soft, indulgent laugh. "My mother spent money as fast as it came in . . . we were always in debt. But the night she was murdered, the painting was stolen. I never saw it again, never thought I would—until that day in Sausalito, that gallery window—"

"How could you be sure it was the same one? If you were only eight years old when you saw it last."

"My name—she had painted my name into the background. You would never see it if you didn't know it was there. But I watched her do it, it was a game—everything for Anna was a game. And I never forgot. Look at the painting tonight, when you go home. Look along the stem of the third rose from the right. It's there."

"Assuming that's true, why didn't you just tell the clerk it was yours? That it had been stolen years ago?"

"Do you know how long that could have tied the painting up legally? There would have been an investigation . . ."

And Charlie didn't want an investigation.

"Why didn't you just buy the painting?"

"I tried to. The clerk insisted on either cash or a local check. I was out of checks and had to go to a bank in the City. When I got back, the painting was gone from the window, and the clerk denied ever having seen it."

"So you returned that night, broke into the back room, and stole it. Just like that."

"It's my property," he said angrily, "and it was stolen from me. It is not illegal to reclaim stolen property."

"You could have used a credit card. Why even leave it behind that long, while you went to the bank?"

"I never use credit," Charlie said.

Right. People with no past don't qualify for VISA cards. And Mom, who was with him that day, hadn't had credit since Pop died.

"You said your mother wanted the painting to be safe from a creditor sale in case something happened to her. Did she expect something to happen?"

"I don't know. Sometimes I think she did. Just before she was killed, she was talking about moving us to Seattle to live with her brother. But I never could link that up with anything."

"Charlie, where do you get your money?"

He closed down. "That has nothing to do with this." His voice took on the edge I'd heard earlier, at the Armistead Gallery.

"It's got everything to do with my mom," I said crossly. "She trusts you, and you've got too damned many secrets."

"Jesse . . ." He sighed. "I've agreed to leave her alone if you clear me. What more do you want from me?"

It was just as valid a question as any of mine. The answer was: I didn't know.

CHAPTER 13

Charlie was taken back to his cell. Mom and I were questioned, then Iverson drove Mom back to my apartment. I had called Marcus from the police station, and even though it was close to two A.M. by then, he'd told me to come over afterward to talk. I took a cab from the Pittsford police station to his penthouse. A private, gold-plated elevator whisked me to the thirty-first floor of the Rochester Towers. Marcus met me at the door.

"I've been at the computer," he said, distracted, the way he usually is when he's been before the screen for hours. His black hair was rumpled; he wore a dark blue sweat suit, but it didn't look like he'd taken time to work out the way he usually does at night.

"Come take a look at this."

I followed him to the computer. Behind it, the sheer blue curtains that sometimes covered a wall of glass were open. (Marcus surrounds himself with blue. Once I asked why, and he couldn't say, except that it was calming.) The lights of Rochester twinkled below. Marcus's desk, another expanse of glass, was heaped high with newspapers and file folders, business magazines and software. It was a working desk, from which he ran an empire almost single-handedly. Not that Marcus couldn't afford help; he just didn't trust it. Alfred was one of the few exceptions. A bright, though surly, young law student, he headed up Marcus's small in-house staff. He'd been with him several months, and had more than proved his worth.

I still wanted to drop him over the Golden Gate Bridge. That, or the Genesee Gorge.

"This is a tough one." Marcus pointed to the computer screen. "Here, sit. I'll get us some coffee."

I took his chair before the terminal. A data base was on the screen. Several printouts lay beside my left arm. One, I saw, had hundreds of Brownes—and Browns—listed by various birth dates. Another had them by places of birth; still others by schools, insurance companies, banks.

"Don't bother with those." Marcus set a cup of hot coffee by my hand. "They're old news. Look at this."

I looked at the screen. He'd tapped into the goddamned CIA. "How did you *do* this!"

"You just have to have the right codes," he said modestly. "And of course, the right equipment."

Of course. A mobster computer hacker. He constantly astounded me.

"The problem is," Marcus said, "if Charlie is some kind of government agent, even the government doesn't know it."

"Did you really think he might be?" I'd considered the idea myself, but discarded it. I guess I preferred to think of Charlie as a crook.

"The man could be almost anything," he said. "Even with the latest information you gave me on Charlie from your trip to California, I can't turn up a past for him since 1969. He certainly hasn't paid taxes—not under the name Charlie Browne. He didn't go to school under the G.I. Bill, and he has no police record, if the fingerprints from his Army files are authentic."

He shook his head. "I've never seen anything like it. Except . . ."

"Except?"

"There was a guy who worked for me. I hired him specifically because he didn't have a background. He had been with a foreign government."

"You think Charlie—"

"I just thought I'd toss the possibility out there. See where it falls. I've got friends inside Interpol and our own State Department asking around for me. The thing with computers, you reach a point of diminishing returns. The only thing you can do then is hit the streets, so to speak. Which brings me to my next suggestion. How about hiring an investigator in California to do some legwork? No one is invisible. Charlie's got to have had neighbors, landlords, people who saw people coming and going—"

"According to Mom, he's lived in various hotels all his life."
I took a sip of coffee, then sighed. "I don't know, Marcus. I just don't know. I was about to tell you to drop the search, when all this happened. Damn." I rubbed my face wearily. "First question: Why was Iverson's assistant killed? The obvious answer is to keep him from telling Charlie anything about the *Hare*. But why? The only thing that makes sense is that the person who stole the painting the night Anna was killed is the same person who killed her . . . and that person shut Burton up to protect himself. Which would also mean that that person was at the party tonight. The hell of it is, I wasn't really paying much attention to the guests."

"What about Iverson himself?"

"Possible. I'm not sure. His brother Robert almost certainly knew Anna Biernej-Browne. There's a painting of her, done by him, in Iverson's private gallery."

"Well, then, we'll just have to find the connection between Robert Iverson and Anna."

"The problem is, Robert committed suicide in 1950—the same year that Anna was murdered."

"Quite a coincidence."

I agreed.

"I wonder how Charlie came to end up here in Rochester, on the very doorstep of a man whose brother knew Anna—if he did?"

"That could be circumstance," I said, playing devil's advocate. "The art world is small, kind of insular. Charlie said Iverson was recommended to help him with the provenance. Iverson is a world authority."

He leaned over me to the computer screen. "Let's look up the brother right now. Robert?"

I nodded. "An artist. He was probably born right here in Rochester."

Marcus performed his magic. In five minutes, he had everything I could ever want to know about Robert David Iverson.

"A suicide . . ." he said, as we both read the data from the screen. "September 9, 1950 . . . at the Iverson estate in Pittsford. He was nineteen years old. Before that, he attended schools in Rochester, then in San Francisco—CityWest Arts, 319 Geary Street. Now defunct." He read some more details,

nothing relative to Anna, and switched back to the main screen.
"Well, no doubt about it . . . your Robert Iverson would have
had the opportunity to know Anna Browne."

I slipped off my shoes and slung a foot up on the desk.
Leaned back in the chair and closed my eyes.

"You know what I wish? I wish I'd never heard of Charlie
Browne."

Charlie's lawyer—a wily man who looked like he might rep-
resent anything from senators to street scum—had given me
the key to Charlie's hotel room. It was after three A.M. when
I cabbed from Marcus's penthouse and arrived at the Sherwood
Arms. Fortunately, nobody cares about these things anymore
in the nicer places. If you've got enough money to be a guest,
you've got a right to be out as late as you want. If you aren't
a guest, there's a certain equanimity, anyway. *We all know
what traveling businessmen need and want*, is the unspoken
agreement these days.

The desk clerk watched me cross the lobby in my short black
dress and velvet coat. I swung my hips and smiled. He smiled
back.

Charlie's room was on the seventh floor. I took off my shoes
and padded down the hall on the balls of my feet, sneaking
up on the place the way that little Indian boy (Red Ryder?) in
the comics used to do. (Please don't ask why; I seldom have
an explanation for these things, they're just something I learned
on the streets as a kid.) I listened a moment before sliding the
key in the lock. Silence.

I opened the door and flicked on the lights, expecting to
find that the place had been tossed by cops, and possibly by
robbers. If the cops had been here, they'd been neat about it.
Nothing seemed out of place. I checked the closet for robbers.
Ever since I read Lawrence Block's *Burglar in the Closet*, I've
been nervous about things like that.

Nope, no robbers. I did find the black canvas suitcase Charlie
had described. I brought it out and set it on the bed. Inside,
beneath several clean white shirts, was Anna's charcoal sketch.

I picked it up and examined it in the light from a bedside
table. Half-finished, as Charlie had said. Rough. No hair, no
ears, just a face—slightly rounded—and strangely, a finger

pointing to one eye. I could see why Charlie, in all his years of searching, wasn't able to find this man. The sketch was too nondescript. There were no distinguishing characteristics, no moles, no scars, not even a crooked nose. Anna had apparently died before she could complete her last message to Charlie.

I rolled the sketch up carefully and stuck it under my coat, then waltzed downstairs and past the desk clerk again. I winked.

"That was fast," he said.

"And short," I replied.

I got back to my apartment at dawn, expecting to find Mom asleep. She was packing.

"I'm going to California," she declared in a *don't argue with me* tone. Her small, pointed chin went up. "I'm going back to where it all began, to the Timmons Gallery, to find out what's going on. I've got to clear Charlie."

She didn't know I'd already been to Sausalito and the gallery. She still thought I'd gone off to *Newsweek*, in New York.

"Sit down, Mom. I've got something to tell you," I said.

The plane trip was not great fun. Mom was silent and brooding. The flight attendants were mostly nonattendant. I couldn't even drink to wile the long seven hours away. When we circled San Francisco this time, I didn't feel that wonderful rush of adrenaline. After landing, I lugged my carry-on—which I hadn't even unpacked from my last trip—and Mom's three suitcases with her makeup and crap, outside to the Marin Airporter, which whisked us off at the less than alarming rate of 35 mph (commuter traffic) to Marvelous Marin.

Aunt Edna met us near the Howard Johnson's in Mill Valley, where the Airporter let us off, and I was never so glad to see anyone in my life. I tumbled into her arms like a kid who'd been adopted by an ax murderess and was meeting her birth mother for the first time in her life.

"Why didn't you come and see me when you were here before?" Aunt Edna demanded. Her hair is carrot red, a bristly mop, and a cigarette dangled from scarlet lips.

"Must you smoke that thing?" Mom complained. I hadn't seen her this grumpy in years.

Aunt Edna ignored her, hoisting up our bags and dumping them into the tiny trunk of her red Fiat convertible. I climbed into the backseat, which was no more than a bench with no leg room, and stretched out sideways. Mom sat up front.

(I wonder how many kids let their moms sit in front. Is it something we all do, in deference to the creaks of encroaching age? If so, I should have been up there, I thought, not her. Five years of hard drinking had left me with more creaks than a Kentucky hills rocking chair.)

Aunt Edna chattered on in her intense way, waving her cigarette for emphasis and oblivious to Mom's sullen mood. I was getting a little pissed at Mom. Aunt Edna is my favorite relative—mostly because she's just like me. Or the me I might be if I were more normal, and not me.

"I hope you're staying a while," she called back. The wind was roaring in my ears, so it sounded like "I hprrsstmmwyl," but I knew what she meant. I'd grown up riding around in the backseat of one or another of Aunt Edna's old convertibles, back home. The activity requires a language of its own, like that between twins.

We pulled up before her quaint little cottage off Throckmorton, in a canyon thick with trees. Aunt Edna loves her trees, and her herb garden, which makes up for the fact that the house isn't much. She swooped to a stop, barely missing her yellow-and-white cat. The cat yowled and ran off, and Aunt Edna laughed as if that were the funniest thing to happen all week. We all disembarked. Later, when Aunt Edna was in the kitchen brewing up herb tea, I said irritably to Mom, "You could at least try to be nice."

"Why?" she grouched, folding her arms. "I don't even like the woman."

"Mother!" I was almost speechless. "She's your sister!"

"So what?"

"So you've been living here with her for the past five years!"

"That's why I don't like her," Mom said.

Christ. "You should have stayed in Rochester, then, the way I asked you to."

"With Charlie in jail? I can be a lot more help to him here. Besides, I hate Rochester. Always have. We *should* have stayed in a hotel. Howard Johnson's would have been just fine."

But the truth, and she knew it, was that neither one of us could afford a hotel. I especially couldn't, since my last trip here. And anyway, Mom always got along with Aunt Edna all right, before—

Before Charlie.

And then I thought: *Men.*

They do it to you every time. You're going along, right as rain, everything just fine, and some man comes into your life. From then on, watch out. One day you're happy, the next sad. One day you're confident, the next your morale is completely trashed.

Men.

I went off to the kitchen to help Aunt Edna. She'd been sensible enough to live the past twenty years without a man, something my mother would never understand.

Dinner couldn't have been worse over at San Quentin. The food was okay, but I kept expecting Mom to bang on the table with her cup and demand to see the warden.

I'd never known she felt like a prisoner, living here.

That was what she'd said to me earlier in the bedroom. "I feel like a prisoner here. All that cigarette smoke—and she makes me participate in her stupid, crazy schemes— Honestly, Jesse, why do you think I was so desperate to meet a man?"

"I don't know," I said, bewildered. "Why were you?"

"I was hoping my Prince would come," she said acidly. "And save me."

The Cinderella Complex. Mom still had it? Good God.

I put an arm around her. "Look, Mom, if you don't like living here, we'll work something out. You don't have to marry Charlie."

"That's not the point, Jessica. I *love* Charlie, now that I know him." Her eyes began to tear, and her chin wobbled. "I just don't want to end up being a Prison Pen Pal."

I tried not to laugh. "Oh, Mom. It'll be all right. I'll help Charlie out of this, I promise."

"You don't even believe in him," she wailed. "You think he killed that man."

"No, I don't."

"You do, I know you do."

"Mom . . ." I sighed. And I asked myself: Did I think that Charlie had killed Iverson's assistant?

No. Not really.

But did I think he was a con?

I was certain of it.

How destructive that might be to Mom's future, I wasn't sure. Hell, maybe a little excitement with someone like Charlie was just what she needed. And who was I to talk, hanging out with the likes of Marcus Andrelli, not to mention (at odd times) a self-contained street gang like the Genesee Three?

God, I hadn't seen those kids in weeks. Abe, Rack, Percy . . . I wondered what kind of con *they* were running these days.

I missed them.

I wondered how I might put them to work helping Charlie.

I said, "Mom, it'll be all right. But you've got to trust me. After all, I may need your help—and you'll have to be at your best." (Appeal to her Mother Guilt, that's it. If Mom thought I needed her, she'd rise to the occasion.)

She managed a smile.

"There now, that's better." I felt like our roles had been reversed. "Look, after dinner, I've got to go to Sausalito and see some people. Do me a favor, will you? Try to get along with Aunt Edna while I'm gone?"

"I'll do my best," she agreed. "But Jesse, you know Edna. And I absolutely refuse to traipse all over San Rafael tonight, feeding the homeless."

I grinned. Aunt Edna hadn't changed a bit. "Just remember, Mom . . . if Aunt Edna hadn't taken you in when you ran away from home after Pop died, you might be homeless too."

I thought she'd smile, but she didn't. She let out another wail.

CHAPTER 14

We finished dinner early. I left Mom and Aunt Edna facing off in the kitchen like a couple of cats—Mom with her fur standing on end, daring her sister to say *one word, do one thing* irritating—while Aunt Edna dragged on a cigarette with studied nonchalance. I borrowed her Fiat and drove the ten minutes to Sausalito, happy to get the hell out of there.

There were several things I needed to accomplish on this trip. Almost all of them began with Ben Jericho. During dinner on his houseboat the other night (was it only four nights ago? It seemed like a year) I'd filled him in on Mom and Charlie, Anna's murder, the *Hare*, and what little I knew then about how Charlie had "found" it at the Timmons Gallery. I hoped that with all his many friends, not only on the San Francisco P.D., but locally, he'd be able to help me out. So far, I hadn't heard back from him.

Before Mom and I left Rochester, I had checked the *Hare*, pulling it out from under my bed. Sure enough, there was Charlie's name along the stem of the third yellow rose from the right. So it was his painting, and about that at least, he'd told me the truth.

I'd walked down after that to Genesee Street and found the Genesee Three. I chewed them out for not keeping a better eye on things.

"My mom was trounced on my stairs the other night. Where were you, anyway?"

There had been a couple of drive-bys in the neighborhood in recent months. Since then, the Genesee Three have set themselves up as a kind of informal neighborhood watch. Their self-appointed mission is to see to it that nobody (except, presumably, themselves) breaks any laws or robs any local citizens.

Ordinarily, they've got no problem with that: The Three are black, tough, and crooked. Beyond that, Abe's a smooth talker, Rack's a martial arts expert, and Percy thinks he's Burt Reynolds in *Deliverance*.

I told them that as far as I was concerned, lately, they weren't doing too hot.

Abe said he and Percy were down at Midtown Mall that night, running a pickpocket scam. Rack was supposed to be "minding the store"—walking the neighborhood beat—but he'd had to go home. A family emergency. His mom, who's on disability from working two jobs all her life while raising seven kids alone, had been ill.

I'm not entirely unreasonable. And the last thing I wanted, at this point, was to have the *Hare* stolen. I looked into their bright, shiny, larcenous, teenaged faces and gave them another chance at being friends.

They didn't look especially grateful. Abe rolled his eyes, Rack cracked his knuckles just to see me wince, and Percy said, "Huh."

So here I was in California, and I had all this shit to do out here, the only problem being, I thought, that Charlie had already followed all the obvious clues. Maybe Ben Jericho would be able to recommend a good P.I., somebody who knew his way around better than I.

First, however, the Timmons Gallery. Marcus was right; there were times when the personal touch was required. Just stirring up the waters might elicit some response.

The gallery was just closing, and the kid I'd met before wasn't around. An older man, short and slight and not nearly as amiable, was turning on lights in the window for overnight.

"What did you say your name was?"

"Jesse. Jessica James."

"And you say you have business with Mr . . . with the owner." He came back to his desk, and I noticed he wore a truly ugly pair of yellow shoes.

"Yes."

"Is he expecting to hear from you?" The man's expression said he doubted it.

"No, but I'm sure he won't mind."

"The thing is, Miss . . . the owner lives out of town. He

likes his privacy, and as his employee, I'm supposed to help protect it. Why don't you leave me your card—"

"Of course." I pulled out the one I use for free-lancing, crossed off my Rochester number and wrote in Aunt Edna's. "Have him call me here." As an afterthought, I wrote on the back of the card, *The Hare.*

The clerk nodded, fingering the card and giving me a close look through steel-gray eyes. He didn't smile or say any of the usual clerk-to-customer things, didn't go out of his way to be anything but unfriendly.

That was okay, I thought as I let myself out the door. He didn't like me. I didn't like his shoes.

I ran into Ben Jericho crossing the street, on the way back to Aunt Edna's car. He had a couple days' growth of beard, a deeper tan, and the smell of not-very-fresh fish on his jeans.

"What the hell are you doing here?" he said.

"I was just on my way to see you."

He stood smiling down at me. Cars were honking. We moved onto the sidewalk.

"I'm just in from a charter. I was on my way to the no name for a beer before I go home. Join me?"

"Sure."

Tom, the bartender, looked up and grinned when he saw us together. "I heard you were out here, Jess. Long time no see."

"Several months. You still remember how to make a Genesee Screw?"

"Oranges and beer? In my worst nightmares. Except that out here it's an Anchor Steam Screw."

"Baby's milk," I said.

Ben ordered beer for himself, and without asking, a Coke for me. Since it wasn't dark out yet, and still warm, we wandered through the narrow bar to the back patio, displacing a cat from a cushioned bench. Tom swears that cat's been at the no name since 1954. Kerouac used to hang out in the no name, too, they say, and a few other famous writer types in the fifties and sixties. Now it's mostly local boat people. On Friday and Saturday nights there's live jazz, which brings in a whole other crowd.

I was remembering how I'd met Ben on one of those Friday nights, and how we'd started talking during a break in the music. He'd told me a little about his past on the force in San Francisco. It had taken a few more accidental meetings and a few more drinks to really draw him out. It still wasn't easy for him to talk about Janet.

"I tried to call you in Rochester last night," he said now, "about that information you asked me to get. You always out in the middle of the night?"

"It's a long story. What'd you find out?"

"Not much of anything yet. The local cops don't seem to know who owns the place . . . some corporation in the East, they think. I was calling to tell you that. And to talk."

A "corporation in the East" was the same information I'd gotten from Marcus. According to his sources, the corporate names were just that—a list of names. He was trying, now, to find faces to go with them.

"Did you ask around at the San Francisco P.D.?"

"I did. Nothing. Jess . . ."

"Yeah?"

He toyed with his beer a minute, then took a deep swallow and put the bottle down. "I really think you should drop this thing. There's something screwy going on."

"Oh? Like what?"

"I'm not sure. But you know that name you gave me to check out? Charlie's mother—Biernej-Browne?"

"Yeah."

"Well, that stirred up something over in the City. Doors started closing in my face, people I've known for years stopped talking."

"What people?"

"An old watch commander, for one. Phil Kroeger. He was around in the fifties, a young cop just starting out then. Now he's a year from retirement, and when I mentioned that name he looked nervous as hell."

"Hmmm. I wonder why."

"And there's another guy—used to be a captain, now he's retired. He and I talk about old times a lot, over in Chico's Bar. I thought sure he'd be able to tell me more about what happened back then with the Biernej-Browne investigation?

Shit, he acted like I'd asked him to help me rob the Bank of Tokyo."

I remembered that there were no police records of the investigation into Anna's death. Just the finding: Death by person or persons unknown.

"You think there might have been a cover-up?"

"Well, it's always possible. And the City had a smaller force then. Things were looser, not so many watchdogs."

"You know, I think maybe I've been spinning my wheels with this Timmons Gallery angle. It might be better to focus on Anna Browne. Her murder—and how it fits in with what's happened to Charlie now."

"Has there been some new development?"

"Charlie's in jail." I told him about the murder on Iverson's estate. "I need to look into Charlie's past. And I'm hoping to find out more about Anna: who attended those salons she held, who she hung out with, dated, whatever. If Charlie's father died when Charlie was a baby, Anna must have had men in her life. And women friends. Someone still alive, who'd know or suspect what actually happened the night she was killed."

There was the sketch, too, from Charlie's suitcase. The man he believed had killed Anna. I wanted to see if anyone recognized it as someone from those days. Charlie had already shown it around, of course, years ago—but I'd learned in reporting that it never hurts to ask things again and again. Sometimes you could jolt a person's memory, come up with a question that opens a whole new avenue of thought.

I drained the last of my Coke. "I'm hoping you can recommend a good P.I., to help me with the legwork. Charlie said he'd come up with the cash to pay one."

Ben thought a minute. "The only one I know who's really good around here is Sam Crewe. She has an agency down there on Bridgeway"—he gestured with his head to the south—"but she's in L.A. on a case right now."

"There must be somebody else. Hell, San Francisco . . . half the fictional detectives in the world are out here."

"Oh, there's plenty in real life, too. Trouble is, most P.I.'s, even the good ones, don't put as much energy and time in a job as you would yourself. Or"—he grinned—"as I would if I was helping you."

"Meaning?"

He shrugged. "I don't have a charter for another week. It might be fun to muddle around in that sort of thing again."

"What about Melissa?"

"Well, she's with a baby-sitter anyway, when I'm out at sea. I could just extend things a bit. In the meantime . . ." He stood and relinquished his cushion again to the cat. "Missy's spending the night with a friend. How about coming back for coffee? We could sit on the deck and talk a while . . . or something."

It was tempting. More than that. The idea of spending an hour or two on the deck of Ben's houseboat, listening to some mean horn and watching the lights blink on across the Bay—not to mention the "or something"—made me downright crazy.

So of course I declined. I walked with Ben to the Fiat, gave him a ride back to Issaquah, rounded up the old mental wagons, and, fully protected by my insecurities, headed on over to Mill Valley.

Considering what I found at Aunt Edna's, I should have stopped along the way for a good stiff drink.

CHAPTER 15

When I got back to the cozy little cottage in the Mill Valley woods, Little Red Riding Hood and the Big Bad Wolf were going at it tooth and nail.

They were fighting over whether to plant Aunt Edna's new herbs at midnight or wait until morning.

"She's so *New Age*," Mom said scathingly. "And she tries to force me into these things, all the time." She and Aunt Edna were standing, hands on hips, at opposite ends of the kitchen table. I looked to see if any blood had been drawn, but the tablecloth seemed okay.

"Mom, you're the one who hooked me up with Samved in Pittsford. You can't get any more New Age than that old fraud."

"Why, Samved's not a fraud! He's nationally known, an Enlightened One, a renowned therapist—"

I snorted. "He watches *Jeopardy*," I said.

"Hah!" Aunt Edna snorted too. "I told you, Kate, that man was a screwball."

"He's helped Jesse!" Mom said.

"He's helped me out of $3,000 over the last year."

"Well, you aren't drinking, are you?"

"I'd give my soul for a drink right now."

Aunt Edna cleared her throat. "As I was telling your mother, basil is best when it's planted in the light of the new moon. Most things are."

"Okay. So what's the big deal?"

"The big deal is that your mother refuses to help. She prefers to sit here and mope all night about Charlie—"

"I am not moping," Mom said.

"—and I'm only trying to help by giving her something constructive to do."

It sounded like a fine idea to me, and I said so.

95

"I think it's a fine idea."

Talk about the evil eye. If looks could kill—"You always stick up for her, Jessica!" Mom said.

"I do not."

"You most certainly do, you always have. You *always* liked Edna better than me!"

"Mom, you're my *mother*. I *love* you."

"That's not the same. It was Edna you liked, always going off with her, riding around in those unsafe little old cars of hers—"

"Oh, give it a rest," Aunt Edna said. She blew smoke rings at the ceiling. "You were working. The kid was lonely, that's all."

"Mom," I said reasonably, "you know that's true."

But I wondered how many times I'd rubbed it in afterward. *Aunt Edna took me out today*, I'd brag when Mom got home from work each night. I'd wait until she had her feet in that old galvanized tub of Epsom salts, and then I'd let her have it. Mom would flash those green eyes at me the best she could, tired as she was, and I'd know with satisfaction that I'd struck home.

Any attention, they say, even anger, is better than none.

"Well, you're getting even with me now," I said.

"And just what is that supposed to mean?"

"With Toni, of course."

"Toni?" Mom sounded completely bewildered. For some reason, that really ticked me off.

"Don't pretend you don't know what I mean—the two of you all cozy and cute together. You never had that kind of time to spend with *me*."

Aunt Edna continued to blow smoke rings.

"You are the most irritating child sometimes!" Mom said.

I wasn't sure which one of us she was speaking to, but decided to proceed as if it were me. "I am not a child. I am a thirty-one-year-old woman who had a drunk for a father, an absentee for a mother, and now that mother has shown up in my life and dumped her problems all over me, and I am trying my best to solve them and will *do* so, if she will only get out of my hair and leave me alone." My voice rose in direct proportion to the length of my pronouncement.

"Jesse!" That from Aunt Edna. "Apologize! You shouldn't talk to your mother that way!"

Aunt Edna came around the table and put her arms around Mom, who was sniffling. "Sharper than a serpent's tooth, a thankless child!"

I jammed my chin out and glared. "And why do you two always do this to me?"

Christ Almighty! *Sisters*. They would always have each other, no matter what. And now—as usual—I was the odd man out.

I grabbed up the car keys from where I'd dropped them on the kitchen table. "You two are driving me crazy. Mother, I apologize. Aunt Edna, I apologize." I stomped out the back door and into the herb garden and bellowed at the new moon. "Moon, I apologize!"

Then I climbed into Aunt Edna's Fiat and drove away. "Don't expect me before morning!" I yelled back into the wind.

I was still steaming as I pulled up to Issaquah Landing ten minutes later. Seven minutes later. It takes ten to reach Sausalito when I'm not mad.

Several houseboats were dark, but light spilled through the stained-glass windows at Ben's. I could hear the World Series on TV, and as I stepped onto the deck I could see him through the glass upper half of the Dutch door. He had a maroon sail spread out all over the floor, and was working on it—mending it, I guess—and keeping an eye on the game at the same time. Logs blazed in the cone-shaped fireplace.

I knocked. He looked up, saw me, smiled, and came to open the door. Suddenly, I didn't feel lonely anymore.

CHAPTER 16

Sanctuary. Rosy light filtering from the dock through stained glass, onto a wide, soft bed. The houseboat gently rocking. Sweet music on KJAZ, a gift: The D.J. wasn't jamming it up tonight.

Ben's warm back against my hip.

I stretched, glanced at the clock radio—3:05 A.M.—and sighed contentedly.

I hadn't been unfaithful to Marcus in all of the year and a half I'd known him. Not that I'd thought about it that way—and not that faithfulness was something he'd ever asked of me. It just worked out that way.

I thought that I should feel as if I'd done something wrong. Instead, I felt all right. More than all right. I tried not to analyze that for a change.

The only hitch was Missy. She was staying overnight with a friend in another houseboat several doors down. She was coming home early, Ben said, to change clothes for a trip to Marine World. I promised myself I'd get up and leave before she arrived. I drifted off, and awoke with a start sometime later.

Footsteps, on the deck.

Missy? Already? God, no!

I heard the knob turn on the Dutch door, and wondered giddily whether to jump up, grab my clothes, and hide in the bathroom—or to huddle like Inspector Clouseau under the sheets.

But then I realized it was still dark out. Melissa wouldn't be coming home yet. I remembered stories Ben had told me about crime on the houseboats. More over at Gate 5 than here, but even so—

I shook him awake.

"What? What is it?"

"Shhhh. Somebody's out on the deck. At the front door."

It took him less than two seconds to come fully awake. He sprang from the bed, his bare feet slapping the floor. A hand reached inside a night table drawer and came out with a pistol that gleamed in the light from the dock. I began to crawl from the covers, but he put out a hand.

"Stay there," he said softly.

He was pulling on shorts. I slid from under the covers, padding quietly across the room for my clothes.

Ben stood at the bedroom door a moment, listening. Then he slid through it and was gone. I followed.

A loud *whuump* sounded from the living room. I ran down the hall and jerked to a stop in the doorway. A figure plowed through the dark. It rammed into me, hairy and sweaty, and knocked me half off my feet. I fell against the doorjamb. Pain shot through my shoulder. Something heavy flew across the room and thunked, then tinkled, like a million pieces of glass had exploded in the air. The figure grunted. It stumbled. Another mass barreled my way. A muffled crack sounded, like a fist connecting with tissue. It took me a moment to realize the tissue wasn't mine. The figures fell, and there was a scuffle on the floor, a thud, a groan. I fumbled along the wall, feeling for light switches, and found one, but only the kitchen light came on. I made out Ben, in his white shorts, locked in battle on the floor with someone fully dressed in jeans and a dark sweater. They rolled into the shadows at the far end of the living room.

A crack of bone, and a gun went off, shattering the night. For a moment, all movement stopped. Then it began again. I looked frantically around the small kitchen for a weapon at easy reach. There was nothing on the counter, no time to rummage in unfamiliar drawers. I ran to the cold fireplace, grabbed a large hunk of wood from the box, and swung into the writhing mess as the intruder's back came into view. He grunted and stumbled to his feet away from Ben—then swung at me, knocking me down. Ben grabbed him from behind, and I caught a glimpse of the guy's face. It was the blond kid, the clerk from the Timmons Gallery.

He slammed down with a heavy-booted foot on Ben's bare

one. Ben gave a grunt of pain, but didn't let go. The kid
rammed backward with an elbow, and Ben *whuffed* and fell,
but took the kid with him. The kid was no lightweight, but no
real match for Ben. They fought some more, with Ben on top,
then the kid, and then, just when Ben had him, the living
room lights came on.

"Daddy!"

It was Melissa, standing in the doorway, her face white and
shocked. I saw through the windows that lights blazed in houseboats on either side. A few assorted people, awakened no doubt
by the shot, stood on the dock in nightclothes. One of them,
a man, ran down the plank after Melissa, yelling, "Don't go
in there!" But he was far too late. She was already in.

Ben released his hold on the intruder. The kid rolled, heaved
himself to his feet, and ran past Melissa, knocking her out of
the way with a fist. He raced through the door, up the ramp
to the dock, through the people standing there, and went flying
with a loud splash into the Bay.

Melissa had fallen but was back on her feet. An ugly welt
rose on her face. Ben was enraged. After a quick check to see
whether she was all right, he went running after the kid. I
heard him dive in.

I ran to Melissa. The side of her face was red. She was pale
and shaking. "I don't suppose you'll be around to pick up any
pieces!" she yelled. Her eyes were thick with tears.

I stepped back just as my arms would have gone around her.
"What?"

"My dad just stopped having nightmares last year. Anything
happens to you, like with Mom, *I'm* the one who'll have to
live with all that again!"

I sank into a chair, my legs suddenly weak. "I didn't know,
I didn't think—"

She whirled toward the door, running after Ben. "You never
do, do you?" she cried.

CHAPTER 17

I couldn't do anything about Melissa, any more than I could do anything about the way I'd behaved with Mom. I was a selfish bitch, an unthinking jerk. As Pop had so often said while in his cups, "Jesse, girl, you can't do anything right." I sat at the breakfast bar, stared at the broken glass and toppled lamps on Ben's living room floor, and thought.

Ten minutes later, Ben came back, dripping bay water and shaking out his hair. There were cuts on his back and arms, and scratches on his face. "I lost him. Too damned many places to hide, with all that craft out there." Melissa was at his side, being protective even as he fussed over her, pulling ice from the freezer and making a pack with wet paper towels, holding it against the bruise on her face. "You okay, Jess?" He studied me a moment over her head, and I nodded.

"Better get into some clothes," I said. He was shivering.

I remembered Ben saying a few days ago: *Who needs violence?* I'd brought it back into his life. I'd walked into that perfect reality he'd created for himself and Missy, and blown it all to hell.

He worried over Melissa some more, and she worried back. I'd like to be able to say the kid was an overprotective, jealous little witch, but that wouldn't be giving her credit where it's due. She and Ben had lived through hell those first few years after Janet died.

Finally, he disappeared into the bedroom to change. Missy sat silently on the couch, rubbing her face with the ice, while I waited for her father to come back.

He returned in jeans, still drying his hair with a small towel. "I didn't get a good look at him, did you?"

"Briefly. It was the clerk I saw at the Timmons Gallery, the first time I came out here."

"No shit. What the hell was he doing here?"

It wasn't the kind of question that expected an answer. I gathered up my jacket and Aunt Edna's keys, and said, "Look, I've decided to go ahead and work this thing out on my own."

Ben looked curiously from Melissa to me. She glanced away. "What's going on?"

"Nothing," I said quickly, "nothing at all. I just didn't think, when we were talking earlier, that all this might end up with somebody breaking into your home. It isn't right."

He frowned. "Missy, did you—"

She opened her mouth, but I spoke. "No, she didn't. This business here tonight just made me realize that this is *my* problem and I need to handle it."

Ben started to argue, but I turned to the door. "I'll see you around, okay?"

I left him with a puzzled expression. Melissa's was more of relief. I can't even imagine mine.

CHAPTER 18

"Gary doesn't work here anymore." The young girl at the Timmons Gallery had a ball of curly yellow fluff for hair. She looked like an extra in *Madonna Goes Coed*, and innocent enough not to be involved in whatever was going on here.

I looked like shit, a woman old before her time, jaded, cynical, and a bit humbled by my latest apology to Mom and Aunt Edna when I got back to the house at five A.M. that morning. I'd left Aunt Edna without a car all night, one more thing I hadn't given a thought to. "What if she'd had an emergency in the middle of the night?" Mom said.

"You mean, like, what if she had to make a midnight run for mulch?"

I'd had to apologize for that too.

I dragged my attention back to the clerk. "Do you know where Gary lives?" Gary Weist, she had told me.

"Somewhere in San Rafael," she remembered. "I guess you could ask the manager."

"An older man? Small, with ugly yellow shoes?"

She laughed. "Mr. Dehn. Would you believe he actually has them delivered here, by the boxload?"

I was awfully tired—but why did that ring a bell? "Look, I'm in kind of a hurry. You don't have any idea where I can reach this Gary?"

"Not really. You know guys these days." She peered into the mirrorlike metal of an antique cash register, and ran a long, red-tipped nail over the corners of her mouth to smooth any flaking lipstick.

"I'm not sure I do," I admitted. "What about guys these days?"

"Well, it takes them a while to grow up. Like, till they're

forty or so. You know, the Peter Pan Syndrome?" She straightened and winked.

"You mean they don't work steady, have checking accounts, pay their own rent?" I guess I knew about that after all. I'd had someone in my life like that, not too long ago.

"And," she said, "when they do have money, they spend it all on dope, or other stupid stuff. Gary has an Elvis collection—would you believe?" She rolled her eyes.

"You've seen it?"

"Nah. I used to watch him looking through the classifieds all the time, hunting for that collector's junk." She grinned. "Wait." Digging down into a trash basket by the desk, she came up with a handful of newspapers. "I found these classifieds when I came in. There are some job ads marked."

The paper was the *Independent-Journal*, a Marin County daily, and several ads under Food Service were circled.

"There was somebody else here this morning looking for Gary," she offered as I glanced over the ads. "A man."

"Oh? What'd he look like?"

"Real good-looking. Kind of sun-bleached brown hair. Big. A great smile."

Ben Jericho. Damn. Why couldn't he leave things alone?

"What did you tell him?"

"Just what I told you . . . except that I didn't remember that paper until just now."

I thanked her, took the paper, and started making the rounds.

I found Gary Weist sometime around noon, waitering in a San Rafael restaurant. Actually, I didn't find *him*. I found his brand-new employer, who was kindhearted enough to give me a home address when I told my story about how the kid had left me (his former roommate) without paying his half of the month's rent. "I'm about to be evicted," I said with just the right amount of drama. "I've got to find him—he owes me almost five hundred dollars!"

The guy—an Italian (Italian men, I think, love it when women act weak; the Virgin in every woman, and all that crap)—clucked sympathetically, and wrote the address down on a paper napkin for me.

I smelled pasta cooking. I hadn't stuck around at Aunt Edna's for breakfast, and wished I could sit down, order, and relax. But I'd just told the guy I didn't have any money. The wages of sin.

On the way to Gary Weist's apartment in the Canal district, I found a Taco Bell. I brought a couple of tacos out to the car and wolfed them down while I looked up the kid's address on a map. The tacos reminded me of Melissa, and the dinner she had fixed, that first night on the houseboat. I remembered how frightened she had been after the trouble there last night, and thought about how this bastard kid I was about to see had knocked her down and bruised her face—how he'd blown her right out of her newly safe world. I thought about how I'd helped him to do so. And by the time I got to his place I was in a real bad mood.

The kid's apartment was on the canal, and run-down. Green paint peeled from the stucco siding. Weeds grew around its foundation, and a rusted bicycle with only one wheel leaned against the recessed wall by the front door. The door itself had been covered with plywood at some time. It was water-stained, almost colorless now, and warped.

Music pulsed through a cracked window—Elvis, unless my ear had gone bad. I hate that whole Elvis cult that's grown up around his bones. It's so stupid—like idolizing an old lover who's died and will never have the opportunity to become a pain in the ass. If Elvis were alive today he'd be as old as my mom, fat as a truck, and his brains would be scorched. Either that or he'd be Born Again, and boring as hell.

The kid wasn't too happy to see me. He opened the door like he expected a friend, and then his face fell, his mouth drooped into a sullen line.

He tried to bluff it, though. "I . . . I'm busy right now."

"Drying your clothes, I'll bet."

The door began to close, fast, but I leaned all my weight and pushed right on through.

"Hey, what do you think you're doing?"

"I thought that was obvious. I'm coming in. After I'm in, I'll just listen nice while you talk."

"Christ, lady, talk about what?"

I crossed a cluttered living room to his stereo equipment and pulled the plug.

"Hey!"

I cast a look around, unable to think for a moment. I felt like I was at Graceland—buried with Elvis, along with his crap. Posters, statues, a velvet painting, a six-foot-replica of the King in cardboard, a set of *Love Me Tender* beer steins—

Then I saw that the kid had a real nice record collection. I ran my finger along it: honest-to-God record albums in plastic covers. Originals, it looked like from the recording dates . . . '57 . . . '64 . . . '68 . . . one called "Speedway," with Nancy Sinatra, would you believe.

Must have cost him a fucking fortune.

I started opening up records and dumping them on the floor.

"Hey!" The kid hurtled across the room and grabbed at my sweater, pulling my arm. I dropped a platter called "The Elvis Christmas Album" and slammed him against the wall. Peace on earth, goodwill to men.

He was taller than me, but I was stronger than, at five-four, I looked. Not only that, I'd grown up on the streets, holding my own with boys.

I slammed a knee at his crotch and got out of the way as he jackknifed over, screaming. While he was busy with that, I grabbed up an armful of records and found my way to his crummy little kitchen.

Ah. It did have a garbage disposal. I wondered if vinyl would grind.

I flipped about five of them out on a counter. They clattered and went rolling. I turned the garbage disposal on and held a record above it.

"No! Don't do that!" The kid was in the doorway, still half bent over, his face all red and teary. I broke the record— "Roustabout"—in several pieces and shoved the smallest ones down the drain. The disposal went crunch . . . gurgle . . . whine. It sounded like a junkyard compressor, but it kept on running.

The kid yelled frantically, "What the hell do you *want*, lady?"

"Information." I picked up another album. "Elvis"—1956.

"God, that's an original pressing! Do you know what the fuck you're *doing*? That thing cost me a thousand bucks!"

Well, to each his own, I supposed. Give me Ella any day.

I held "Elvis" above the sink. "Why were you on Ben Jericho's houseboat last night?"

"I don't know any Ben Jericho."

"Right. You were just taking the Annual Houseboat Tour." I slid the record from its protective vinyl. Tested its flexibility.

"Oh, lady, come on, don't do that," the kid whined.

I snapped the album in half, then in half again, and shoved it down the hopper. Then I grabbed the kid by the shirt, pushing him up against the old Coppertone fridge.

Funny how easy it is to intimidate people. Sometimes all it takes is a quick, decisive offense. The kid could have made a break for it, been out the door anytime. Hell, he'd handled himself pretty good with Ben; he could have knocked me flat on my face. But it's like they tell you in the self-defense classes for women: Act like you're in charge, unpredictable, even a little crazy. It's amazing how it works. I've seen the strongest men crumple.

I shoved a thumb into his throat, and with the other hand, grabbed his crotch and hung on like a leech. He tried to get away, but every movement hurt more. His arms flailed at his sides like a butterfly when it's pinned. His face turned red, then drained of blood and became white.

"Okay, lady, shit, okay, let go! Look, it wasn't anything personal!"

But I saw his hands come down. He thought he was being clever; he was going for my throat.

"Neither is this." I let go and punched him in the gut.

He grabbed at his stomach and doubled over. "Christ, you are one mean bitch!"

"Believe it." Just ask Mom and Aunt Edna. Ask Melissa Jericho, if no one else.

I yanked him upright by his Dutch-boy cut. "You inconvenienced me last night. And you hurt a little girl, gave her more grief when she's already had her share."

I pushed him into the living room. Swept a pile of newspapers off a green vinyl chair. "Sit." I shoved, and he sat. I went back to the stereo, knocked everything off the shelf with one motion, and squatted in the mess on the floor. Picked up an album. "Aloha From Hawaii Via Satellite," I read aloud. 1973. A sticker on the front: *Chicken of the Sea Tuna Fish.*

"How much did you pay for this thing?" I removed the album from its jacket.

"Fifteen hundred bucks," he groaned. "Oh, please . . ."

"Okay, well, I'll tell you what." I wobbled the record between my palms. "You start talking. While you talk, I'll just amuse myself here. When you finish telling me everything I want to know, I'll be amused enough. Got it?"

He sat miserably, his head in his hands.

"The first thing I want to know is where that painting of the *Hare* came from. The one you had in the window at the Timmons Gallery a week or so ago. The one Charlie Browne tried to buy."

His heated look could have melted tar, but we had reached that point where he knew he was giving in, and I did too. Whether my premise about a strong offense had worked or whether he was just tired from the night's events, he didn't believe he could fight me and win—and for that reason alone, he was right.

"Browne?" he said hoarsely. "The one who asked me to hold the painting while he went for money?"

"That's the one."

He sighed, rubbed his face, and leaned back, staring at the ceiling remotely as he spoke in a monotone. "The painting came in one day with this shipment of stuff from the owner's house. It—it wasn't supposed to, I guess, because when the owner came in the next day, he almost shit a brick. He grabbed it out of the window—"

"Wait a minute. This was before or after Charlie Browne was there the first time?"

"After. Right after, I think. He wasn't back yet with any money. But the boss, he was on one of those surprise tours, you know, like they make to see you're not screwing up, and he had a fit over that painting. I told him I already had a buyer, but he yanked it out of the window himself, took it in the back, and hid it in a closet. He told me to destroy it after I closed up that night."

"But you didn't." I wondered why this twit had even been trusted with the job.

"I . . . no. You could see it was worth something, and my girlfriend, Gail, she's got this thing about rabbits, and I knew she'd like it . . . What the hell. I'm leaving here soon. I wanted to give her something."

"But you didn't take it with you that night."

"I meant to, I just forgot. I was in a hurry to meet Gail, and I left it there, and the next day . . . it was gone."

"Did you tell the owner?"

"Shit, no. I pretended like I'd destroyed it, just like he told me to."

"You said the shipment, with the *Hare*, came from his house?"

He closed his eyes. "Yeah, somebody who worked for him found it while he was getting these other paintings ready to go out. The guy, the assistant, said he couldn't reach the boss, so he was just gonna send it. He'd found it in the cellar, all covered with cobwebs, but he said that sometimes this old stuff has value, and even if it's not signed collectors'll still buy it, because they never know—"

"Spare me the art appreciation course."

"Jeez!" He shook his head, then winced. "So he said to put a $70,000 price tag on it and see what happened."

"What's the owner's name?"

"I don't know—"

I heard a loud crack, and the kid's face screwed up. His eyes began to water. "You can break the whole damned place up, and I still won't know!" he cried.

I looked down and realized what I'd done. I'd broken "Aloha From Hawaii" over my knee. Shit. What a loss.

"Adversity toughens the soul," I said. I lined up several more albums. "Now, why don't you just tell me what you were doing last night on Ben Jericho's houseboat?"

"I'm telling you, lady, I don't know any Ben Jericho! I just know the owner of the gallery called and asked me to do a job for him. He said he'd pay me well, and I needed the bucks, because after you showed up the other day he didn't want me working at the gallery anymore."

"And the job was—"

"To follow you that night and shake you up a little. That's all, I swear. I wasn't supposed to hurt you or anything, he just wanted you scared."

I got up, kicked a path through the mess of records, and

walked around a little. Thinking. Finally, I smiled. "Okay. Well, that about does it then, I guess."

The kid looked relieved. He wiped his eyes.

"Oh, except for one thing." I leaned over the chair and grabbed him by the hair, my knee firmly planted in his groin. My face was only inches from his. I could feel him shaking, and didn't like the feeling, but I didn't back off. In fact, I twisted his hair with my fist. "I need the name of that owner."

"Christ, you gotta believe me, I don't know his name, it's some deep dark secret or something!"

"Where does he live?"

"I don't know, someplace in the East, I think!"

"Where do you and the other clerks reach him?"

"We don't. Him, or that assistant of his, they call us."

"But you've seen this man. The owner. He was in the gallery just last week."

"Well, yeah, but—"

I pressed with my knee and yanked with my hand. "What the hell does he *look* like?"

He yelped and dug back into the chair with his ass. "T-tall. D-dignified, kind of, a little mustache, about seventy—he's got some kind of heavy position at a gallery back East, an authority or something. I swear, that's all I know."

Shit. Dignified? Mustache? Authority?

"What about that employee, the one who found the painting? You know his name?"

"Burton," he snuffled. "That's his last name, Burton."

Iverson's assistant, Burton.

Double shit.

I let the kid go and straightened, rubbing my palms on my jeans and heading briskly for the door.

"Look, lady," he whimpered, "don't tell him I said anything, okay?"

"Why?" I stopped beside the cardboard cutout of Elvis and looked back. "You got more business with this guy?"

"No—but there's no telling what somebody like that might do."

"No telling." I stared Elvis in the face, starting to feel mad again. Then I pushed on his cardboard chest, knocking him flat on his heels. He bobbed a little on the floor, then lay still.

"The King is dead," I said.

Back at Aunt Edna's car I stood for a minute, bent over the hood, choking back vomit. Wondering: *What happened to me back there?* Not all of my anger had to do with Melissa Jericho; the motivation wasn't that noble.

Goddamn. I was losing it.

I climbed into the Fiat, turned the key with fingers that shook, and tried to remember where I was. Which way to drive.

South. I was in San Rafael. I had to get out on 101 and drive south.

I pointed the car and moved into the flow. Horns blew. I think I went through some lights. Somehow, I ended up on 101. It was automatic after that.

Think, Jess. Think of the problem at hand.

The owner of the Timmons Gallery lives in the East. He has a big-time position back there. An authority. What's more, he bears an amazing resemblance to Everett Iverson.

Hell, let's face it. Mustache, authority, Burton and all—he *is* Everett Iverson. The man I'd thought was perfect for my mom.

Beyond that, I couldn't think. There were too many things going on in my mind, having to do with who murdered Anna, and why Iverson had his brother's painting of her enshrined in his house. Why Burton was killed. And the *Hare.*

I got back to Aunt Edna's to find that Mom had received three dozen sterling-silver roses—from the man of the hour, Everett Iverson. She was bubbling like a teenaged girl.

"He's coming out here in a couple of days. He wants to take us to dinner."

I'll bet he does. Having hired Gary Weist to intimidate me, Iverson probably wanted to see if I'd taken the hint and dropped my investigation yet.

I found myself in the uncomfortable position of switching horses midstream.

"Mom—what about Charlie?" I said a little wistfully.

"What about him, dear?"

"You haven't just forgotten him, have you? I mean, just because Iverson sends you flowers—"

She laughed. "Oh, Jesse, that doesn't mean anything. He's just being nice. Surely you didn't think—why, Charlie's the man I love!"

I couldn't tell her that I, more than anyone, knew how unreliable an emotion love could be. How you could go along with your thoughts all geared toward one person, and then—

I looked at Mom, getting all rosy over a bunch of flowers. Swell.

Well, it was all my fault. I'd left her alone with Aunt Edna too much. Washed her out of my hair while I played hotshot and went off to fight the wars. Not only that, but ever since she'd knocked me on my ass that first night in my apartment, I'd been fighting her. Every step of the way.

James Dean's brother, in *East of Eden*, said to him: "What have you ever done to make Pop love you? You can't just fight against people all your life, you have to fight *with* them."

I put my arms around Mom and held her. It was time to make up.

"Tell you what," I said generously. "Let's rent a movie. We'll make some popcorn, sit around, and pig out tonight. Then we'll talk about how to help Charlie—together."

She patted my back. "Oh, Jesse, I'm sorry, I can't. I'm going with Edna to feed the poor."

I dropped my arms. "Tonight? Mom, you have to go tonight?"

She nodded happily. "Practically speaking, it's still the new moon," she said.

I spent the evening with a movie anyway: *East of Eden*. I must have missed something first time around, I thought.

CHAPTER 19

The next morning, I called when Alfred was out to lunch back there, and got Marcus on the phone. I told him about my conversation with the kid the night before. How according to the kid, Everett Iverson was the owner of the Timmons Gallery. And how the late Burton, Iverson's assistant, told the kid he'd found the *Hare* a few weeks ago in Iverson's cellar, covered in dust.

"Sounds like it's been there a long time," I said. "Maybe even since the night forty years ago when Anna was murdered."

"Well, I'm still running him through the computer, and so far, Iverson's past seems straightforward enough. College—a master's degree, then a doctorate—honorary degrees and several awards. Nothing about him owning galleries, either in California or anywhere else. Of course, the ownership of Timmons, as we already know, is a mare's nest. I'm still trying to sort it all out."

"Anything yet to link Robert Iverson directly with Anna?"

"Not directly. But didn't you say she held weekly salons for artists in the area?"

"And San Francisco was a fairly small city in the forties and fifties. Even now, it's incestuous at some social levels."

Still, I was having a hard time seeing the creator of those childlike, almost spiritual paintings in Iverson's home gallery, as a killer. I said as much to Marcus.

"Bottom line," he pointed out, "is that the *Hare* disappeared the night Anna died. And until a few weeks ago—if your informant is correct—it was hidden in the Iverson family cellar."

"So let's say Robert Iverson knew Anna. Let's say, even, that for whatever reason he stole the *Hare*, brought it home to Rochester, then got cold feet and hid it away in the cellar.

Does that necessarily mean he was cold-blooded enough to kill Anna?"

"Could have been a crime of passion," Marcus said. "Unpremeditated."

"So he bumps her off and then takes the *Hare* to remember her by? To remind him of his crime, and her death?"

I could hear him tapping his pen against paper. I imagined him at the huge glass desk, feet up, ankles crossed, rubbing thoughtfully at his brow. "We talked about this before, Jess. What you need is to find people who knew them both. See what kind of relationship they had, if they even knew each other at all."

"I'm working on that." Actually, until last night, I'd hoped that Ben would work on that. Oh, well. Best-laid—and best-laid plans—ofttimes go astray. "In the meantime, will you see if you can find any other connections to Everett Iverson out here? I really want to nail that son of a bitch. First, he puts the moves on my mom, then he hires somebody to scare me off—"

"What do you mean, he hired somebody to scare you off?"

"I took care of it. Don't worry."

"Jess, I don't like you being out there alone."

"I'm not alone," I said, matching his sharp tone. "I've got friends—" Well, I'd had one friend, at least, until last night.

"Who?"

"An ex-cop. No one you know."

There was a momentary silence, then he changed the subject. "Charlie is still in jail . . . which surprises me. His lawyer, I hear, is quite a renegade. Had charges brought against him in the sixties for sneaking a prisoner out of jail right under the eyes of the guards. Finally proved the guy innocent of all charges, and got him off scot-free. Now he pops up all over the country to defend anyone from crooked politicians to rock stars. Keeps a low profile personally, though."

"How in the hell did Charlie find somebody like that?"

"Good question. I'm still drawing blanks where your mom's true love is concerned."

"Let's hope he's her true love."

"Oh? You've certainly changed your tune."

I stuck my leg in the air and inspected my toes. "Oh, hell,

STOP! *DANGER...* *INTRIGUE...and* *SUSPENSE AHEAD!*

1. Detach the Free Gift seal at the right.

2. Follow the trail of footprints to the next page.

3. And affix your Gift Seal in the space provided inside to receive:

FREE GIFT

A free 362-page Agatha Christie Bedside Companion.

A free preview of the mystery classic...
And Then There Were None!

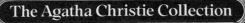

The Agatha Christie Collection

Follow the trail
into Agatha Chris

FREE PREVIEW! The Bedside Companion is your **FREE GIFT** just for viewing Agatha Christie's renowned mystery classic, **And Then There We None,** for 15 days risk free. It's one of the most captivating murder mysteri ever written! Will you discover who dunit before the author reveals the solution?

And Then There Were None demonstrates the exciting mystery entert ment that awaits you in **The Agatha Christie Mystery Collection.** The C lection brings you Agatha Christie's novels in hardbound collector's edition that are not available in any bookstore. Each book is bound in simulated leather — rich, Sussex blue in color, and decorated with distinctive gold em bossing. The covers are padded and soft to the touch. The bindings are sew (not glued), and the pages are of acid-free paper that will last for generation All in all, each volume is a masterpiece of the bookbinder's art and will disp elegantly in your home.

You might expect to pay $20 or more in bookstores for luxurious volumes like these. Yet they are yours for only $11.95 each (plus shipping and handli

NO OBLIGATION — EVER! Send for **And Then There Were None** and enjoy it for 15 days risk free. If you like, return it, owe nothing, and that wil that. If you keep it, you'll receive additional volumes in **The Agatha Christi Mystery Collection** about once a month — and always with 15-day previe privileges. Keep only those volumes you want. Cancel any time. And whate you decide at the outset, **The Bedside Companion** is yours to keep **FREE.**

footprints below
's World of Mystery!

I don't know. There's a bunch of silver roses in the living room from Iverson, and Mom woke up singing. At this very moment she's getting her hair done and buying new clothes for dinner with Iverson. And at this time last week she was doing the same for Charlie. How come I feel suddenly that I'm raising her, instead of the other way around?"

"I don't know. Different personalities, maybe. You ever wake up singing, Jess?"

Not often enough, I thought.

"Jess?"

"Huh?" My big toenail, I thought, inspecting it carefully, needed clipping. No wonder my Nikes hurt when I walk. I began to pick at it.

"Everything okay?" Marcus asked.

Ow. The nail was coming off, too far down. It hurt. "Yeah," I said vaguely, "sure, what could be wrong? I'm in sunny California, sitting here in a loft surrounded by trees and bees—"

"I meant with us."

"Oh, that."

A longer silence this time. Then Marcus said briskly, "I'm flying out there in a couple of days."

"You are?"

"I've got business appointments lined up back-to-back on Thursday, but I'd like to see you Thursday night."

"Oh. Okay."

"I'll send a car for you—"

"No, don't." I'd had enough of limos for a while. "I'll meet you in the City. You staying at the company penthouse?" Andrelli Enterprises owns corporate apartments in several cities. Marcus had offered Mom and me the one in San Francisco for this trip, but I'd turned it down.

"On California Street, yes."

"What time?"

"Seven?"

"Okay."

"Try to contain your excitement."

"No, really, it's just—"

"What?"

"Nothing." Why did it always have to be so . . . so programmed, lately, with Marcus? I was beginning to feel like I was being fitted into the slots of his schedule, falling into the cracks between appointments. And to think that when I'd first met Marcus Andrelli a year and a half ago, it seemed that falling for a mobster might be fun.

"I'm bringing you a surprise," Marcus said.

"Oh, yeah? What?"

"If I told you—"

"I know, I know, it wouldn't be a surprise." Hmmm. Well, if I knew Marcus and how predictable he'd become lately, it wouldn't be all that much of a surprise. A diamond bracelet that I'd never wear . . . a pair of matching earrings . . .

"It should be arriving on the noon ferry in Sausalito, Thursday," he said.

I sat up. On the *ferry*? Didn't sound like earrings.

Then, suddenly, I knew. *Tark!* The big guy. Marcus's bodyguard of twenty-three years. Tark and I had been partners in more than one adventure over the past year and a half. And Tark was an activator—while Marcus sat more and more in the ivory tower. I loved Tark. With him, it was junior high all over again . . . running with the boys, hopping trains, jumping off bridges, heisting cars . . .

Well, I didn't do all those things with Tark. But you get what I mean.

So . . . Tark was back from Italy! And Marcus was bringing him along. I felt so good, suddenly, I'd have planted broccoli by the light of the moon.

I was still smiling when we said good-bye.

CHAPTER 20

Scrounging in the fridge for breakfast was a disgusting task. It was packed with herbs and tofu, raisins and nuts. Well, I'd be in top fighting form when Mom's honored guest arrived. Lean and mean.

"Everett will be here in two days, dear," Mom had said. "Won't that be fun? He's taking us all to the Alta Mira for dinner."

The Alta Mira. Aunt Edna had taken Mom and me there for lunch after I helped Mom move in here. Perched on a hill in Sausalito, the Alta Mira is old-style chic rather than trendy. It also has one of the best views in town. Dinner meant we'd have to dress our best. Shit. All I'd brought was jeans.

I ambled off to Aunt Edna's room, hoping I might find something suitable and not too froufrou. An earlier glimpse had shown me a futon (for sleeping on the floor), bamboo blinds, and a poster of Cesar Chavez. So Aunt Edna, despite the Buddha in the corner, hadn't been lost completely to the New Age.

But the room was so small I had to walk over the futon to get to her closet. In an open, beat-up brown carton on the floor I found Aunt Edna's jeans, some almost certainly left over from Berkeley days. Aunt Edna graduated from Berkeley in the seventies at the age of forty-two. Back then, she wore Levis, fatigues, and work boots everywhere. Some, as I'd suspected, were still here.

But the rest of her closet had now been taken over by things like

hot pink sweats.

God. Hot pink and orange *everywhere.* That, and that awful purple/green/red color in silky, flowing tunics. If Mom had become Betty White, Aunt Edna was a short, skinny Bea Arthur. The froufrou nineties had struck her down, just like everyone else.

I couldn't find anything in between that and the jeans, and I backed away, trying to reach the door before the virus got me—the premise here being that I can't face clothes that wake me up before I've had my morning coffee.

Grabbing a spear of fresh chive, I went out to the garden, munching it. Thinking about Everett Iverson. I needed more information—ammunition—to come up with a plan before he arrived. Marcus was supposed to call back tonight with his latest computer magic.

I sat on a redwood log in the garden a while, but couldn't think. The racket drove me nuts. Bluejays squawking, bees having noisy sex with marigolds . . .

Give me a nice city street any day, with things I know and understand, like drive-bys and sirens with red lights flashing.

Birds? Birds are fussbudgets, always nattering at you. And they're dangerous, too. You never know when they'll attack. You think not? Tell the truth, now . . . have *you* seen Tippi Hedren since Alfred Hitchcock's *The Birds*? Rumor has it they got her leaving the wrap party and she's never returned from Bodega Bay. The other rumor is that Melanie Griffith, her kid, is really the daughter of a crow.

(Oh, okay, so I'm bitter. I'd like to look like Melanie Griffith too.)

I finally took the bus to Sausalito and got out and walked around. There weren't any bikers today, but the black suits with cameras were out in droves. My restlessness grew. I didn't know why I'd come down here. Yes I did. I wanted to talk to Ben about last night. Then again, I didn't want to talk to Ben about last night. I just wanted to run into him.

No I didn't. I never wanted to run into Ben Jericho again.

I walked along Bridgeway, drawn to the water. At home in Rochester I do my best thinking along Lake Ontario—sniffing the fishy air, watching storm clouds move in from Canada. There's always so much drama back there. It gives the intellect a nudge.

Here, though, not much happens at all. Boats bob on the Bay, but what's new? Boats always bob on some bay in California. It's a constant. The only thing that threatens the normal scheme of things is a now-and-then earthquake, and even then life gets back to normal pretty quick. Sails flap gently in an undramatic breeze, sunshine streams, and sea lions squawk for the tourists as if paid by the mayor to perform. Tourists in polyester and starchy pin curls pile out of the ferries (which always reminds me of the Johnny Carson joke about Nancy Reagan: "She fell down and broke her hair"), and the gulls wheel—

Well, now, there's a menace for you. I've never seen anything more scary than a hungry gull with a sharp eye out for food.

I got a turkey-and-cheese sandwich and thick black coffee at the Venice market and walked along the sidewalk that rims the Bay. Finding a free wooden bench, I sat on it and washed the sandwich down with the coffee, wanting a beer (another great line, this one from W. C. Fields: "Somebody left the cork out of my lunch").

Eight miles across the water floated the City—in caps, if you please, although that, Aunt Edna tells me, may be becoming passé. At any rate, San Francisco looked white and pristine—like a movie set. Taintless, undefiled.

It wasn't a movie set. People killed people over there. At this very moment, someone might be getting shot in San Francisco, which, as a city of crime, is a piker, since at this very moment a whole passel of people were probably being snuffed across the Bay in Oakland.

Forty years ago, someone had killed Anna Biernej-Browne in San Francisco. Someone had snuffed her in her studio after a party—and now Charlie, her son, was in jail for allegedly killing Burton, the first man in forty years who had been about to tell him something about that murder. Or at least about the *Hare*, which had disappeared the night of her murder.

Only to surface a few weeks ago in Everett Iverson's cellar.

Why had the *Hare* been found in Iverson's cellar? The only answer, it seemed, was Robert. Robert Iverson had been in San Francisco the summer Anna was murdered. He had painted a portrait of Anna—a romanticized portrait, at that. So—he had known her. (Loved her?)

Had he killed her?

Had Robert killed Anna, stolen the painting, and hidden it away later in the cellar of his family home in Rochester? And was guilt over this the reason he had committed suicide three months later?

Whatever the reason, it seemed that Everett, his brother, was now trying to scare me off from digging into the past, from discovering what Robert had done. Not that I could blame him for wanting to protect his brother—he had obviously loved him a great deal. The part I got hung up on was the murder of Burton, Everett's assistant. If Charlie hadn't done it—then who? Again, the answer came back: Everett Iverson. And he'd left Charlie holding the bag, while he was on his way out here to wine and dine my mom.

I couldn't stand the ruminating anymore. I fed the rest of my sandwich to a gull to keep it from eating my eyes, and hopped on a ferry to San Francisco.

CHAPTER 21

I got off at the Ferry Building and walked across Embarcadero, then took a streetcar to Nob Hill. I'd been thinking that Laurence Higgham—Marcus's contact at the gallery there—might be a good place to start. He had known about Anna and Charlie; he might know other people who were around during Anna's time. But Higgham wasn't in. I left my name and Aunt Edna's phone number with the maroon-and-gold-plated guard.

I wasn't all that disappointed. The person I really wanted to see, I had to admit, was in Pacific Heights.

Avery Carlisle was in, and I didn't have to wait this time. The gates opened almost immediately. The voice on the security phone told me to take the main path to the left of the fountain and follow it to a greenhouse. I did so, thinking again how great it was here. A getaway at the very edge of the city—near the sea, yet still only minutes from downtown.

Along the path I passed two small clearings, shrines of sorts. One had a Buddha at its center. The surrounding garden was oriental, while water flowed from a bronze sculpture of lily pads. The second clearing had a three-foot statue of St. Francis. Perched on his arm, and on the ground around his feet, were birds. Real birds. I stopped a moment and remembered all the old stories from Catholic school. About St. Francis and his love of nature. How he came from a wealthy merchant family but went off somewhere to fast for weeks on end. How he'd shown up once, after a fast, stark naked—at an upscale party his father was giving. I don't remember his agenda, but it was some sort of political statement, and I remember how Sister Bartolomeo had read that story in school, and how it had thrilled me. St. Francis the Hippie—just like me.

I was eight years old, I think, at the time.

Now I looked at St. Francis and felt something akin to coming home. Even though I don't follow the old traditions anymore, I'm always glad to see there are people who do. They provide me with something comforting and solid that I'm too stubborn, or too perverse, to provide for myself.

I found Avery Carlisle outside the greenhouse with a couple of students, a boy and girl in approximately their late teens. The three were talking animatedly. Carlisle, who wore a blue work shirt and soft blue work pants again today, said something. The girl giggled. The boy blushed, but he didn't look upset. There seemed to be a rapport among the trio beyond that of students and teacher. Carlisle turned to see me, and invited me into the group with a motion of his hand.

"Ms. James. I'm delighted to see you again." He took my hand as I joined them. "I'd like you to meet two of my favorite people. Joseph"—the boy smiled, even white teeth flashing in an olive face—"and Sara." She was tiny and dark. Both students wore what I now guessed was standard at the Carlisle Foundation—loose white shirts, and white pants or skirts. Sara giggled again and looked shy.

"These two young people," Carlisle said, "are perfect examples of what the Carlisle Foundation is all about."

I'd have shaken hands with them, but Carlisle was still holding mine.

Joseph shrugged boyishly. "Whatever we do is because of you," he said.

I looked curiously at Carlisle, who shook his head. "I provide the milieu, Joseph. You work with it, just as you work with your clay."

"But you brought us here in the first place," Sara said softly. "No one else would have."

"On the contrary. There is always someone ready to help. We find different people at different times, but when we ask for it—the help is there." Carlisle released my hand and rested his on her white-clad shoulder. "People are only channels. Remember that, Sara. The source is elsewhere."

Sara smiled and nodded, but I could see she wasn't buying it. For whatever reason, Avery Carlisle had a friend for life.

"Now, off with you . . . it's time for your still-life class." Carlisle hadn't looked at a watch—in fact, didn't wear one.

But the words were no sooner out than the chimes in the bell tower sounded the hour. Sara and Joseph said good-bye to me and ran off.

"A neat trick," I said, "that time thing."

Carlisle chuckled. "An *old* trick. When you've lived here as long as I have, you begin to know the hour from the slanting of the shadows beneath the trees. Even from the way the leaves sing." He took my hand again and drew me inside the greenhouse. It was nicely warm after the day's cooler weather, and the humidity felt good against my skin. The scents were heavy—earth and water, perfume, foliage, moss. Filtered sunlight made it seem like another world.

"Now tell me," Carlisle said, "why are you here? I'm very happy to see you again, of course."

"You are?" I love fishing for compliments.

He wagged a finger in front of my nose. "No fishing for compliments," he said.

I must have looked startled. He laughed softly. "Reading minds is something that comes with age, too."

"What was all that with Joseph and Sara?" I asked. "What did you do for them?"

He drew me down a path between huge plants that looked like rubber trees, although they were probably a more exotic species. I wasn't sure he was going to answer my question, but at one point he stopped and pointed to a bed of dirt and rocks. It wasn't very spectacular. I said so.

Avery Carlisle agreed. "Doesn't look like much, does it? I keep it here as a life lesson. Those are the only kind I teach anymore—I leave the art to more talented and energetic people than I. But at some time early in their first year, I bring the students out here and tell them this: 'When you turn over soil, you inevitably turn up rocks. It's part of nature. Imperfection exists in all things. The important thing is a judicious hoeing—a preparing of the soil for better things to come.' "

"A good lesson," I said. "But when Joseph and Sara said you had helped them, it sounded like something more."

"Some of our students here have had difficult lives. Joseph came from the inner city, Sara from an upper-income family. Both were abused in one way or another, and both reacted by getting into trouble with the law. I heard about them through a friend, and discovered they had a talent for art. When they arrived here—separately—both were on probation. I merely provided them with a place to learn. To figure things out. Given half a chance, people will often do this for themselves, I've found."

"Do your students pay more here than at other art schools?" I was thinking of the grandeur of the buildings and the grounds.

"Absolutely not. Absorbing the cost of the grounds and facilities is part of what we give our students as a foundation. They pay fees comparable to other schools or colleges in the area. We also have excellent scholarships for students who can't pay but show exceptional talent. Like Joseph."

"Do you have a lot of students like Joseph?"

"Not a lot, but now and then they do come. I always feel I have something to learn from them, too, and I welcome the opportunity. Besides," he said passionately, "it's somewhat of an adventure—seeing what will grow, once the soil is prepared."

I'd had someone like Avery Carlisle in my life once—when I was fourteen. That was the summer I was picked up for stealing cars. *Acting out*, the psychologists called it: doing it for the thrill and because life was so rotten at home—not for any real gain. Aunt Ruth (not my real aunt, but I'd come to call her that) had taken me in as a foster child for the summer. Ruth Donovan was a woman in her fifties, an architect, who lived in an inherited mansion but spent her summers poking around in ruins like an archeologist, wearing khaki and jeans. She took me on working field trips with her, and taught me something about how women can take care of themselves.

At the same time, I picked up a taste for living well while still having my feet firmly planted on the ground. Aunt Ruth put me up in a bedroom the likes of which I'd never seen except in movies, with a frilled canopy bed, a mirrored dressing table, and a bathroom with gold fixtures. At dinner I learned how to use tools for fine dining rather than the kind I'd been using to break into cars. On warm summer evenings she'd take me to concerts in Highland Park, and during the hot days it was to air-cooled museums and art galleries. I felt like Shirley Temple, the orphan, being adopted by her best friend's rich family. Pretty soon I was having dreams of how it might be, going to college, getting a job, creating some sort of better life for myself. It didn't have to matter that my pop was a drunk and Mom (as I saw it then) was inept.

So I knew what Carlisle was talking about. Sometimes kids need a change in venue—some breathing space from all the troubles, to sort things out. By September, Pop had sobered up long enough for Mom to convince the social workers it'd be okay for me to come home, and I'd kept my nose reasonably clean after that. But Aunt Ruth was the one most responsible. She'd given me, in that short summer, another outlook—other soil in which to grow. It's the sort of thing you take with you: the thought that there might be another way to go.

There was something I'd wanted to ask Carlisle, however. "Why does everyone dress alike here? It's almost—"

"Cultlike?" He didn't seem offended. "That's the problem with surface evaluations," he said, gently reproving. "I assure you that building individuality is one of our greatest concerns here. We aren't a cult, Ms. James."

"No . . . actually, I didn't mean that. I was thinking that it seems like a kind of . . . coed monastery."

"Hmmm. Well, yes, a natural parallel, I suppose. It's true we encourage a meditative atmosphere. We have, actually, one radio and one television on the entire grounds. Our students have access to them at any time, and at first it's rather interesting to see what happens when each new class arrives. For a while it's Saturday morning cartoons, ballgames, sitcoms . . . but they show little interest after being here a while."

"Forgive me . . . but doesn't a kind of . . . oh, I don't know, a kind of a brainwashing take place, when people are in an environment for a long time that changes their thinking in some strong way?"

"Absolutely. Well, children growing up in families are brainwashed, you might say, by the beliefs of their parents. And they're induced to believe certain things by the television they see every day. Members of traditional churches are said to be 'indoctrinated'—another term for conditioning. Anytime a person turns the practice of individual thinking over to one set dogma or belief, rather than remaining open at all times to new ideas and possibility—that's a kind of brainwashing, I believe."

We had begun to walk around the long bedding tables, and Carlisle stopped now and then to lovingly straighten the little green sticks the plants were bound to. Some I didn't recognize, others were simple flowers that I remembered from people's gardens, walking home from school as a child. They were mingled together, with no seeming rhyme or reason. Certainly no caste system, since orchids stood side by side with asters.

"Here at Carlisle we place great emphasis on individual thinking," Carlisle went on. "There would be no art without individualism, after all, and art is what we teach. And as for this period of retreat, as one might call it, from the outside world—our students have all grown up in a world of turmoil, a world where countries send their best hope out to be killed in the name of a flag, where small children are gunned down on school playgrounds. Our students have only a short time here, one to two years at the most, and that time is a kind of haven for them. It strengthens them, I think, for moving about in an unsure world when they graduate."

"I once heard the actor Peter Ustinov," I said, "tell an interviewer that at some point in his life he created his own country in his mind. Then he created a constitution, the first article of which was: 'No chicken's neck shall be wrung.' He said that when things happen here on earth—having to do, for instance, with politics, wars, injustices—he views them from the standpoint of *his* country, a standpoint quite different from the usual automatic response people have been conditioned to spew out all their lives."

"Exactly. He was talking about the way so many of us go around unaware—brainwashed—all our lives, I believe."

"And about having another frame of reference for humanity. A gentler one. It sounds like you're doing something along those lines here—creating a kind of oasis of peace, for people to exist in for a while. It's a wonder they ever leave."

"Oh, it's one of our requirements," Carlisle said firmly, "that they leave. After all, what good is peace if it's not taken into the world?"

"There are orders of nuns and monks who believe that praying for peace is enough. They shut themselves up in cloisters all their lives."

"A metaphysical principle," Carlisle said, nodding. "And a

great heroic deed on their part. But for me, to bring the deed into the world is the thing. It's so important what people *do*, you see." He spoke earnestly. "What people do, good or bad, can change their lives and others so dramatically. . . ." His voice trailed off.

"So you send them back into the world, having lived with all this silence and lack of turmoil for so long. But what about the *Paradise Lost* theory? That people, once removed from all this utopia, will lose it? That they won't be able to survive?"

"Many of our people come back for two-week visits now and then. Refresher courses, you might say. But I'm not sure one ever completely loses peace, if one has the kind of mind that seeks it out in the first place. The desire for it may take different directions, various outlets, but it's always there."

"Are your students confined to the grounds here?"

"Oh, good heavens, no! We believe, more than anything, in balance. The students are free to leave, to go into the city at any time. We urge them to go on nature walks, visit their families, tour the museums and galleries—but we ask them to look for beauty instead of the ugliness that's all too readily available out there. We give them homework, in fact, along those lines. They have to come back and report upon the good they've found."

I wondered what it would be like, to be part of this. To spend some time here.

I felt almost hungry for it, in fact.

Shit. Hanging around Avery Carlisle was making me weird.

Well, actually, Tark had started that. The big guy. I wasn't as smart as him, and I didn't read Kierkegaard or the other philosophers—at least not often—but I suppose I was thinking more and more about things as I muddled my way through life.

"Come, look at this," Carlisle urged. He took me into an adjoining section of the greenhouse, one with desert plants.

"Is that a Christmas cactus?" I'd seen something like it at Aunt Edna's, and she'd told me that was what it was. This plant, however, was huge. It had broad flat "leaves," with jagged ends, and all in all, it didn't look like much.

"Similar. A night-blooming cereus. It blooms, usually, only twenty-four hours each year. Then it dies."

"The whole plant?"

"No, just the flower."

"So the rest of the time, the plant just sits there like this and looks at you?"

At my doubtful expression, he laughed. "But you miss the important thing. Such a noble deed, to choose to be a cereus."

"You think the cereus chooses to become a cereus?"

"Well, there is the theory that souls choose the person they want to come back as—welcoming all the trials that person will have, for their growth. Whether plants might do this too, who can say? Certainly those twenty-four hours are magnificent ones for the cereus. A trumpet flower—like a lily—blazing its glory as if proclaiming the coming of the King."

I shook my head. Buddha, St. Francis, and now plants who choose what they want to be. It was all too much for me.

"I really came to ask you some questions about Anna," I said. "And about someone named Robert Iverson."

"Of course." He smiled. "We'll go inside. Would you like to see Anna's paintings?"

"You have some?"

"Nearly every one, except for those she sold in the final years. Charlie left Anna's work with me for safekeeping years ago, when he began to travel."

"Charlie must think a lot of you, to do that."

"Perhaps," Carlisle said enigmatically. "Perhaps."

CHAPTER 22

I followed him inside, down white-walled corridors blazing with natural light and red tile floors. Arched windows overlooked a courtyard lush with glossy greenery and exotic pink, yellow, and orange flowers. A feathery mist drifted between the plants, low on the ground. Where the sun touched the tops of shrubbery, moisture rose. In a center courtyard, a class of five young people sat before easels, quietly sketching.

We went down several more corridors with classrooms on either side. Here, other students worked at easels, or sculpted clay or stone figures. In one workroom—the only one with its door closed to the corridor—metal structures were being shaped by women and men over torches, wearing welding masks. I paused a moment to watch, and Avery spoke proudly beside me. "In there," he said, "you will find the flowering of creative souls who took shop in high school and found the building of bookcases too confining. It's a miracle, what they do with molten steel."

After a few more corridors, the arches opened onto a large room at the back, a kind of solarium, although its skylights were shaded from direct sun by the overhanging fronds of palm trees. Their long skinny trunks did nothing to obstruct the dramatic view of gardens through wraparound windows. There were no plants inside the room, but plants would have been an unnecessary adornment.

It took me a moment to see Anna's paintings. They were placed so naturally throughout the solarium, they seemed a part of it, as if they'd grown there stroke by stroke. In place of one small windowpane, near the floor, was a canvas of a tiny brown rabbit on his hind feet, with boxing gloves. He might have been peeking from the shrubbery outside the glass. Another startled me, it was so real. I had turned to look about and was confronted by a soft brown eye on a section of wall that slanted my way. It belonged to a gray rabbit in a top hat. The other eye winked slyly, mischievously.

I saw now where Charlie's air of devil-may-care came from. And I was reminded of Robert Iverson's paintings, so whimsical, as if the artist had lived on another plane where life was meant to be outrageous fun. Another thought struck my mind.

"Charlie's father," I said. "Who was he?"

Avery Carlisle smiled, took a seat on a crescent-shaped stone bench, and shook his head. "I see what you're thinking, and it's natural enough. But Robert Iverson was much too young to have fathered Charlie. He'd have been twelve, perhaps, when Charlie was born."

"You knew Robert Iverson, then?"

"Oh, indeed. Robert was an excellent artist, one of the many who gathered around Anna in those days. She liked Robert especially, I think, because of his whimsy. It was so like her own."

Carlisle turned in his seat to a slender white column, where several switches were hidden behind a panel. He turned one on, illuminating each painting with warm light as if he'd turned on the sun. There were fifteen to twenty canvases, all told.

"Charlie's father," he continued, "was someone Anna knew during the second world war. The usual war story—he was shipped out before they could marry, and died somewhere in Germany, I believe. It wasn't easy for Anna, although back then, women with children seldom ended up on the streets. There were other things that could be done . . . men with money." He smiled kindly.

"Are you saying Charlie's mother was a prostitute?"

His eyes widened. "Most certainly not. You have to understand that life was quite different in those days. Men were expected to take care of women, and they did so with a sort of caring that one doesn't often see today between the sexes. Then, too, Anna was a beautiful woman, with great spirit and fire—men flocked to her side, hoping to be warmed by that fire. It was, I would say, a fairly even exchange."

I wondered. In my experience, women who were "taken care of" by men generally paid a price, and you could forget the fair exchange. Maybe it was different in the forties—but I didn't think so.

"Was Everett Iverson one of the men who 'took care' of Anna?" I asked.

"Robert's brother, Everett? Why on earth would you think that?"

"A painting of Anna's, *Hare Amongst the Roses*, was found a few weeks ago in Everett Iverson's cellar. It had disappeared the night she died, and it's occurred to me that Robert Iverson might have killed her and taken it, or Everett got hold of it in some other way. Directly, perhaps."

He shook his head. But he seemed to be thinking. There was something he wasn't saying.

"What is it?" I asked.

"It's just that . . . well, Everett Iverson was out here in those days, several times, visiting Robert. I'm sure he must have met Anna. However, he couldn't have been giving her money. I recall having the impression that Robert—and his brother—were quite poor. We were most of us struggling in those days."

"Strange. Everett Iverson told me that his estate in Pittsford had been in his family for many years. It must have taken money to own and maintain a place like that."

"Of course, he may have had property, but little cash. That, too, was common in those times."

"I suppose. Tell me, what was Robert like?"

"In appearance, he was pale . . . pale blond hair, dreamy gray eyes. Eyes that saw other worlds. Completely without hearing, of course. A childhood illness, if I remember correctly. Some sort of reaction from medication. Because the hearing impairment came late in childhood, Robert's speech wasn't affected. Still, he was shy. He would sit in a corner at Anna's parties and observe. Highly intelligent—although not, perhaps, about himself."

"Why do you say that?"

"He seemed unhappy a good deal of the time. I always felt that he might have done more, if he hadn't been held back by what he saw as his limitations."

"Could it be that his illness wiped the family out? Financially, I mean. There weren't the kinds of social programs then that there are now."

"That's certainly a possibility," Avery agreed.

"Do you know if any of the people who were here then are still around? People who went to Anna's parties, and who knew her and Charlie?"

He shook his head. "It's doubtful. That was a long time ago, and there have been three major wars since then. People move around. I'm sure many are gone—passed on."

"Three months after Anna's death," I said, "Robert Iverson committed suicide."

"Yes," he said pensively. "I remember that. Robert was so intense . . . all that energy and creativity . . . for a while, I believe, he channeled it into his feelings for Anna. He must have painted dozens of portraits of her."

Like the one I'd seen in Everett Iverson's hidden gallery room.

"About Charlie. Did you know that he's in jail?"

"Yes. His attorney called, just the other day. I regret now ever having sent him to Everett Iverson."

"You sent Charlie back East, to talk to Iverson about the *Hare*?"

"I'm afraid so, yes. Iverson is one of the world's topmost authorities in art, and Charlie has been almost obsessed with tracking down the provenance of the *Hare*."

"Well, it looks like Iverson himself had the *Hare* . . . possibly for many years."

Carlisle sighed. "So I understand, from Charlie's lawyer."

"Do you think it's possible Robert killed Anna and stole the painting?"

"Robert? No. I do not." He said it firmly.

"What do you think, then? Was it Everett?"

"That's one explanation . . . one Charlie could live with, I suppose, although . . ."

He left the thought unfinished, instead taking me over to the opposite end of the solarium, to show me a piece that Anna had done when she was only twelve years old. It was a painting of a hare, over a photograph—a technique, he said, that's used by several artists today. "Anna was experimental. Always looking for new avenues to explore."

From the expression in his eyes when he spoke, it was clear that he had cared for Anna, along with all the young men who had flocked to her side.

"Have you ever married?" I asked impulsively.

He turned away from the painting. His eyes twinkled. "No, never," he said with warm humor. "When I was in my teens, I was already losing my hair. And, I was short and scrawny, not at all what the girls wanted their men to be. They wanted them tall and good-looking, like the heroes in the romance books and the movies." He chuckled. "Well, not much has changed. Even in business and politics, the most successful leaders are the ones with height."

"You haven't done too bad," I observed, looking around.

"Inherited wealth," Avery said wryly. "Next to intellect and wit, it's the great equalizer."

"You inherited all this?"

"When I was thirty. It was held in trust until then by my father, who thought I was insane as a young man, wanting to be an artist."

"You've done a lot of good with it."

"I've tried."

I left Avery Carlisle a few minutes later, taking away with me something new, something I didn't yet understand.

Later, I realized what it was. I was thinking strange things: that there might, in small pockets or corners of the world, be people who routinely lived in peace.

I'd never even contemplated such a thing before.

CHAPTER 23

It was Thursday. I arrived far too early at the ferry dock in Sausalito. But today was the day. Marcus had said, "I'm bringing you a surprise. It'll be arriving on the noon ferry."

The "it" was a person—I was sure of that by now. I'd been thinking a lot about Marcus's surprise. It was Tark.

Had to be.

I couldn't wait. I hadn't seen the hulk for months—not since he'd gone to Italy with Bernadette in July. Before that, we'd done a lot of shit together. When I first met Tark a year and a half ago, I never dreamed we'd be friends. He was a mob bodyguard, after all. But Tark turned out to be solid, somebody I could count on, somebody with a level head. Add to that assorted muscles and a steady gun hand, and you couldn't beat the combination.

I paced restlessly along the fence, looking down into the water. *Tark.* He had broken away from Marcus last summer, not sure he wanted to be the "apostle" any longer to Marcus's "genius."

"I'm forty-two years old, Jess," he had told me. "It's time I found out who I really am."

But he and Marcus had been boyhood friends, and Tark was loyal. I'd known he couldn't stay away long.

The ferry came into sight, tooting across the Bay from San Francisco. It was a twenty-minute trip, but seemed more like forty. I was fidgety, thinking of all the things I'd say to Tark. How I'd probably hug him, causing him all sorts of embarrassment, but I wouldn't be able to stop myself.

The boat was a little closer, a little larger now. It left a white stream in its wake . . . you could almost see the passengers pointing at Alcatraz as they steamed by. I nibbled on the Mrs.

134

Fields chocolate-chip cookie I'd bought down the street. Feeling butterflies.

Tark was home. Everything would be all right now. With me. With Marcus. Life would go back to being the way it was.

For some reason, that seemed important to me.

The ferry was near enough to cut its engines and glide the rest of the way in. I walked down the sidewalk toward the gate. It was locked, so I stood behind it, waiting impatiently for a man in a pea coat and watch cap to open it up.

The boat came gently to a halt. The ramp was lowered, the gate opened. People began to disembark. I watched them, tourists, mostly, with cameras and tote bags—some carrying babies, some with bags from department stores in the City or from Fisherman's Wharf.

So far, no Tark.

I waited. Until almost everyone, it seemed, had left the boat. Where the hell was he, anyway?

Then I saw my "surprise." And laughed out loud.

Typically, they were the last to abandon ship—which had the added attraction of assuring that their backs wouldn't be exposed. They shuffled down the noisy steel ramp, looking tensely from side to side like they thought they might be jumped.

"Whew!" one of them said when he spotted me. "We sure ain't in Kansas anymore."

"We ain't even in the Melting Pot," the second one added. "Never saw so many white-bread faces in all my life."

"Looked at us like we belonged on a tramp steamer, headin' back to Kenya," Abe agreed.

It was the Genesee Three—calling it the way they saw it, as always.

Well, to be fair, there are a few black faces in Marin. There's Marin City, after all, just the other side of Sausalito. A lot of good people there, some of whom grew up working in the shipyards during World War II. Some upscale new blacks, as well—professional people. So it wasn't color that had made people look at The Three that way.

It was, I thought, their clothes.

Abe was dressed in what was probably his version of California Living: a long, gauzy cotton shirt with a brown-and-orange African design; an orange cotton kerchief twisted into a headband; jeans; and sandals. Ordinarily a dandy, I'd never seen him so dressed down. Percy, whose hair had been reverting to its seventies-style Afro the past few months, wore a shiny, skintight black tee with no sleeves and a neckline nearly to his navel. He looked like he was out here to do a remake of *Dirty Dancing*. Rack wore his usual black leather jacket, black leather pants with studs, and boots.

The Genesee Three. My guys.

They looked, truly, bizarre.

"What in the world are you doing here?" I hugged each in turn. They weren't Tark, but they'd do as the next best thing.

"Vacation, Jess." Abe broke away from my hug, looking gruff and embarrassed. "Andrelli brought us on his jet."

"I figured that. But I didn't even know you knew him—at least, not all that well."

"Only recently met the man," Rack said. "Guess he's not too bad."

They'd had their doubts in the past. I wondered what had brought them around. What it was all about. They wouldn't tell me, I knew from experience, until they were good and ready.

I reached for a box Abe was carrying, to help.

"Hey, hey, hey." He laughed, holding it up and away from me. "This here's a secret, Jess. No can see."

"A secret?"

"I'm not supposed to let you at it until you're sitting down, relaxed, and in a good mood."

I peered more closely at the box. It was from Saks, in New York. Hmmm. "Just one peek?" I said.

Abe chuckled. "No way."

I looked up into his dark face, into his cool, smiling eyes, thinking I might wrest the box away—

Abe has astounding eyes. Most of the time they're world-weary. They've seen it all. But now and then, when Abe's relaxed, they turn warm . . . and they're astoundingly beautiful then. (Eyes are a thing with me; I notice things like that.) Abe's eyes are green, but a deeper, bluer green than Mom's or mine.

I think that somewhere in his background is an Irish Gypsy. Or a horse thief. Maybe even the same one as in mine.

We piled into Aunt Edna's car, with the top down. Rack scrunched in next to me, while Abe and Percy sat on the back, above the rear bench seat. Their odd canvas suitcases, each in many colors, were stacked at their feet. I pulled out of the parking lot, then wound around onto Bridgeway.

Rack looked at the boats that were docked to the right and said, "Kinda nice out here."

Percy grumbled, "Not one brother. Not one brother, since the airport."

"Nice cars, though." That from Abe. "Volvos, BMW's, Porsches . . ." Abe had some experience with cars. At heisting them, mostly.

Rack said, "Don't worry about puttin' us up, Jess. Andrelli says we can stay at his place in the city."

I grinned. "Forget it. I'm taking you home to Aunt Edna." I wouldn't miss this for the world.

Aunt Edna took one look at The Three, at their singular sartorial splendor, stuck a cigarette between her teeth, put her hands on her hips, and said, "What am I supposed to do with you?"

Abe pulled matches from his pocket and lit her cigarette with finesse and panache. One thing about Abe—he's got panache. Better, he knows when to use it.

Rack cracked his knuckles. "Nice vegetable garden out there," he said.

Aunt Edna's eyes slid his way. "You like gardens?"

"I like food."

She didn't crack a smile.

Percy said, "You got a hoe? A spade and stuff?" This from a kid off the streets who, to my knowledge, had never seen anything in his life but concrete and steel.

"I do."

"Well, then. Guess we've got everything we'll need."

Aunt Edna raised a carroty brow. "I suppose that means you're staying."

Percy jutted out his chin. "Not if we're not welcome."

"Who says you're not welcome?"

"Nobody."

"You hear anybody say that?" Aunt Edna turned to me.
I shrugged. "Not me."

Abe said, "Well, if it's what you'd like, Aunt Edna . . ."

"I didn't say I'd like it."

He grinned. "You say we go, we go."

"Go where?"

"Back to the city. Andrelli."

"You like cities?"

"I live in one. They're not all bad."

"You like the country?"

"Only been there once. I liked it fine."

"You'll like it here, then," Aunt Edna said.

It was dinnertime. I had opened the box from Saks. The
guys were out in the garden, poking around. I went through
the kitchen and stood in the doorway until Abe glanced up. I
wasn't sure whether to laugh at myself or hide.

Abe whistled softly. Rack nodded appreciatively. Percy was
drinking iced herb tea. He took a while, then he shrugged.

I cleared my throat and stepped forward. My bare feet
dragged on the grass. "Marcus doesn't really expect me to wear
this tonight, does he?"

"That's what the man said." Abe was looking at the dress
like a designer would, up and down, turning me around. "Nice
lines." He straightened a shoulder pad.

I tugged at the skirt. "It's so damned short. And all these . . .
these . . ."

"Sequins?"

"Yeah, sequins. I feel like somebody named Patty-Jean, from
Nashville."

"You look fantastic," Abe said. "You always look good in
black. Relax."

"Fantastic . . . yeah, that's one word for it," Percy said.
"Might help, though, to wear shoes."

"That does it!" I started back for the house. "You see what
I mean? It's just not me."

"So what's wrong with that?" Abe argued. "Maybe it's time
for a change."

I paused and turned back. "You think so? Why?"

"No reason. Nothing wrong with change, though. Is there?"

"No . . . no, I guess not."

"Not once in a while, anyway," Abe said. "Go for it, Jess."

"I just wish Marcus . . ."

"What?"

"Oh, nothing." I frowned, went back in the house, and took the dress off. Stared at it, piled there on the bed. Why was Marcus always doing these things? Making me out to be something I'm not?

We'd have to have a talk.

CHAPTER 24

Marcus and I were high atop the City, but in San Francisco, height is relative. NYC has those hundred-story things, while in San Francisco they just pile thirty, forty floors or so on top of the hills, and there you are—in some ritzy-glitzy supper club above the fog, surrounded by stars.

No fog tonight, and a jazz combo played Gershwin and Cole as the City flirted and winked below. I imagined I was Ginger Rogers—not that I could dance. I can't follow, and can't lead. My mind works overtime, wondering which way my partner will go next. I always outthink him and spin the opposite way.

Marcus made up for that, whirling me and my sequined black dress around as masterfully as Fred Astaire. He looked, actually, like Armand Assante, his Roman nose and strong black brows lifting now and then with a cool, arrogant air. I found my breasts (such as they are) being squashed against his chest, the starched white shirt of his tux against my cheek. His scent, as they say in the romance books, was freshly, erotically, male.

A girl can handle only so much of that. "Can't we sit this one out?" I grumbled.

One corner of my dance partner's mouth lifted in a small, satisfied smile. His too-dark eyes were knowing. "Having trouble breathing?" he murmured with a soft laugh.

I pulled away and huffed back to our table, pretending to ignore the diners who watched our passing and smiled. Marcus held my chair, grinning, but I yanked it away as I sat. He took his own seat and curled his lips some more at my juvenile irritation, lifting a bottle of nonalcoholic champagne from its bucket and filling our glasses.

"I think you should know," I said perversely, frowning at the tasteless champagne, "I've been . . . seeing someone while I've been out here."

The satisfied smile disappeared. "Ben Jericho. Ex-cop, lives on a houseboat, owns a sailing charter. That someone?"

Bubbles went down the wrong way. "You are totally without shame!" I choked. "How can you have me followed and then *tell* me about it?"

"Not that it makes a difference—and isn't it interesting that that's the first thing you thought?—but I haven't been having you followed. You told me about Jericho after you were here last winter."

I'd forgotten. "But I didn't sleep with him then—" I bit off the words—too late. "I didn't mean—" My tongue tripped over itself.

Marcus sighed. "I know you've been trying to put a distance between us, Jess. You have been for a long time."

"It's—it's not just that."

"Ben Jericho is too normal for you," he said with an air of certainty. "You'd never be able to handle it."

"You think that's why I've been with you? Because you're not normal?"

"I think you're with me for a lot of complicated reasons. That's one."

I was silent. One of the things I liked about Marcus—one of the things that aroused me, in fact—was the way he would look at me the way he was doing now—steady, unwavering—and say what he thought. I would shuffle around, tap-dancing, scared shitless to say what I really felt, and there he'd be. Knowing it all the time and not letting me off the hook.

If Marcus touches me at a moment like that, anywhere—if the tip of his finger even breezes past my nose—I'm gone.

I dragged my eyes away, inched back in my striped velvet chair, and looked off to where the combo was playing. The bass player's dark fingers strummed a riff through "I'll Get By." He teased the strings in a frankly sensuous way, now and then meeting a woman's eyes and giving her a playful grin. Around the room, men and women leaned a few inches closer to each other. A woman in a tight white dress swayed in her seat. Her partner, an IBM type with steel-rimmed glasses, relaxed enough to toy with her hair. I wondered how many of these couples were real couples, and how many were just passing the night away, rather than be alone. I thought of all the one-night stands I'd had back when I was drinking. Lust to dust.

And okay, here's the truth. (Tell me you don't agree.)

As a reporter, I've got all this time and performance pressure, and I don't want it in bed too. I want slow. Easy. Nice. A lot of men these days, whether they work for somebody else or themselves, have time and performance pressure—but they carry it over into sex. They're too damn busy in bed worrying if they'll do good, then hurrying so much that they forget to do good, then worrying whether they've done good.

Oh, sure, there are women like that too. But men are the worst.

I blame it on football and credit cards.

Yeah, I do. Look at it this way: Men don't think twice about getting up the morning of the Big Game and deciding over breakfast to go out and buy a VCR. After all, they've got that piece of plastic, and this is the Age of Instant Gratification, right?

The problem comes when impulse buying slops over into impulse dating. I mean, let me tell you, women are not VCR's. You try instant gratification with any self-respecting woman, buddy, you ain't gonna see no replay. And that's a fact.

Anyway, about Marcus and me. Marcus is too sure of himself to worry about performance pressure. He knows he's good; he doesn't have to prove it. Marcus and I once made love through an entire World Series, lying on the floor in front of the TV, with the sound eventually turned off. Marcus might not have a lot of time to play, but when he does he takes it slow and easy, so when it's over I don't feel like I've been his ten-minute aerobic workout for the day.

Now if I could only figure out what to do about all the other shit that comes between Marcus and me, I'd have it made.

"Sometimes I feel trapped," I said quietly, "by all the things you give me. By all this . . ." My hand made a futile gesture at the glitzy room.

Marcus pushed his plate back and laid down his fork. He leaned forward, folding his arms on the table. "I'm still learning about you, Jess. For a while I thought you'd like diamonds and limos for a change. I know how it is when someone's been without money all their life. When it comes along, they want to see and do everything all at once. I wanted to do that for you. But almost since I met you, you've been sober—"

"Hah."

"—most of the time. And you've been growing fast. On the one hand, you're sarcastic and cynical about the so-called good things in life. On the other, you have a yen a mile wide. I can't keep up."

"You haven't had time to keep up."

He sat back, arms still folded. "All right. That's fair. But has the fault all been mine?"

I thought about it and answered honestly, "No. But what do you mean, a yen? For what?"

"To know things. To have other kinds of advantages you missed growing up, to learn about music and art . . . you think I haven't noticed?"

"Yeah, I guess I thought you hadn't noticed."

"Well, do me a favor. Don't make that mistake again."

"I've tracked down an address out here for Iverson," Marcus said as we tackled thick steaks and baked potatoes.

"A business?"

"No, a house. At a very prestigious address."

"No shit. I wonder why he's staying at a hotel. I wonder why he's even coming out here—other than to find out how much I know, and keep me from learning more."

"I've got a source who says he's meeting with directors of art museums from China. The meeting seems on the up-and-up, something about a cultural-exchange show to be held here late in the year. The other directors check out as being who and what they say they are, and the meeting's been scheduled now for several months. It would seem to be coincidence that Iverson's arriving while you and your mom are here."

"Did you turn up any more businesses for Iverson? Other galleries?"

"Not a damn thing. If he's got any, including the Timmons, he's covered his tracks nicely. I've got someone running checks on the four named corporate owners of Timmons, but so far, they're crystal clean. Presidents of companies, chairmen of boards . . . three own other galleries as well. A diversification;

nothing unusual in that. As to background, they've come from all around the country, and the only thing they apparently have in common with Iverson is that they each have a longtime interest in art. Either they attended art schools as young men or have owned galleries for twenty, thirty years. They may have crossed paths with Iverson socially or through business, but I've turned up no other obvious link between them yet."

"Iverson's gone to a hell of a lot of trouble to maintain a low profile, though."

"You still don't have anyone on it personally? Someone to go around and talk to people?"

"Not yet. I'm working on it."

"What about your friend?" His mouth twisted on the word, as if it were sour. "Jericho? He must have connections in the area."

"He does." I shrugged. "I don't want him involved."

"Oh?"

"Oh." Talking about Ben reminded me of Melissa. I didn't want to think about that, and I said something sure to turn the conversation around. "Have you seen your son since we talked last time?"

Marcus went from warm to distant in three seconds flat. "No."

"You think about it at all?"

"No."

"So nothing's changed."

"You know it will never change, it can't." He picked up a spoon and fiddled with it impatiently. "Look, can we drop the subject?"

"He needs you, Marcus."

"I am the last person in the world he needs. If my enemies knew Chris was my son—"

"They don't have to find out. He wouldn't tell anyone. Marcus, the kid is so fucking great—so grown up for seven years old—and he's already kept more secrets in his little lifetime—"

"Do you know how much it hurts me," Marcus said in a low, harsh voice, "that you've seen him and I haven't? That you visit him when I can't?" His fingers gripped the edge of the table, his knuckles white. I wanted to push him just another inch more, make him so hungry for the kid he wouldn't be able to stay away any longer—

I almost did . . . push him, that is. Then I realized his eyes were moist and he was trying hard not to let me see. He sat across from me, staring numbly at the tablecloth—King of the New Order of organized crime in upstate New York, master of nearly all he chose to survey. Six feet tall, darkly handsome, dressed in a tux that would have cost me a month's income, a man who had it all—

Except for one small boy. The child of a beautiful woman who had come into Marcus's life eight years ago and then left it to protect their son. Chris lived in Brighton, less than an hour from Marcus's apartment, but he might as well be in another country.

Nothing Marcus or I might do could fix that. And why I insist on pushing the matter, why I even go to see the kid every month or so, is beyond me. I don't like kids. (Did I mention that?) Or dogs.

The combo was playing "My Funny Valentine." Crystal clinked. People spoke in hushed voices or danced. For some people things are incredibly simple, I thought, or at least they seem that way.

I straightened and said matter-of-factly, "About Ben Jericho. He's referred me to someone, an investigator in Sausalito. She's due back in town in a couple of days, and if I haven't made any progress by then, I'll talk to her."

"Why not let me put someone on it?" Marcus said.

"Like who? Tark? Tark isn't back from Italy, is he?"

"No, but he's making noises in that direction. There seems to be trouble in paradise."

"Between him and Bernadette?"

"Well . . . I think her family's the problem. They haven't quite forgiven her for turning on Paulie. Of course, they've never known the whole truth."

Paulie Gandolo was Bernadette's brother, a scum-weasel-slimebag if there ever was one. He was in prison now, and Tark and Bernadette had played a large part in putting him there.

"If I told him you needed help—" Marcus began.

"No. Let him be until he sorts things out with Bernadette."

I wanted him to do that. I wanted Tark happy—and I wasn't sure he could be, coming back to work for Marcus. Tark needed, at forty-two, to be his own man.

Even at thirty-one, I knew how that could feel.

"What about getting The Three to help?"

I snorted. "You mean the Bobbsey Twins Invade Mill Valley? They were with Aunt Edna and Mom when I left—playing Pictionary. I never saw three thugs gel out so quickly in my life."

Marcus grinned. "I did promise them a vacation."

"Yeah, and I still want to know why. They won't tell me a thing."

"They handled a job for me, that's all. It was important. I was grateful."

"Must have been some job."

He didn't elaborate.

"Marcus, if you get those kids in trouble—"

"Oh, look who's talking now. Housebreaking, ball-busting, you name it . . . they've done it. And half the time with you as point man, leading the parade."

"Yeah, well, it keeps them out of real trouble. By the way"—I changed the subject again—"what about Avery Carlisle? You run a profile on him?"

"Everything he told you checks out. And I talked to Charlie. He confirms that Carlisle gave him a job after college. He sought Carlisle out because of his reputation, not the other way around. They've seen each other often over the years, but nothing points to his being other than a mentor and employer to Charlie."

I couldn't help feeling relieved. "Where is Everett Iverson's house out here?"

He named a street I wasn't familiar with. "On Nob Hill. But Jess, I hope you're not thinking of going there alone."

"No way. Not a chance."

Tomorrow night, I thought. While Iverson's waiting at the restaurant for Mom and Aunt Edna—who most certainly will not be arriving there, if I have anything to say about it, not without me—I think I'll do a little sightseeing on Nob Hill.

* * *

Over dessert, Marcus said, "I didn't actually have business out here this week. It was an excuse."

I glanced up from the mocha mousse I was putting down faster than I used to put down drinks. "I don't understand."

"I've felt you drifting away again," he said, his eyes steady on me the way I mentioned before. "I thought I'd better do something about it before you were gone."

I put down my fork and wiped my mouth with the napkin. "You came out here to see me? That's the only reason you're here?"

"That's it."

I dropped the napkin. Bent to pick it up, which meant, thankfully, that I had to address the floor. "I don't believe it," I mumbled.

"Nevertheless."

When I sat straight again, I pushed the mousse around with my fork, making little swirls like chefs do with the chocolate sauce. The kind that look like those Austrian swag drapes. Aunt Edna used to have those, back when I was a kid, and I was always fascinated by the way they pulled up and down, never once losing those swags, and once I remember—

"Jess?"

"Huh?" Aunt Edna's drapes departed in a mist.

"Will you please look at me so you'll know I'm telling you the truth?"

It took me a while, but I finally looked. They were still there—those probing brown eyes. Marcus touched my cheek—a whisper of air against my skin, nothing more.

I was gone.

CHAPTER 25

When I got home to Oz the next morning, Glinda Goodwitch was there.

On second glance I saw that it wasn't Glinda Goodwitch, it was Mom—in a pouffy layered pink thing with rose petals cascading down one breast and thigh.

Must be the dress she'd bought for dinner with Everett Iverson, I thought. Being as short as she was, the hem came nearly to Mom's ankles. Aunt Edna had half-basted it, and now she was putting tucks in the waist, an unlit cigarette dangling from one side of her mouth, straight pins from the other. Her carroty hair was more frizzed than usual. Mom was standing on a step stool, arms akimbo to keep from getting stuck. She did look for all the world like Glinda Goodwitch preparing for takeoff.

She looked vulnerable, too. "You can forget the alterations," I said brusquely. "You are not going anywhere with Everett Iverson tonight."

Mom gave me a look that would have flattened me at the age of twelve. Now, it only made me shudder.

"I will not put up with your being difficult today, Jesse."

Aunt Edna muttered something through the pins in her mouth that sounded very much like, "She probably didn't get laid."

I ignored both comments and sat on the kitchen counter, taking an apple from a wooden bowl. It was red and shiny. Too shiny. I could see my sour frown in it. "Is this thing real, or if I eat it, will I fall into a deep sleep and not wake up until this nightmare is over?" A welcome idea; the time had come to level with Mom about her date for tonight.

Mom glared. "What is the matter with you? First Charlie,

148

and now . . . Jessica, what have you got against Everett Iverson?"

I took a deep breath and then a bite. "Okay," I said through chews. "This is the scoop, and you don't have to take my word for it. Marcus will confirm everything I say." I had no doubt that having met Marcus only once, she'd trust his word, as a mobster, over mine. "Everett Iverson is a liar and possibly a murderer. He owns the Timmons Gallery, and he had Charlie's painting of the *Hare* hidden in his cellar in Pittsford—probably since the night forty years ago when Anna Browne was killed. It's almost certain he killed his assistant, Burton, to keep him from telling Charlie that the painting was found in his cellar —"

"Jesse!"

Mom was pale. Her arms had dropped, and she must have gotten stuck by a pin. She was rubbing at the inside of one elbow. Aunt Edna was listening intently, but not with any great surprise. I don't think anything has surprised Aunt Edna since Reagan bamboozled the masses and got himself elected to two terms.

I went on, figuring I might as well get it all out at once. "We don't know, of course, who killed Anna. But one scenario says that it was Everett himself, although we don't yet have a motive. The other says it was his brother, Robert—who knew Anna and had a thing for her—and that Everett's been protecting his brother's memory all these years by keeping the *Hare* hidden. His killing of Burton may have been unpremeditated, and committed—again—to protect Robert's memory. Either way, I've got other plans for tonight, Mom, and you and Aunt Edna cannot go out with that man alone."

Mom was speechless. Aunt Edna spit the pins into her palm, stuck the unlit cigarette behind her right ear, and rode into the gap, questions flying.

"Suppose everything you've just said is true. What now? Will Iverson be arrested?"

"Not yet. We haven't got any real proof of the above. The fact that the painting was in Iverson's cellar is hearsay, now that the assistant is dead. Even so, possession of the *Hare* wouldn't necessarily prove murder."

"If you haven't got proof, what makes you think Iverson's involved at all?"

"Trust me. It fits. And Everett Iverson had me attacked on Ben Jericho's boat the other night, to scare me off so I wouldn't find out any more. That is a fact."

Mom let out a moan. Her hands went to her mouth. "Attacked . . . oh my God."

Aunt Edna took her elbow and helped her down from the stool. Mom sat on it, pink puffs of chiffon billowing around her like a collapsed parachute.

Aunt Edna said matter-of-factly, "You spoke about proof. What are you planning to do, Jesse?"

I shrugged.

"Out with it." Aunt Edna narrowed her eyes. She took the cigarette from behind her ear, pulled a lighter from her jeans, and lit it. Smoke rose in a blue haze around her head.

I glanced uneasily at Mom. She wouldn't like my plans for tonight at all. She'd argue and fuss, flutter and complain. But she might as well hear it. There didn't seem any other way.

"I figure I'll just go have a look at his place," I said, "while he waits at the restaurant for you and Mom tonight. Marcus turned up an address for Iverson, in the City."

"But Everett clearly told me he was staying at a hotel," Mom said. "Jesse, are you sure—?"

"I'm sure. I don't know why he hasn't mentioned a house here, but I'm planning to find out. Now all I need is for the two of you to pretend you're still meeting him tonight, so he'll be at the restaurant in Sausalito at six o'clock. That'll give me time to get into his place on Nob Hill before he finds out you aren't showing and comes home. Provided he does actually come back to the house, and not the hotel."

"Won't he be suspicious when we don't show up?" That from Aunt Edna.

"Not if you call the restaurant when you're about twenty minutes late and tell him your car broke down. Tell him you had to walk several blocks in heels or something, and that you don't feel up to going out after all that. Tell him thanks, but maybe next time."

Aunt Edna was shaking her head. "Won't do. He'll insist on coming over to see that Kate's all right."

"You can convince him that's not a good idea. If anybody can do it, you can—"

But Aunt Edna was still shaking her head. "He doesn't know you suspect him of all this?"

"I don't think so."

"Well, we don't want to put him on the alert. I say we go to dinner." She fended off my protest with a wave of her arm. "What the hell can happen to us in a crowded restaurant? And if we're there with him, that will give you plenty of time—"

"No, Aunt Edna—"

Mom stood up with a silken rustle, shoulders back, spine straight. She had clearly been making decisions of her own while her sister and I talked. "Edna is right," she said firmly. There was a glint in her eye I didn't exactly like the look of. "Nobody has my daughter attacked and gets away with it. And I simply will not allow you to break into the house of a possible murderer and risk getting caught." She gave a curt nod in her sister's direction. "Edna and I will keep Everett busy for you. You just go do what you have to do, dear."

I stared. "Mom, uh . . . I'm breaking into the man's home. You're not even going to warn me against this?"

Her chin went up. "Don't be silly. You're a grown woman, Jesse. And you've been breaking into places since you were twelve years old. I have every confidence in you, dear."

Aunt Edna nodded her agreement. "Nail the bastard," she said.

When I left them a few minutes later, it was with a feeling of awe. Mom was standing once more on the stool, impatiently getting pinned. "Hurry up," I heard her say. "We've got to plan what to do to that wretched man when this is over." Aunt Edna muttered back, "Quit wiggling, for God's sake, or I'll stick you in the butt." Mom said, "How dare he try to hurt Jesse? I'll fix his hide." Aunt Edna answered, "Don't worry, I know just the thing."

With much trepidation, I put their plans for revenge behind me and went in search of the Genesee Three. I shouldn't have. Put their plans for revenge behind me, that is. It was not one of my smarter moves that day.

CHAPTER 26

I found The Three out back in the vegetable garden. Perce was bare from the waist up, muscles rippling with sun and sweat. He was wielding a hoe. Rack was on his knees in the dirt, planting something green. His dark tight curls were full of dust and twigs, and his face was smeared. Abe had reverted to type, and looked a bit of a dandy, in pristine white pants and shirt. He sat on the wooden bench, reading a book called *The Findhorn Garden*. He looked up. "You should read this, Jess. Fascinating stuff. All about how plants have spirits in them, and you gotta talk to the spirits, get them to cooperate, then you get these forty-pound cabbages and things."

Rack said doubtfully, "Spirits? I don't see no spirits. Just little white bugs and ants and stuff."

"Devas," I mumbled.

"Huh?"

I cleared my throat. "Devas. The spirits. They're called devas."

Abe raised a brow. "That's right. How do you know that, Jess?"

I gave a shrug. "Samved told me. When all my plants were dying last year. He said I was cutting them back too much and they didn't like it. I'm supposed to ask their permission first. People torture plants for their own ego, he says, lopping them off that way just to make them pretty."

Rack was sitting back on his heels, staring thoughtfully at the bare-root plant in his hand. "You believe that?"

"I don't know." I remembered Avery Carlisle, and his success in the greenhouse. How he seemed to have such reverence for his plants. "I guess it can't hurt."

"You do it, Jess?" Abe asked.

I flushed. "Of course not. Don't be dumb." I didn't think I

had to mention the time I brought an ivy back to life by reading it *Tales of the City*. I mean, c'mon, everybody knows these things are flukes. To believe they work is really nuts.

"Boy, I sure am glad you guys came out here," I enthused. "Listen, Aunt Edna and Mom are going to dinner with Everett Iverson tonight. I want one of you to go with them. Make sure everything's okay."

"You mean go along, like an escort or something?" Abe looked disappointed in me. "Lady, you do come up with the dumbest ideas."

"Meaning what?"

"Meaning, how do you expect them to explain one of us? A visiting cousin? In this here white-bread county?"

Rack snickered. "We could stand behind them, wavin' a palm."

"You want Iverson to be suspicious, that oughta do it," Percy said.

"Well, somebody can at least follow them. Sit at a table alone. Just watch and see what goes on. Make sure they don't go off in a car with him afterwards or something."

I was remembering all the neat capers we'd pulled together in the last two years. How much fun they were.

Abe nodded slowly. "I could do that."

"Great. And I've got this other idea, too. While Mom and Aunt Edna are at dinner with Iverson, I'll be breaking into his house in the City. I want Perce and Rack to go along. One of you can be lookout—like when we did that party scam together last year, and then that night at Harrigan's—"

Rack looked pained. "We be on vacation, Jess."

"Yeah, right." I chuckled. Rack liked to kid. I still had a smile on my face when I turned to Perce. But Perce was taking up his hoe again. He shook his head.

"I don't know, Jess. Aunt Edna says the planets aren't in the right conjunction for anything too physical right now—"

"Besides," Rack added, "we promised your aunt we'd take over for her at the shelter tonight so she could go to dinner. You wouldn't want us to let her down."

"Oh." I opened my mouth, then closed it. They were serious. "Oh . . . yeah, of course. Okay."

"You'll be all right, Jess. You've done this sort of thing a lot.

And with Iverson off with your mom and Aunt Edna, what could go wrong?"

I swallowed my irritation and thought: What, indeed? Shit, I could do without these guys any day.

I still felt kind of let down.

CHAPTER 27

It was a little before six that night. I drove Mom, Aunt Edna, and Abe to the Alta Mira, dropping Abe off a short distance down the hill so Iverson wouldn't see him. Abe would arrive at the restaurant a few minutes after them and sit at a table alone, keeping an eye on things.

The plan was that after dinner, all three would wait until Iverson had left the restaurant, and then take a cab home. He would think I was picking them up, which would abort any idea he might have of offering them a ride. I didn't want Mom and Aunt Edna alone with him in a car, their destination at his whim.

I also wanted to see how he reacted to me. If he gave any sign at all that he knew I'd found out about his owning Timmons and the *Hare*, and that he had sent Gary Weist to rough me up on Ben's houseboat, I'd have to rethink leaving Mom and Aunt Edna with him at all.

But Weist must have kept his mouth shut. So far as I could tell, Iverson didn't suspect a thing. He met us in the parking drive, wearing a self-assured smile and a superbly cut dinner jacket. He helped Mom from the car. She primped and fussed with her hair, blown about by the ride over with the top down (preferable to being cooped up with Edna's poison smoke, and Aunt Edna had to fend for herself. This she did with her usual grace—clambering up from the bench seat, cigarette between her teeth, hiking up her orange skirt, and slinging an unladylike leg over the side of the car.

"So good to see you again, Jesse," Iverson said. He leaned on my door. "I do wish you were having dinner with us. Couldn't you see your way clear—?"

I smiled. "Thanks, but I've got a hot date. Rain check?"

"Of course. We must talk sometime soon. I'd still like you

to write a piece about my foundation's work with hearing-impaired artists, if you will."

"I'd be happy to." There was a car behind me, waiting for the parking attendant, and I was in the way. I smiled and waved at Mom and Aunt Edna. "Have a good time," I said.

They smiled back. Iverson did too. I varoomed the Fiat's motor, which was good for turning one or two of Aunt Edna's red hairs gray, and peeled out of there.

The ride across the bridge was fun . . . top down, a brilliant sunset, cold, brisk air—

Tight stomach. Rush of adrenaline. Clenched hands on the steering wheel.

There was nothing like breaking into someone's house. Not even sex felt as good.

CHAPTER 28

Iverson's place was in a high-rent area near Coit Tower, with a dramatic view of the Bay. It faced the water. A short driveway led to a garage, and the rest of the house, a stark white cubicle with all glass in front, was piled on top of that. I parked the Fiat a block down the street and made my approach on foot. It was a steep climb beneath thick trees that hadn't yet lost their leaves.

Coming up a flight of stairs alongside the garage, I met with a wrought-iron gate. It was ajar, as if someone had left hurriedly and forgotten to lock it. I pushed it open carefully, testing for squeaks, but the gate was well oiled—as most things are, I guess, for the rich. I entered what seemed to be a large, glass-enclosed courtyard. It was filled with reflected light from the city. The glare rebounded off white panels, and when I put my hand against one, I found it was cold and smooth. Marble. Looking up, I could see clouds through a transparent ceiling. City lights struck the cumulus and bounced back down to me.

My eyes adjusted, and I saw that I was in a kind of scaled-down Greek villa. This courtyard had marble floors and pillars, square arches, and palms of varying heights. A rectangular pool was lined with miniature statues and short, potted cypress trees. The effect was one of being outside. Beyond the glass walls was a million-dollar view. Squat little ferries twinkled as they made their passage across the Bay, carrying commuters at this time of evening, I supposed. The surface of the water was smoked glass. To my left, fog moved in from offshore. It poked over and under the Golden Gate Bridge, half-obscuring the lights of Marin. To my right, Oakland and Berkeley blazed. The Bay Bridge lights hung like garlands on a Christmas tree—a sentiment that lacks originality yet is so apt, I couldn't think of any other.

Water whispered. I made my way cautiously along the slippery edge of the pool. It gave off an invisible icy mist, and when I brushed by a short palm, it rattled like old bones. I shivered. Despite the great view, this place gave me the creeps. It felt like a tomb.

An arched passage led into a living area. It, too, had a view, this one facing the tall, gem-lit city buildings as they curved around toward the Bay Bridge. The window, one solid sheet of glass, brought more light in. It also made it a bad idea to turn on a lamp; there were no drapes that could be closed. I wondered if you had to be an exhibitionist to live in a place like this. That, or so completely ego-driven, you thought you were the only person in town.

I pulled out a pocket flashlight that Abe had given me, but didn't turn it on. Reflected light showed me that this room had four cushy sofas grouped together around a central fire pit. A touch told me they were leather. White leather, matching the thick white carpeting beneath my feet. Marbleized mirrors covered one wall. On another I could just make something out in the dim light that gave me a start.

Heads.

Heads of strange, exotic animals, I realized, drawing close and flicking the penlight briefly at each one. Not the usual bag of the weekend warrior—deer or moose. A zebra. And one that I thought might be a gazelle. Another I didn't recognize, with ornate horns and a tiny, fragile face that even in death looked gentle—a face that said its owner would never have thought to fight back when the hunter's rifle bore down.

In a small black frame I saw a certificate of accomplishment from a place in Kenya: the Four-O-Five Club. It sounded familiar, and I remembered, then, a PBS show a while back about the Four-O-Five Club and other places like it. They were expensive and select. They stocked acres of land with animals bought at auction from zoos, then arranged "hunts" for their members. The term "hunt" being something of a stretch, since there's nowhere for the animals to hide and they lose the instinct to run. Often they're kept on flat, unsheltered plains and become domesticated, thus allowing the hunter to get within a few feet and aim lazily before pulling off his shot.

The animal has as much chance as a carnival balloon at the hands of a master dart thrower.

It was then that I realized there were smaller animals, too. Whole bodies—on shelves, displayed. An anteater? Something prehistoric-looking. And several kinds of lizards. Their ridged backs threw ragged shadows against the white wall as an advertising searchlight flashed from somewhere across the city. There were bodies of cats, too. White cats with shiny eyes. Little gray cats with orbs as black as the night. They looked so alive I touched one. It was hard and cold. I remembered touching the face of a dead woman, once, someone whose death I was partly responsible for. Mary Burghoff. She was at the morgue, and my hand reached to touch her face before I could call it back. I think I had some weird hope she was only pretending to be dead.

On a glass shelf next to the cats were several small figures I recognized as voodoo dolls, the kind that are supposed to ward off evil spirits. Beneath them, books about life after death . . . and the transmigration of souls.

I looked at the cats again, and my flesh puckered. I felt sick, like I'd stepped into a graveyard and found that nobody had bothered to bury the deceased. I moved on swiftly, down a short corridor. Turning left, I entered a bedroom straight out of a movie set. Except for a large window and one wall of pictures, the rest was mirrors—with one gigantic round bed in the middle of it all. It was surrounded by sheer black netting with silver threads. A spread looked like it must have used up several families of leopards. I pushed the netting aside and touched it. It felt soft yet bristly—too harsh to be fake. I snatched back my hand.

Things only got worse. I turned on the tiny flashlight, shielding its side glow with my other hand. There was a dark furry chaise lounge before the window. Without a doubt, mink. Its glossy surface brought back memories of the kind of coat I used to think I might want someday when I grew up—like next year, maybe. Now, with all the animal-rights stuff, you can't wear fur without getting stomped, spit, and painted upon.

At the foot of the chaise was a gaudy but probably real elephant foot encrusted with colored stones.

I turned to the wall of pictures. They were photos, all in black and white, and all of men with naked torsos. They posed—showing off muscles and other protrusions—along the entire wall. The photos were glossy, eleven by seventeen, I guessed, or larger. Each was framed in silver, and mirrored back my shifting figure as I passed from one to the other. They seemed all to be of different men.

A little dazed, I stood looking around—half-forgetting what I was there for. This wasn't the house of the Everett Iverson I'd seen at his staid, conservative estate in Pittsford. Nor was it the home of the ladies' man I'd thought him to be. Had I stumbled into the wrong place?

I'd have left at that point, certain that I'd botched things as usual. Either that, or Marcus had given me the wrong address. But a large framed painting on the far wall caught my eye. A misty city, it seemed. The style had a familiar look. I stepped closer, directing the penlight to the canvas. Now I saw that the buildings of the city were starbursts, the fog a woman's white veil. It flowed from her face, which was part and parcel of a blue-gold sky. A small smile touched her lips. Her dreamy eyes disappeared, then reappeared as I shifted the beam of the flash.

The painting was signed: *Robert G. Iverson.*

Looking down, I realized that it hung on a door. I turned the round steel knob, but it wouldn't budge. I don't know what made me so crazy to get into the room behind that door. Something instinctive, sucking me in. I wondered, crazily, if there was someone behind it. The family loon? I had thoughts of finding Robert Iverson there, babbling and white-haired, but alive.

I needed something to work on that lock. After a brief search, I found another door, and behind it, a bathroom. Flashing Abe's slight beam around, I saw an array of creams and oils on a marble countertop. I lifted one after the other, shining the pinpoint of light on each label. Musk. Rose. Gardenia. There was a gold-and-crystal bowl filled with fresh, new, unopened condoms. They were sprinkled over with potpourri. For no particular reason, I lifted a piece of the shredded wood to my nose. The scent was of jasmine and flowery climes.

My gaze drifted up, and the penlight followed it. Surrounding the gilded mirror were four framed, five-by-seven photos of Everett Iverson. In each, he was with a different man. The pictures seemed of recent vintage; three of the subjects had gray or graying hair and other signs of age. One who stood out from all the rest sported a thick blond mane and mustache. His features were heavy and hard, denoting years of tough living.

I studied the photos, concentrating on Everett Iverson. No sign of the dignified ladies' man here, either. In some shots the men's arms were around each other; in others, they did various interesting things.

Criminee.

No wonder Iverson took a hotel room when he came out here on business. He was leading a secret life in California— one that didn't fit with the sedate reputation he'd built for himself back East, or the flirtation he seemed to be having with my mom.

And speaking of Mom, I'd have to hurry. The dinner with Iverson must be over by now. If she and Aunt Edna had done as I'd told them and gone straight back to the house, Iverson might arrive here at any moment. Or would he go to his hotel room? There was no way of knowing.

I yanked open a drawer and found tweezers, nail files, and other helpful tools. Taking them, a one-ounce bottle of rose oil, a tiny cake of soap, and a condom, I started out of the bathroom, then paused, thinking I'd heard a noise. A car door? It had sounded like that. And footsteps somewhere near. But after several moments of straining, I heard nothing more. A neighbor, probably. The houses were close together here.

I returned to the locked door and knelt down. Holding the penlight in my teeth, I went to work.

It took me longer than it should have, and all the while I grunted and cursed the Genesee Three. Rack would've had this lock open in five seconds flat. Perce wouldn't have bothered; he'd have broken the damned thing down. Not that I wanted that. I didn't know yet what I'd do about Everett Iverson, but in the meantime I didn't plan to leave behind any evidence of my visit.

Several tense minutes later, the lock popped. The sound— not much more than a snicker—was sweeter than April rain.

I stuck my tools in a pocket and opened the door cautiously, no longer really expecting Robert Iverson (the family loon), but so weirded out, still, from Everett's animal collection, it would only have surprised me a little to have found his brother stuffed and mounted on a wall.

I turned the knob, stepped inside, pulled the door half-shut behind me, and switched on the flashlight again. There, in a room slightly larger than a walk-in closet, were perhaps three dozen paintings. All were stacked neatly upright on the floor. None were hung. Packing materials and flat empty crates were scattered around.

One painting in particular drew my eye. I walked toward it, fascinated.

I have a strange kind of memory. I may not remember what day it is, or where I left the keys to my car. But things pop up from the gray cells without warning, and not always at the right time—things that not everyone knows, or even wants to know. Like, who cares that on September 15, 1963, the manager of the Giants, Alvin Dark, took Willie Mays and Willie McCovey out, to play an all-Alou outfield, with Matty, Felipe, and Jesus Alou? It was the first time three brothers had appeared together in the same major league outfield, and I guess that was big news at the time—but like I said, who really cares now? It's not like it's in the Hall of Fame or anything. So why I remember it, I don't know. I just do.

I remembered the painting directly before me now, too. The cells shifted and I was back, suddenly, at the Armistead Gallery in Pittsford, talking with an assistant there, doing research for an article. This was when I was at the *Weston Free Press*, so it was more than three years ago. And this assistant—an older woman with short, wiry, gray hair—was telling me how she'd just recently returned to the work force again after having been retired several years.

"I have my garden," she chatted away, "but it isn't enough. I missed the serene feeling an art gallery or museum gives one."

The woman was a wealth of ancient information. Holding up a catalog, she pointed to a photo of a portrait, a portrait of a woman's face exploding from a chrysanthemum, the skull cracked down the middle in a neat zigzag. "This painting," she said, "is a C. W. James." Then, brightening, "James, like you! What a coincidence. It was part of a collection that was stolen from here in the forties," she went on, eyes on the photograph. "You may remember reading that in the forties and early fifties, there was a rash of thefts from museums around the country. The authorities suspected that the thieves responsible were operating out of this area, although they never found proof."

I wasn't writing about art-theft rings at the time, but about grants and scholarships—and anyway, the woman's story was old news, so I didn't think any more about it. However, I remembered now that this woman was no longer at the Armistead Gallery when I went back to do final interviews with the rest of the staff. I should have wondered about that, but I was really fucked up in those days, drinking and such. I thought she had simply moved on, the way people do. Or gone back full-time to her garden.

Now, looking at the canvas before me, I was almost sure that wasn't true. On this canvas, a woman's face exploded from a chrysanthemum. It was cracked down the middle, with neat zigzags beginning at the nose. The signature in the corner: C. W. James.

I leaned with my back against the doorjamb and slid down to a squatting position, thinking.

I'd never met Everett Iverson before the day I met him at the Armistead Gallery with Charlie and Mom. But he was certainly the director of the gallery at the time I interviewed the gray-haired assistant. He'd been director there, I knew, for many years—twenty or more. And if a recent hiree (someone given to chatting freely) happened to bring up the subject of a one-time local art ring around Iverson . . . might he not get a little nervous? Take her off the payroll?

That is, if he happened, in the forties and fifties, to have been part of that ring himself?

Of course, there could be other, legal, reasons for the director of a major museum and art gallery to hide stolen paintings this way. Couldn't there? I didn't know. And I didn't even know for sure that the rest of the paintings here were stolen.

Shit. I wished I knew more about the art world. All I know about anything is self-taught, things I learned growing up in the streets and, lately, from working for papers. In college, I was too busy busing tables to get into the extracurricular or "fluff" courses. And after that, until a few months ago, I was drunk half the time. From my usual vantage point then, the only kind of art I'd seen was by Armstrong—with my face up against some cold linoleum floor.

I was lost in thought, sitting on my heels, wondering what to do next, when I heard it. A small noise—closer now—coming almost certainly from the bedroom. I froze.

Iverson?

All sorts of thoughts raced through my mind. Iverson's reputation and cover were in the process of being blown—by me. His whole life, the structure he had so carefully built around himself, was in danger of crumbling. Not only that, but this was the man who'd undoubtedly killed Burton, his own assistant, to keep him from telling Charlie where he had found the *Hare.*

He might even have killed Anna Biernej-Browne. I'd never been able to see his brother Robert as a killer—not the same young man who had painted the childlike paintings I'd seen. But Avery Carlisle had said that Everett Iverson was out here in those days, visiting. Had he met Anna, murdered her that night, for whatever reason, and then taken the *Hare?* So that instead of killing Burton to protect Robert's memory, it had been his own life and reputation he was protecting?

But if Iverson was an art thief, why would he only have taken the *Hare?* Anna must have had any number of paintings in her studio that night—and with her dead, their value would probably go up.

As all this thought took place, I was inching toward the door in a squatting position and finding that it wasn't easy. My legs were stumps of petrified wood, my fingers Popsicle sticks. I remembered how, as a kid, I was always afraid at night of the bogeyman in the closet. Now the bogeyman was outside the closet.

Shit. What had I done, coming here alone?

The bedroom lights hadn't yet turned on. But I heard a light scraping, as of drawers being opened and shut.

I bent shakily onto one knee, blew softly on my fingers to melt the ice, then grasped the door, inching it open another crack. And nearly screamed at a dark form, only a foot away from my face. I shoved the door as hard as I could, knocking the person off his feet, and ran for it. I was halfway across the room when my foot struck something hard. I stumbled. Went falling. Tried to get up. My arm was yanked from behind. I twisted around, leveling a kick at the shins. The man dodged it with expert ease. But in doing so, he had to let go of my arm. I scrambled to my feet and made for the door again. He grabbed me by the shoulder and spun me around. The beam of a monster flashlight blinded me. I heard a grunt. An exhalation. My opponent stood back.

"Well, Jesse! How the hell are you, anyway?"

CHAPTER 29

My attacker wore jeans and a heavy black sweater. He had turned off the monster flash, but his silver hair gleamed in the light from the city below. He was incredibly handsome in this light, the lines on his face (not that there were many in the first place) smoothed out by shadows. The startling blue of his eyes wasn't visible in the half-dark, of course, but the wicked gleam was clearly there.

I could see why Mom had fallen for Charlie Browne.

I rubbed my arm where he'd grabbed it, feeling in a foul mood. "What the hell are you doing here, Charlie?"

"The same as you, it seems—looking for something on Iverson."

"You escape from jail?"

He grinned. "Out on bail. Good behavior."

"Oh, right. Good behavior. Why didn't I know that?"

"Testy, testy."

"I love being attacked in a strange apartment in the dark."

"You weren't too bright about it," Charlie noted seriously. "What if I'd been one of the bad guys? What if I'd had a gun?"

My eyes flicked down to the shoulder area, then the hip. There wasn't much room for a hidden weapon. Charlie's jeans and sweater clung to his tight frame. On the other hand—he did wear black leather gloves.

"What if you *are* one of the bad guys?" I said.

Charlie laughed. "Jesse, Jesse. One of these days I'll make you trust me. You'll see."

"One of these days, wars will end, peace will reign, hell will freeze—"

He laughed again, softly, not in the least perturbed. "So, what've you found? Anything?"

166

I thought about it. Say no? Get him out of there? Not let him see the paintings? I didn't trust Charlie Browne.

On the other hand, it might not hurt to pretend for a while that I did.

I kicked the elephant foot—the thing I'd fallen over—out of the way and led Charlie back to the closet. I flashed my small light around the room, illuminating the paintings stacked on the floor. Charlie turned his own flash on and palmed through them, pausing now and then to whistle. Instant recognition.

"Some of these," he said almost reverently, "have been on various lists of mine in the past."

"Lists?"

"To find."

"Oh, to find. Of course."

He held one up, a bright splash of vivid color. "A Whitfield! God, Jesse, this has been missing for thirty-seven years!" My flashlight beam tilted up, revealing an expression of excitement. A gleam in the blue Paul Newman eyes.

"So now what, Charlie?"

His face swung round to mine. He stared a moment, the baby blues going blank. Then he grinned kind of boyishly, and shrugged. "Guess we'll have to tell the authorities." He chuckled softly. "Or maybe not. What do you think, Jess?"

"I think there's several million dollars of stolen art here. The police would want to know."

"Of course. You're right. On the other hand . . ." Charlie's tone became silky smooth. "There's no reason they've got to know right away."

"Uh-huh."

"I mean, look at it this way. They find out, all they can do is come in here and arrest Iverson for art theft. We still don't have any proof he killed Burton. Not enough to clear me, anyway."

"It might at least point the investigation that way."

"Which could take forever, if Iverson's covered his tracks well. And he has. Where was he, after all, when I was found with Burton?"

"With me." On the terrace, then in the gallery, looking at Robert's painting of Anna.

Charlie nodded. "He was waltzing you around the manse. No proof he was anywhere near the stables when it happened."

I remembered something. "Wait a minute, Charlie. I saw someone. Someone either coming from or going to the stables, right around the time it must have happened. I was on the terrace—"

"Who?" he said tersely. "Who did you see?"

"I don't know . . . it was too dark. A form. A shadow. I thought—Will you let go of my arm?"

"Sorry. I didn't realize. What was your first impression?"

I remembered, with irritation and disappointment. "I thought it might be a dog."

Charlie sighed. "That's what I mean." He began to straighten the paintings, putting them back the way we'd found them. "We need to approach this from another angle."

"You got something in mind?"

"A little scam, perhaps. Use Iverson's obvious greed for this sort of thing against him." He flashed his larger beam around the closet, giving it a last look. "Wait a minute, what's that?"

There was a stack of paintings against a back wall that Charlie had only given a surface look to. Now, his light illuminated the wall itself.

"I don't—"

"Over here."

I followed and saw him run his fingers over the edge of a door. It was nearly invisible; the canvases had hidden its knob. We moved the paintings out of the way, and opened the door. There was a light switch just inside, on the left. Charlie flicked it on.

"Holy Christ."

There, in a small room, hung floor-to-ceiling, were portraits of a woman. They were sick, deranged—unframed, and hideous. Dark slashes fought with bloody crimsons and putrid greens, along with purples that looked like angry welts. In one canvas the woman stretched out a skeleton arm. A death's head glowed whitely from the bones of her hand. In another the skin on her face was torn, scarred, hanging down in strips. Her teeth were bared, as if in the agony of death. In still another canvas, blood dripped from nostrils and ears. A black-handled dagger protruded from a bony chest.

In each portrait, the woman's hair was dark and flowing, the eyes vivid blue in hollow sockets. In each portrait, she held a hare.

Charlie walked from one canvas to the other, his face pale, his eyes filled with anguish. "Anna?" he whispered. His voice was suddenly much too full. It made my own throat close. I stepped closer and touched a nearby painting, tentatively, then the next. The artist's torment seemed to reach with those bony, decaying hands to grab me. I pulled back, afraid.

All of the portraits were signed by Robert Iverson. Yet they were so unlike the fragile, fanciful paintings in Iverson's home gallery in Pittsford, so lacking in the fine spirit and talent that went into those paintings, they could only be called obscene.

What in the name of God had happened to make Robert Iverson do such a thing?

"Charlie, let's get out of here," I said, feeling sick.

I don't think Charlie heard me.

"C'mon," I urged. "The man was demented."

He wiped impatiently at his eyes, which were moist. "How could anyone see her like this? My mother was a kind, beautiful woman—she didn't deserve this."

I didn't think so, either—nobody deserved this. On the other hand, I wondered if Charlie, at eight years old, had been smart enough to see his mother as she was—all the many personalities she might have contrived, in order to survive.

"I found her, you know," he said softly, sounding almost like that eight-year-old boy.

I was silent.

"She had a party that night. She sent me to a neighbor's house to spend the night, and I came home early, and there she was. . . .

"I thought she was asleep. She had wrapped her hair the night before in one long, silky braid, like a piece of licorice, I remembered calling it, and she had laughed. When I found her, she was just lying there on the floor, by her easel, and the braid was draped over her chest. I bent down and shook her and said, 'Mother? Mother, wake up'—"

His voice broke. "Damn the man! What could she have done that made him hate her this way?"

"Charlie, stop it. For Christ's sake, Robert Iverson *killed* himself. And now we know why. He was mad, that's all. Let's get the hell out of here."

He stared around the room a moment more, rubbing a hand over his face, making an obvious effort to collect himself. "You're right," he said. "We've got to move."

I pushed him ahead of me, turned out the light, and shut the door behind us. We put the canvases back against the door, the way they were, and went through the first closet into the bedroom. Charlie paused and looked around in the half-dark. "Everything the way you found it?" His voice was returning to normal.

"I think so. No, the elephant's foot." I crossed over and righted it.

"Let's check in the front room too. Make sure we don't overlook anything. We'll wipe down whatever you might have touched—You remember exactly how things were?" He pulled out a handkerchief and wiped the closet doorknob on both sides.

"Yeah, I remember. I remember everything. But, Charlie?" I faced him.

"What, Jess?"

"I'm just wondering. How come you're so good at this?"

"At what, Jess?"

"Wiping doorknobs, breaking the law."

Charlie grinned. He was returning to his old self. "Practice, Jess."

"I figured that. I just want to know where you got this practice."

"Oh, here and there."

"Right. Here and where?"

"I watch a lot of TV."

"Uh-huh."

He patted my shoulder. "You worry too much, Jess. Where else were you tonight?"

"Bathroom." I made a gesture. Charlie went ahead, training his flashlight on the counter and walls. It hit on the pictures of Iverson and his friends. Charlie leaned forward, squinting, and stopped at the second photo down on the right. The man with thick blond hair and the heavy, dissolute look. "Uh-*huh*. Rune Jenners," he said with satisfaction.

"Who?"

"Guy in this picture with our pal Everett. Rune Jenners."

"You know this Jenners?"

"I know *of* him. Jenners is one of the owners on record of the Timmons Gallery. Not to mention several other galleries around the world. He's under investigation—suspicion of art theft, several, in fact, over the past thirty-odd years. If Rune Jenners and Iverson have been this close—" He paused, looking more carefully at the photos of Iverson with the other three men. "I wonder . . ."

On the street, a car door slammed. "Charlie, I think we'd better get out of here. It's getting late. What if Iverson shows up here, instead of going back to his hotel after—" I closed my mouth, remembering, suddenly, that Charlie didn't know about Mom and Aunt Edna.

"After what, Jess?" His tone was sharp. "Do you know where Iverson is?"

"Uh—well, yeah, he's, uh—he's out with Mom."

"*What?*"

"Simmer down. Aunt Edna's with them too—"

"Christ Almighty, Jess, you let them go somewhere with Iverson?"

"I've got somebody watching after them, Charlie. Jeez, it's okay." My reassurances sounded false even to my ears. "Anyway, they should be back at Aunt Edna's house by now. I'm sure they are. Let's go, Charlie."

I went ahead of him through the dim, graveyard living room, making sure everything was as it had been before I arrived, and keeping my ears tuned for any more outside sounds. We made it to the street okay, and then to the Fiat. Nerves, I thought. No one had discovered us here.

Charlie climbed into the passenger seat, scrunching his legs into the Fiat's small space. His knees nearly came to his chin. "I took a cab directly from the airport," he said. "I figured there wasn't any time to waste."

I decided to be firm. "Charlie, whatever happens from here on out with Iverson, we've got to keep Mom out of it. She's not like us—she doesn't lie well, doesn't know how to tap-dance."

Charlie grunted. "Obviously, you don't know your mom very well."

My first instinct was resentment. What'd he mean, I didn't know Mom? Who the hell did Charlie Browne think he was, anyway?

But Charlie, I discovered an hour later, was right. I didn't know Mom anymore at all. Because when we got back to Aunt Edna's house, both she and Mom had disappeared.

And Abe was nowhere around.

CHAPTER 30

"Where are they, Charlie? Where the hell are they?"

It was after ten o'clock, and the maitre d' at the Alta Mira had told me on the phone that Mom, Iverson, and Aunt Edna had left over an hour ago. If Mom and Aunt Edna had done as they were supposed to and come straight home, they should have been here, with Abe, by now.

Charlie glowered at me. "This was a dumb-ass scheme, Jesse. You should have known your mother—"

"Look, I'm sure they're okay." I wasn't sure at all. "If they did go with Iverson somewhere, Abe's looking after them."

But Abe would have had to follow secretly. He could hardly jump into Iverson's car and say, "Hey, man, goin' my way?" What if he hadn't been able to follow? What if he'd lost them?

"Iverson would never take them to that house," I said. "He wouldn't want them to see how he lives. So they've just gone somewhere for drinks, right?"

Charlie didn't answer. He was pacing, pacing back and forth in the yellow kitchen, his face deeply lined with worry. Now and then he ran a hand through his hair, leaving it upended. Whatever else I believed about Charlie, it was clear he cared a lot for Mom. He looked like a little boy who'd lost his best friend, the one he always went to camp with.

I knew how he felt. The thought of Mom in Iverson's hands made my throat ache. "She'll be all right," I said, mostly to reassure myself.

I tried to remember how tough Mom was in the old days, standing up to Pop. Her chin and hands trembling. "I will not give you another cent. Everything I've got left is for rent and bills." This scene occurred almost weekly, with Pop drinking up most of his pay after work on Friday and then coming home around midnight for whatever Mom had managed to salt away.

"Give it to me!" he'd roar. "I earned it, it's mine!"

"Not one cent!"

Once, Pop almost hit her. But never quite. It was the verbal abuse that went on and on. That was what got us—both her and me.

When Pop died, she blamed me for a while, because I was drunk that night and he came to my rescue. (He was drunk, too, which was why he drove into a tree.) I didn't learn until I came out here last year that she was actually blaming herself back then, and that because of the guilt, she had taken it out on me.

All those years she had stayed with Pop, telling herself it was love? All that time she just hadn't known what else to do. When she heard he was dead, she admitted to me last year, the first thing she felt—the first tiny flicker—was relief. It scared the hell out of her, held up a mirror to a truth she didn't want to see and couldn't accept for a long time.

But Christ, Mom was tough. The courage that had taken her through those years was still there, underneath the Golden Girl exterior. I should have remembered that before. The Kate James who had been formed by adversity in the old days wouldn't just meet Iverson for dinner tonight and pretend to sociability, knowing he might have killed Burton and left Charlie to take the rap. She'd take him on, her chin thrust up, her green eyes narrowed to slits: giving him the evil eye. She'd make him pay.

And Aunt Edna? She'd go along with anything. They were a pair, her and Mom. I'd heard stories of them as kids, always into scraps together. When the chips were down, there was no deadlier duo in town. Both of them raised on the wrong side of the tracks, back in the days when Irish women, no matter how poor, starched their lace curtains and hung them at the windows like a proud, national flag. Pride. They had that, letting no one else in. Fighting their fights together, sticking up for each other . . .

I remembered a story Aunt Edna told me about a time when some neighborhood toad took to bothering them on their way home from school. Mom and Aunt Edna were only a year apart, in third and fourth grade, respectively, at the time. This other kid was a fifth-grader, I think, a menace-in-training with a scout knife. Aunt Edna started loading rocks from the driveway in her little red purse every morning, thinking she'd use it as a weapon. Mom was the one who bopped him, though. With her geography book. "I got him with Sudan!" Mom cried, finishing up the story. "It was wonderful! He never came near us again."

My eyes began to smart. Neither Mom nor Aunt Edna were kids anymore, and the enemy this time would likely brandish more than a scout knife.

Why had I let them go to dinner with Iverson—a man who had sent an employee to rough me up on Ben's houseboat, and who had almost certainly murdered his own assistant, Burton, to cover up the theft of a painting? For a man in his position to take those risks, he'd have to be on the edge, his personality beginning to crumble.

And I should have known better.

I'd told myself that as long as Abe was around, Mom and Aunt Edna would be all right. But what could Abe do if they'd recklessly gone off someplace where he couldn't follow?

"Where else would they go?" Charlie murmured, as if to himself.

"The hotel!" I remembered. "Damn, what am I thinking of? Charlie, he's got a room at the Devon Hotel in the City. He's taken them there."

Charlie grabbed the keys to the Fiat and headed for the door, looking grim.

"Wait. I'm going with you."

He paused, turning back. The worry lines deepened. He put a hand on my shoulder and spoke heavily. "Your mother would never forgive me if you were hurt. Jesse, we're talking about a killer here. Kate and Edna are alone with a killer."

"I know, Charlie. I know that." I grabbed his arm. "C'mon. Let's go."

He hesitated, holding back a moment. "It may not be easy."

"Easy, schmeasy," I said, thinking of Mom and Aunt Edna taking on the fifth-grade bully. What good were genes, anyway, if they didn't help out in a pinch?

Finally, Charlie nodded. I gave him a push and he preceded me out the door.

And that's how I ended up an hour later on a windy ledge thirty stories up, somewhere above San Francisco Bay.

CHAPTER 31

"Goddammit, Charlie. I am not going out on that ledge. What do you think this is, Hollywood? I am not Robert Wagner. I am not even MacGyver. I am not, repeat not, going out on that ledge."

We were on the thirty-first floor, on a small balcony outside the apartment next to Iverson's suite of rooms. Charlie had talked to the manager downstairs, after the desk clerk told us Iverson had come in around nine o'clock and left orders not to be disturbed. The clerk had refused to ring through for us.

"Was there anyone with him?" I had asked.

"Two older women," the manager confirmed. He tugged at his pointed beard, then twisted his small white hands, holding them high against his chest.

Charlie took the man aside. I don't know how he pulled it off. I didn't ask. But the next thing I knew, we were in an empty room next to Iverson's, and now we were on its balcony, with a narrow ledge between us and Iverson's balcony—which was almost close enough to touch and swing over to, but not quite.

I shuddered, trying not to look down.

Charlie put the heat on. "Getting timid in your old age, Jess? I remember Kate telling me stories about how you used to jump off bridges into the Genesee River with the boys in eighth grade."

"They weren't thirty stories up, Charlie. They just looked that way at the time."

"It's not really that far," Charlie urged. "I'll be holding you. Trust me, I won't let you fall."

Trust Charlie. Trust a man I barely knew, a man with a mysterious past who was out on bail on a murder rap—

I looked down, in spite of myself. Cars pulling up to the curved entrance or driving along the street looked like tiny Christmas toys. The wind gusted, tearing at my hair and the loose sleeves of the blouse I hadn't taken time to change. Oh, God.

"I still don't understand why we don't just knock on the door. Or get a key from the manager and walk in."

"The manager says there are dead bolts on all the hallway doors. We'd let Iverson know we were here, and there's no assurance he'd let us in—at least not before harming—Jesse, we've got to know what's going on in there first, make sure Kate and Edna are all right."

"So I'm supposed to go through the bedroom . . ." I tried to recall everything we'd gone over on the way up here. Stalling.

"All you've got to do is take your handy-dandy little weapon there and pop the lock on his bedroom door, just like I showed you on this one."

I hefted my "weapon." On the way out through Aunt Edna's garden, I had picked up a stainless-steel trowel of lethal proportions. I don't think I did this in conscious imitation of Aunt Edna and her purseful of rocks. It simply seemed like a handy-dandy thing to do, since Charlie didn't carry a gun. I'd bullied him into hiding the trowel under his windbreaker as we made our way through the hotel—and although doing so had given him considerable amusement at the time, he had to admit to its usefulness now.

Charlie had decided I should use the trowel to force the lock on the sliding doors into Iverson's bedroom.

"Yeah?" I said. "And while I'm doing that, what the hell are you supposed to do, Charlie?" The wind seemed to be blowing in all directions at once. Foghorns moaned across the Bay, sounding afraid and forlorn. Like me.

"I'll tap on the living room window," Charlie said.

"You'll tap on the living room window. Fucking impressive." I stuck my hands on my hips. "Charlie, are you *crazy?*"

"No. He won't be expecting anybody to tap on the window."

"You *are* crazy."

"And while I'm tapping on the window, you'll be going in the bedroom door."

"Just like that. He won't even hear me, what with all the noise—you going tippy-tappy on the window and stuff."

"Trust me."

That again. Trust Charlie Browne.

"Charlie—this is so complicated. We should call the cops —"

His voice rose impatiently. "I told you not to come. Dammit, you're wasting time—"

"Never mind! Christ!"

"Then *go*, Jess! Don't think about it. Either that, or get back inside and wait for me."

"I'm going, I'm *going*."

I stuck the trowel in my belt, slid a leg over the balcony railing, and planted my right foot on the narrow ledge that ran along the side of the building. With Charlie gripping my waist with one hand and my right arm with the other, I swung my other leg over the rail—and got rocked by a gust of wind that felt like a freight train bearing down. I tottered. Charlie held on.

"Go, Jess," he said quietly. "I've got you. I swear I won't let go."

I took a breath, finished the swing, and got both feet planted nervously on the narrow ledge. With the toes of my Nikes against the building, my heels hung over the edge. I wobbled. There was nothing to hold on to but the fine crevices between bricks. An illusion of safety, at best. Fear swept through me, first hot, then cold. Charlie's grip was all that stood between me and the street, thirty floors below. It took only a moment to realize I'd better move fast. I leaned sideways, reaching for the railing of Iverson's balcony. It was inches away, but I couldn't quite touch it. Charlie leaned far out, his hand hanging on to my wrist. I realized that he no longer held my waist. I began to fall backward, away from the building. My wrist, sweaty now from exertion, slipped a fraction of an inch from Charlie's grasp. I jerked my head around in time to see him lean farther and grab my wrist with both of his. He was strad-dling the railing now, clutching it with the strength of both legs. No hands. I didn't see how he could help but be pulled over the rail by my weight. "Ch-Ch-Charlie . . ." My teeth chattered. It came out sounding like a Spanish dance: *Cha-cha-cha*.

"It's okay, Jess. Easy does it."

I reached again for the railing, shaking so hard I missed it twice. Then I got it—grasped it firmly—and gave a nod to Charlie that hammered in my head like a death warrant. He let go of my wrist. I swung that arm around, gripped Iverson's rail, followed with one leg, then another—and went falling—falling—falling—falling—

Onto the right side of Iverson's balcony, not the wrong. For a heart-stopping second, I hadn't been sure.

Then Charlie was hoisting himself onto the opposite rail. He stood straight, with arms outstretched, his windbreaker flapping, and my stomach went into my throat as I saw what he was planning to do. I wanted to yell out, "NO!" but at his signal I stumbled back, making room. Charlie gave a leap and crossed the space between balconies easily, as if terra firma were two short feet below. He landed beside me with unbelievable stealth on both feet, without even a stumble. I watched the whole thing with awe.

Was Charlie a cat burglar, then? He'd done that awfully well.

I didn't have time to think about it. Charlie positioned himself at Iverson's thinly draped living room window. It was fairly large, but not full-length like the door I was to go through. I stood before mine, met Charlie's eyes, and saw him raise his hand to tap. He nodded, synchronizing his movements with mine. I slid the garden trowel into the crevice of the bedroom door just above its lock and nodded back.

A woman screamed.

Charlie's hand went still. I faltered. We looked at each other, fear in our eyes. Charlie gave a shattering yell like the kind they teach you in martial arts. He kicked the living room window in.

Glass went flying. Charlie swung through the opening the broken window made, and that was the last I saw. I was breaking through the bedroom door, the garden trowel raised in my fist.

CHAPTER 32

The door gave easily—too easily, but there wasn't time to question why. The bedroom was pitch dark. All kinds of racket came from the front room. I heard Mom's voice out there, garbled with Aunt Edna's. Both were high and panicky. I heard Charlie. I stumbled against a bed, losing balance and falling into its smothery softness, then pushing myself up and racing around it. My eyes adjusted a little to the dark, and I spotted a crack of light around a door. I made for it, yanking at the knob, but nearly dropped dead as something came around me from behind. High-tension wires, strapping themselves around my upper body. I struck backward with the garden trowel. A muffled howl. The wires loosened, but not enough. I struck again. A string of curses. The wires tightened this time, and I realized they were arms. With my fingers, I discovered flesh and bone at my waist. A hand. I swung upward and back, toward where I thought there must be a head. One arm loosened and grabbed my weapon before it connected. I was lifted off my feet and thrown onto the bed. The torso belonging to the arms slammed against me, pinning me down. It was heavy and long, a crushing weight. A hand went over my mouth, stifling my scream for help. I couldn't move, couldn't yell. *Mom! What in the name of God was happening to Mom?*

The door from the living room burst open. I twisted my head as the hand on my mouth let up a fraction. Figures were outlined in the light from the other room. The hand let up some more. I yelled.

"Charlie!"

Lights came on. Charlie stood there, his face and arms bloody. Behind him, two silhouettes. Female. Mom and Aunt Edna. I stared. They stared back. The heavy form above me

180

raised up. Curses were breathed against my face. "What the fuck—!" My eyes swung up to the familiar voice.

It was Abe.

"You think I'd leave Mom and Aunt Edna alone with that creepo?" Abe stormed. "You give me a job, I do it."

"I know, I know. I'm sorry."

We were in the living room. Abe had explained how he'd followed Mom, Aunt Edna, and Iverson in a cab, and how he'd gotten in the same way we did, from the apartment next door. Abe's strength always was in his second-story work. But no wonder the manager looked so nervous when we talked to him. He wasn't above taking bribes from both Charlie and Abe, but he must have been picturing a free-for-all up here. Which is what he almost got.

I gawked at the setting before me: candlelight on a silver-and-crystal-appointed table.

"Where the hell is Iverson? What's been going on here?"

"He went down to the corner, to the Heavenly Cheesecake store," Mom said.

I must have looked confused.

"Dessert," Aunt Edna explained. "Lime curd."

Lime curd. Mom's favorite.

"You'd have been proud of me, Jesse! I pretended to the most awful craving—"

"We thought it was a perfect opportunity," Aunt Edna explained, "to check things out here. After Everett left we went through drawers in the living room, and Abe was in the bedroom just in case he came back—"

"Then I saw a figure outside on the balcony—" Mom said.

"Charlie. But we didn't know that. We were so nervous to begin with—"

"I just couldn't help it," Mom said. "I screamed."

"But Everett's been gone half an hour," Aunt Edna added, "and he was only supposed to be a few minutes."

Charlie had been on the phone through all this. Mom had tried wiping off blood from the cuts he'd gotten coming through the window, but he kept moving around. He was angry. Now he dropped the receiver with a bang. "The desk clerk didn't see him leave. Iverson would have had to go past him, unless he left by the service exit—but why would he do that?"

Abe said, "He had a call just before he went out. Took it in the bedroom."

"Where were you all this time?"

He made a face. "In the closet, all wrapped up in the stinkingest perfumey suits and tuxes—"

"Did you hear the conversation?"

"Bits and pieces. Said something like, 'How long were they there,' and how he'd be over to check it out."

Charlie and I looked at each other. *The house*. Someone had seen us at Iverson's house. Had to be. And going out for cheesecake had been an excuse . . .

Shit. If he was on to us, he wouldn't be back. Neither we nor Mom would ever see him again.

"Let's get out of here," I said to the room in general. I was feeling depressed. "This isn't going anywhere."

Charlie nodded agreement. "I'll talk to the manager about cleaning up this mess," he said. There was broken glass all over the living room floor. The wind was blasting in, making the heavy drapes stand nearly straight out. I was glad we didn't have to go back that way. I wondered briefly what Iverson would think if he really was on a cheesecake run and came back to this scene.

But only briefly. I didn't believe for a minute he'd be back tonight. He'd lay low at his house, most likely, wondering what Charlie and I had been doing there, and how much we knew. He'd wait to see if we made any moves, before he'd surface again.

Charlie had gotten Mom's coat and was putting it over her shoulders. Mom slipped her arms into the sleeves. Charlie turned her around and planted a gentle kiss on the tip of her nose. Mom touched his cheek with her fingertips and murmured something. Aunt Edna rolled her eyes.

"Can we go now? I've just about lost my taste for lime curd."

CHAPTER 33

Charlie, The Three, and I were in Aunt Edna's garden the next evening, talking quietly. Mom and Aunt Edna were cooking dinner. The sun was low, the bees tired out. They made a few desultory dives at my hair, then quit.

Rack was watering some rather sizable green things that turned out to be the broccoli Aunt Edna had planted by the light of the new moon when Mom and I first arrived.

"I'd never have believed it," I said. "Even in California, broccoli doesn't usually grow at this time of year. And look how big it already is!"

"Well, we been talkin' to them, Jess. You know." Rack shrugged his shoulders diffidently.

"Talking?"

"You remember. The spirit things."

"The devas?"

"The devas, yeah, I guess that what you call 'em, whatever."

I shook my head. "I don't get your fascination with this stuff."

Rack looked embarrassed. I remembered him on Genesee Street, back in Rochester, always looking tough. Swaggering. Standing taller than he really was at five-foot-seven or so, creaking about in his leathers and studs, letting people know that despite his size, he was Boss.

"Now and then," he explained, "you gotta stop and reassess things, Jess. Nothin' wrong with that. Long as it doesn't change everything, not for good."

"Hmmm." He was sounding like Abe.

"There's something fascinating about watching anything grow," Charlie said. "It takes one back to early, more primitive times."

"You mean when men were men and women were women?" I sneered.

183

"I was thinking back to when women were warriors, along with men. Why are you always so prickly, girl?"

"Because I always know that sooner or later, some man is going to call me *girl*."

Charlie groaned.

"To get back to business," he said, "you're meeting with this P.I., Samantha Crewe, tomorrow?"

"Yes. A friend of mine set it up."

"Ben Jericho? Just who is this guy?"

"Don't worry. He's an ex-cop, straight as they come. And he and Sam Crewe are old friends. He trusts her. That's good enough for me."

"I don't like it, Jess. This entire plan hinges on Iverson's showing up at the reception at the Asian Museum. If he's skipped town—"

"Somehow, I don't think he's done that. After all, we were careful not to leave any clues behind that we'd found anything legally incriminating. He can't know we saw the paintings in the closet. Did the hotel get that window fixed all right?"

"Yes, and you were right. Iverson never did go back there last night. I wonder if he tried to call the room, to make some excuse to Kate and Edna." Charlie worked his arms, rubbing tension out of them. He winced as his left hand grazed a deep scratch from his window-crashing escapade. "When are we meeting with this P.I., Jess?"

"Tomorrow afternoon. But, Charlie, I'd rather you stayed here with Mom. It wouldn't hurt to hold her hand a little."

He thought about it, then nodded. "Your mother and I have some serious talking to do."

I looked at him sharply. "You calling off the relationship?"

"Not at all. But I do feel Kate should be given the chance to rethink it. She never expected all this, uh . . . excitement that she's had in the past few weeks."

I started to agree, then bit my tongue. Mom was a big girl. She could handle this.

"I suppose you'll be too busy to help when the scam actually comes down," I said to Abe, but meaning Rack and Percy too.

Rack turned the nozzle on the hose so it barely dribbled, and set it down along a row of broccoli. He faced me with his arms folded. Perce rested on his hoe like a Grant Wood painting. Abe roused himself from the book he'd been reading and said mildly, "The brothers and me, we been havin' a little talk."

Rack and Percy nodded their accord.

"We feel we been lettin' you down," Percy said.

"But only because it seemed pretty safe out here," Rack interjected.

"Too damned safe," Percy breathed, "if you ask me." He wiped dusty sweat from his dark brow.

"Even so, we made our pact 'long time ago, to be there when you need us," Abe added.

I scowled. "So you've said. But why? This is so damned frustrating! Why won't you ever tell me why?" They couldn't be under orders from Marcus; I'd known them long before him.

"*Why* don't tell nobody nuthin'," Abe said, his grammar lapsing as it often does when he's dead serious. "Doin' is what counts. And we ain't been doin'."

"Sooo . . ." Rack cleared his throat, stuck his chin up, and shoved his thumbs in his jeans. His ribs were skinny, but that didn't fool me. Rack is a master of several martial arts. In his eyes now was a look that proclaimed more than ever the Genesee Street kid he was. "From now on, anything you need, you get, Jess. Simple as that."

I looked at the other two, who stood firm and square beside him, then again to Rack. Rack was seventeen, probably, now. He'd been fourteen when they'd first entered my life to fend off two men who attacked me near my apartment one night. Abe's age was indeterminate. I've often thought he might have been beamed down through time from ancient Egypt. His frequent flashes of wisdom startled me. Perce? Not for a minute have I ever doubted that Percy, like Rack, should have been in some good school these past few years, getting the kind of education kids in places like Marin County—even upscale Rochester—doze their way through. They'd have shaken up everybody's curve—given the white-bread students who don't have anything to do but watch television and snort a few lines at night something to think about.

Aside from all the punk rich kids they could have brought down to size, they would most likely have won scholarships and gone on to Princeton, Rutgers, Yale. The Three had demonstrated their innate brilliance in all the scams they'd perpetrated over the past several years.

And that, in my opinion, is what's wrong with society today. We don't offer our best and brightest enough *good* schools, the kind that woo them, that seduce them into learning. We herd them like cattle into pens every day, erase them clean of individuality, then wonder why they drug themselves out to get through it, or why they quit and move into more creative and oftentimes illegal schemes.

Nor do we offer them jobs that will let them properly live. Rack supports his mother, who can no longer work, and his six younger brothers and sisters, with his petty crimes. Percy has two elderly aunts, I've learned, and a whole slew of grade-school-age cousins whose parents disappeared. He helps them out so they won't end up on the streets like him. The system, both welfare and legal, has let both those families down—so Rack and Percy do what they feel they have to do. And who am I to judge?

The least I could do, I thought, is let them enjoy this first vacation of their lives—brief as it would be.

"You know what I think?" I said. "I think you should go back to watching the broccoli grow. I've kind of been feeling good, getting along on my own. Proving I can do it, I mean. It's something a person needs to know."

"You don't have to be a hero." That from Perce.

"Like the man said," Abe warned, " 'Show me a hero and I'll write you a tragedy.' "

I blinked. "You reading Fitzgerald now?"

He shrugged, kind of offhand. "Aunt Edna's got a few books in there."

"I know." She'd gotten me onto Fitzgerald too. When I was seven.

"Charlie," I said, remembering suddenly, "there's something I've been meaning to ask you about."

"Shoot, Jess."

"Don't tempt me. I mean your shoes."

He looked down.

"Not those. The ones that came to my apartment, right after you and Mom arrived. The ones that were brand-new but wrapped singly in newspaper, like they weren't from any store."

"Oh. Those shoes."

"What's it all about, Charlie?"

He tried to give me that charming smile, but I thought it was taking an effort. "The strangest things bother you, Jess."

"True."

His eyes took on a wicked gleam. His white teeth flashed. "Codes, of course. There are secret codes sewn into the lining of every shoe."

"Right."

He laughed. "Give it a rest."

"Now you sound like Aunt Edna."

"I wish you had some of her esprit de corps."

"I always thought I did."

"Oh, you've got humor and wit. But underneath that you're an old soul, Jess, weary and jaded. Still . . . there may be hope."

"You gonna save me, Charlie?"

"Just possibly," he said.

We ended up, all five of us, hitting baseballs in Aunt Edna's side yard. Charlie never did tell me about the shoes.

CHAPTER 34

I'd seen all kinds of P.I.'s back in New York State. Most of them looked like grizzled bookies or cigar-chomping gangsters. None of them looked—or cooked—like Parker's Spenser.

Sam Crewe didn't look like Spenser, either. She was a P.I. of a different order. Long brown hair in one thick shiny twist. Long slender legs and a million-dollar white suit, probably Armani, although what do I know of these things? It was exquisitely simple and well cut. Her eyes were large and violet, her manner all business.

I'd been pacing, thinking about this upscale office, the money that must be behind it. Samantha Crewe had a staff of four—a secretary, a bookkeeper, and two investigators, one man and one woman. The man—Trucker, she called him—was in L.A., working on a case for one of the movie studios. The woman, who had crisp blond hair, a tense smile, and looked to be in her fifties, had swept through for a few minutes and swept on out. Marta, she said her name was. She was designing a security system for a fifty-room mansion in the City, and was late. Big money—it had to be. Clearly, the Samantha Crewe Investigative Agency did nothing so tacky as spying on husbands and wives.

"Please sit down," Sam said pointedly. I realized she was talking to me. Was I making her nervous, then? I kind of hoped so; the prospect of seeing Samantha Crewe's cool, poised exterior shaken, pleased me.

She motioned to a chair that looked antique; its seat and arms were green velvet, soft and nicely worn. A black ceramic cat sat on a five-drawer oak file cabinet, and there were polished oak pieces around. No ferns, I had to give her that. An orchid plant was one of the few things on her desk. It had one single, perfect, white-green spike in bloom. The view through triple-sash windows, white framed, looked out on Bridgeway and the sparkling Bay waters. Eight miles away, San Francisco gleamed in the sun.

I'd been pacing, trying not to act intimidated, but chic women make me feel that way. I sat, my back straight, and pulled my worn Nikes underneath the chair to hide them. Ben saw. The corners of his mouth curled knowingly. I stuck my chin out and ignored him. So this was the kind of woman he hung out with when I wasn't around? A straight-arrow, follow-the-rules woman—a female Grady North?

Sam came around her desk and leaned against it in front of us, arms folded, attentive to what Ben was telling her about me and why we were there. What he'd like her to do. When he'd finished, she said, "Jesse—may I call you Jesse?"

I shrugged, without much grace.

"What's the main agenda here? What do you want from this Iverson—a confession to the murder of his assistant? Or proof that he's an art thief?"

She spoke in a finishing-school accent—evenly, with clear diction. The voice said that the person before me was polished and educated. Smart.

I would never like her. Never. "I want it all," I said firmly.

Sam nodded. "I understand. And I try to give my clients everything they want. But I've found it's always best to leave room for compromise. It's not a perfect world."

Where had I heard that before? Grady North, again. It wasn't a word—compromise—that fell easy on my ears. "Clearing Charlie, I guess, is the most important thing," I said.

"Are you certain Charlie Browne is innocent of Burton's murder? What if he's not—or what if the killer is someone else, neither Iverson nor Charlie?"

"According to a friend on the Rochester P.D., the Pittsford police have cleared everyone else at the party that night. I guess it could've been someone off the street. But how many murders are committed by people off the street? Usually it's someone the victim knew."

"You're right, of course."

The telephone rang. Sam glanced at Ben and he got up to

answer it. It was a call he'd been waiting for, though, a friend from the Fraud Unit at the San Francisco P.D.

"You can do it?" Ben said. "What we talked about?" A short silence as he listened. "Yeah, wires for Sam and me, and then the other thing, the guard thing. Uh-huh. Sam Crewe. She's an investigator. A woman." He looked at Sam—gave her, actually, a look that was warm and decidedly approving. "She's, uh, about five-seven. Slender. Dark hair, kind of shiny. Purple eyes, sort of, and, uh, pretty, you know . . ." His voice trailed off at Sam's uplifted brow, and he blushed under his tan. Turning his broad back to us, he spoke softly into the phone. The pink color on the back of his neck slowly faded. When his tone returned to normal I heard him give a description of Iverson, a time—seven o'clock the next evening—and all the other details he and Sam had been talking about earlier. He hung up the receiver and turned back to us.

"Ronnie's setting it up. And he'll bring the wires, so we can get it all on tape."

Sam spoke to me. "You're sure Iverson will go for it—that he'll want this Durbar painting enough to bite?"

"That's what Charlie says, and he seems to know about these things. Iverson's got a real hunger for Durbar, and he's collected all but this particular one."

"And he won't recognize Ben?"

"No reason for him to," Ben answered. "I've never met the man."

"But isn't this entrapment or something?" I said.

"Only if we set out to trap him," Ben said innocently.

Sam widened her eyes, keeping her beautiful face otherwise blank. "If Ben's friend Ronnie—a San Francisco cop—just happens to catch Iverson in an illegal scheme to buy a stolen painting, while he's at the reception for another purpose—suspicion of fraud on the part of another dealer, say—" She shrugged. You'd have thought she was as guileless as the day she was born.

"Ronnie's already working on a case like that," Ben added. "Being at the Asian Museum tomorrow could easily be justified as part of that case."

"Once we've got his offer for the stolen painting on tape," Sam said, "we offer Iverson a deal. He can confess to murdering his assistant, Burton—something accidental, say, that wouldn't put him away too long, might even get him probation, but would clear Charlie all the way. Ben, in turn, offers to get Ronnie to let him off the hook about the stolen Durbar—which would at least save Iverson's position in the art world."

"Blackmail, you mean."

"Certainly not!" Sam's violet eyes widened even more. "Persuasion. A trade-off. It's done in business all the time."

She looked at Ben, he looked at her, and they both nodded.

"It'll play," Ben said, grinning.

"Quite well."

They both laughed. Sam actually threw back her head. Her eyes shone, her red lips curved impishly above the long white column of her neck.

Nice.

I cleared my throat, getting their attention at last.

"Clearing Charlie's name," I said, "getting Iverson for the murder of Burton, that's the important thing. But finding out about the early art thefts would be a real nice bonus. And one way or another, I want to know if Everett Iverson killed Anna Browne forty years ago, or if his brother did."

"We'll do what we can," Sam said. "I'll put Trucker on it; he'll be back tomorrow. He can talk to people Anna Browne knew, or who knew people she knew. But it's been a lot of years—"

"I want Iverson," I said insistently. "On everything."

Her violet eyes searched mine a moment. "It sounds as if this is a personal thing with you."

My glance slid to Ben. I thought about Melissa, and how Iverson had sent the kid to rough us up in front of her. Sam looked at Ben too. They didn't have to speak. It was there between them, some kind of understanding.

I got up and started pacing again while they worked out details. Half-listening, since I'd be an observer at tomorrow's game—no more. My gaze lighted on a photograph of a young woman—obviously Samantha Crewe—with an older man. They seemed to be on a movie set. There were cameras, director's chairs, booms.

I didn't realize Sam and Ben had stopped talking until she came up behind me and said, "My dad. He was an old movie

man. Special effects. He worked on some great movies in the
forties, met all the big stars . . . Gary Cooper, Jimmy Stewart."
She sounded wistful. "He used to take me to work with him,
summers and school vacations, but of course that was later, in
the sixties. I used to think I'd be an actress. Trained for it, in
fact."

"What happened?"

She made a sweeping gesture. "My choice, to follow a different business. But that's what it is. Business. Too much paperwork and too little magic in being a P.I."

"I love old movies," I said. "I watch them on tape all the
time."

Sam Crewe gave me the full benefit of her million-dollar
smile. "I knew we had something in common."

"Remember *Suspicion*?"

"Oh, God, yes. Cary Grant and Joan Fontaine. I saw it
fourteen times!"

"And *The Uninvited* . . ."

"Ray Milland! I was in love."

The meeting ended with Sam and I talking on and on about
old movies, and Ben standing around impatiently, wondering
what he'd started here.

Men can be funny that way. It's okay for them to like two
women at one time—but let those two women like each other,
show they might even be friends, and it takes all the fun out
of the chase.

Which, of course, made it all the more perversely fun for me.

CHAPTER 35

The Asian Art Museum is at 9th Avenue and Kennedy Drive, in Golden Gate Park. There are showings of Asian art throughout the year, and occasionally, receptions for patrons, artists, and museum directors involved in cultural exchanges.

The reception tonight was being held in a small, well-appointed room on the first floor. There were landscapes of the Yangtze Gorge, spanning the dynasties from the Tang to the present. One representative piece was an ink and color on paper by Lin Fengmian. It was behind velvet ropes, watched over by two security guards. Invitations were being checked carefully at the door.

Our scam was well under way. Ben and Sam were circulating, making small talk. Charlie and I were in the second-floor security room. We monitored the get-together on two banks of television screens. Security cams, with the ability to pan and zoom, had been mounted in every room when the Asian Museum remodeled a few years ago. The video cameras' sound was turned down, but we could hear Ben and Sam clearly. They had been wired, with equipment provided by Ronnie.

The scene below was of champagne and hors d'oeuvres, a chamber orchestra, and tasteful, oriental arrangements of flowers. Sam and Ben were dressed to the teeth for the occasion, Sam in an understated gray suit with gray stockings and heels. She looked like the successful art dealer she was supposed to be. Ben wore a tux, as did all the other men in attendance. Along with patrons of the arts were members of the Chinese consulate and others who would donate to or in some way participate in the show that Iverson and the Chinese dealers had been meeting all day to discuss.

That was the good news. Sam had found that Iverson had shown up at the earlier meetings, and was expected here at the museum tonight. He had apparently decided that Charlie and I were no real threat, and had even sent fresh roses to Mom, with a note apologizing for not returning to the hotel. He'd been tied up in a traffic accident, he said, and when he called his hotel room, she and Aunt Edna were gone. He'd been "staying somewhere else," and would call her later in the week.

Well, men have a lot of experience apologizing for not showing or calling when they say they will. I remember one guy I dated who didn't call for a year. When he showed up again he said he'd been working on the Alaskan pipeline. (The pipeline had been finished for over five years.)

Meanwhile, Charlie had come up with the invitations for Ben and Sam. He didn't say how. He had also come up with the 200-year-old landscape by Durbar that they were to use in the scam against Iverson. How he got it, and so quickly, went unexplained too. The only thing I knew was that it wasn't a forgery. Iverson, Charlie said, would spot a phony immediately. Four years ago, the Durbar had gone for $279,000 at auction. Its worth today was estimated at twice that much. The painting was in the director's office near the reception room, wrapped in paper and locked in a steel vault. Ben and his friend Ronnie from the S. F. P. D. Fraud Unit had worked it out with the cooperation of the museum director. Ronnie was even now acting as security guard beside the vault.

Ben had been nervous. "What if something happens to that painting? I can just see myself working that half a mill off with charters the next seventy years."

"Don't worry," Charlie had assured him. "It'll be fine."

For a long time, nothing happened. The chamber orchestra played, Sam and Ben mingled . . . but there was no sign of Iverson. Then we spotted him, walking through the front door in a tux, his salt-and-pepper hair well groomed and glistening for the occasion. He spoke a few words to a Chinese man who had entered with him, then they shook hands and parted. Sam and Ben worked their way toward Iverson.

Two attempts to get close enough failed. He was always in the midst of large groups. Now and then, Sam and Ben were stopped by small talk with people who took them to be genuine dealers.

HARE TODAY, GONE TOMORROW 195

Finally, they stood with Iverson and a few others at the banquet table, loading up their plates with food. When they and Iverson were the only ones left, Sam took Ben slightly aside, turning her back to the rest of the room. She murmured something in Ben's ear.

Charlie closed in on them with the zoom. It was so good, you could see the pores of their skin.

"You've acquired a Durbar?" we heard Ben say. "I can't believe it."

"Shhhh. *The Well*," Sam murmured. "I'm quite excited about it." She seemed not to notice that Iverson had moved closer, nor that he merely toyed with the food on his plate as they spoke.

"An estate sale?"

"No. Just between you and me? The owner is terminally ill. One of my agents had access to the house through a friend, who'd been hired as a private nurse. The painting . . . acquired legs, shall we say?"

Ben laughed. "What a coup for you! Christ, a Durbar. Do you have a buyer?"

"One or two potentials. They're having trouble coming up with the cash."

"You could hang onto it a while, keep it underground."

Sam shook her head. "We need a quick cash sale." She gave a shrug. "Expenses."

"I'd like to see it," Ben said.

She linked her arm through his in a chummy way. "I have it with me," she said in a low voice. "One of the potential buyers is here."

"You brought it *here*?" Ben looked around incredulously.

"Silly. It's in a vault in the director's office. Wrapped. The director thinks it's a minor work that I've brought to have authenticated by someone here today."

"You haven't changed a bit." Ben's eyes were bright with obvious admiration.

Charlie was panning between them and Iverson, who clearly couldn't contain himself any longer. He smoothed his hair with both palms, checked his tie to see that it was straight, and moved in on Sam. "Pardon me."

Sam assumed a polite but bored face.

"I couldn't help overhearing. You have a Durbar?" You could almost see him salivate. "You have it here?"

Sam's voice could have chilled ice cubes. Her nose rose several inches in the air. "I'm afraid you've misunderstood."

"Ms.—"

"Drake. Sylvia Drake."

"Ms. Drake." Iverson held out a hand, which Sam took and dropped quickly, as if it were distasteful in some way. "I'm Everett Iverson, from the Armistead Gallery in Pittsford, New York. I'm an authority on Durbar." He reached inside his suit jacket for a business card. Sam accepted it, still looking frigid.

"I realize this is a delicate matter," Iverson said. "Please . . . don't be alarmed. I have a Durbar collection. Everything, in fact, but *The Well.* You simply must let me see it . . . in complete confidentiality, of course."

Sam was unbending. "I tell you, you misunderstood. The painting I have is a minor work, by a minor artist. How on earth would I have come across a Durbar? There are none in existence for sale."

Iverson said firmly, "I assure you, I am not asking out of idle curiosity." He let the implication lie there: He was prepared to buy.

Sam allowed a glimmer of greed to brighten her wide violet eyes. Iverson clearly noted it.

"Please," he urged, this time with more authority. "This could be a profitable transaction for both of us."

Sam glanced at Iverson's business card, which until now she'd ignored. She nodded. "I've heard of you, Mr. Iverson." She raised an eyebrow and spoke to Ben. "Jimmy, Mr. Iverson is indeed an authority on Durbar . . . along with many other artists of the seventeenth and eighteenth centuries. Stilson, LaCriet."

She had named two painters whose major works, Charlie told her, had been missing for years. Iverson smiled tightly, yet acknowledged the understanding between them: *It takes one to know one.*

"Nice to meet you," Ben said.

But Iverson wasn't listening. His attention was fixed on Sam. She tapped his business card on the nails of her other hand, which was curled loosely, palm up.

"How interested did you say you are in this Durbar, Mr. Iverson?"

"What part of the country did you say the painting is from?" he countered.

Iverson would know that the present owner of the Durbar was an elderly collector living in Chicago. He was seeking one last clue to confirm Sam's story.

"The Midwest," she said "I can't tell you any more than that."

"Of course. Well, Ms. Drake, I would say that I am *very* interested. Shall we just have a look?"

Sam hesitated a moment more. She looked at Iverson's card again, then searched his eyes quite openly. Finally, she nodded. She, Ben, and Iverson headed for the director's office. The scam was under way.

Charlie and I both sighed with relief.

The cameras showed Ronnie in the director's office, standing by a vault, in a security guard's uniform. He was undistinguished-looking, the way a bit player should be—average height, average coloring. You'd be hard put to describe him later, if asked to as a witness. He responded subserviently to Sam's request that he open the vault.

"Of course, Ms. Drake."

"And . . . could you leave us alone?"

"Certainly." The vault was opened, and Ronnie left to stand outside the office door. Sam brought the Durbar into the office while Ben and Iverson waited. She unwrapped it carefully, dragging out the suspense. Then she stood back, allowing Iverson access. Ben, behind him, made appropriate noises of appreciation. Iverson rubbed his narrow white hands, as if preparing for surgery. Charlie had told us that Iverson was one of the few experts in the country who needed no chemical testing or electronic analysis to authenticate a painting. His eye and experience were enough.

He pulled a folding magnifying glass from his pocket and peered at the landscape, studying it for what seemed forever.

Sam waited patiently. Ben stood with his hands in his pockets, making small talk. Iverson studied the Durbar's lower right signature corner. Finally, he straightened.

"Magnificent. No doubt as to its authenticity, of course. How much are you asking for it?" The elation in his voice was unmistakable.

Sam answered without hesitation. "Five hundred thousand."

Iverson shook his head, smiling indulgently. "Much too much."

"But—"

"Under these rather delicate circumstances . . ." He shrugged elaborately.

"All right. Four and a half."

"Three."

"Not a penny under three-fifty."

"Done."

They both smiled with satisfaction, as Ben watched on.

"I must have your check today," Sam said.

Iverson reached for his wallet.

"Wait. Not here. I wouldn't like to have to explain the Durbar to just anyone who wanders in."

Iverson nodded.

"We'll conclude our business in the other room," Sam suggested, "and you can pick up the painting before you leave. Is that acceptable?"

"Absolutely."

It seemed there *was* honor among thieves. Iverson didn't question the Durbar's safety, nor that it would be there when he came back to pick it up.

Sam rewrapped the painting, then took a roll of twine from a shelf and tied it four ways, like a Christmas package. She replaced the painting carefully in the vault, closed the door, and threw the steel lever that locked it.

They went back into the reception room, leaving Ronnie still standing outside the office door.

And that's when it all fell apart.

Sam and Ben had drawn Iverson to an arrangement of chairs in a quiet corner. They were just sitting, with Iverson reaching for his wallet again, when a slight man with a beard approached Ben.

"Ben Jericho! What's the San Francisco Police Department doing here?"

It was Laurence Higgham—the Nob Hill art dealer Marcus had sent me to on my first trip out here.

"What the *hell*?" Charlie's voice was tight, beside me.

"I'm afraid you've made some mistake," Ben said coolly. He turned away, leaving Iverson and Sam alone with Higgham, who stared curiously after him. When Ben was several feet away, with his back to them, he spoke quietly into the wire for our benefit. "The man's an art dealer. We had him under investigation once for art theft."

"Christ, get out of there!" Charlie said, even though Ben couldn't possibly hear. Then, to me, "If Sam is quick, maybe we can still pull this off."

But I was watching Iverson, and it wasn't going to happen that way. Smoothly, he detached Sam's hand from his arm, where she'd rested it. "I'm afraid I must be going," he said.

"I don't know what this is all about," Sam said angrily to Higgham, "but there's been some mistake."

"Indeed there has," Iverson said.

He moved away, heading for the outside doors. Higgham looked at Sam in obvious bewilderment.

Charlie swore impressively. "Shit, it's no good. He never handed over a check!"

"But he offered to buy it! What about intent?"

"That won't hold up in court. Not without closure."

With an angry motion, he switched off the cameras to the director's office. I continued to watch as Ben wove his way through the reception room, heading for the stairs that would bring him up here. Sam's frustrated gaze followed Iverson's departure through the front door.

I said, "Charlie—" I turned to the chair beside me. It was empty.

Charlie! Where the hell was Charlie?

I looked into the screen again, scanning the reception room. Charlie wasn't there. Finally, I turned the cameras back on in the director's office.

No sign of Charlie Browne.

And the cameras in the vault showed that the Durbar was gone.

CHAPTER 36

A few hours later I was resting on the bed in Aunt Edna's guest room, eyes closed, trying to contain my anger.

Iverson had disappeared. He hadn't returned to his hotel room, nor to his Nob Hill house. He was presumably on the run. I had Marcus tracking him down, checking out airports and other hotels, all the usual things. Charlie, Mom said, had called shortly before I got back to Aunt Edna's. "He'll be out of touch a few hours, Charlie said." *A few hours.* Charlie had his hands on a painting worth half a million dollars. I wondered if we'd ever see him again.

A weight lowered the mattress. It was Mom, sitting on the edge of the bed, hoping I'd wake up so she could talk. I used to do that to her when I was a kid. She would grumble and complain, rubbing her sleep-filled eyes, but she'd talk to me —no matter how tired she was from working an all-night shift at whatever greasy cafe.

I glanced at the clock. 2:34 A.M. "What's wrong, Mom?"

She was wearing a soft yellow robe. Putting on something soft and yellow is something Mom does when she's feeling insecure. "I'm not sure anymore, Jesse. About Charlie."

I was amazed that she ever had been. "What aren't you sure about?"

"That I should marry him. I never realized until we talked the other day, but there really are an awful lot of questions Charlie can't answer. It makes everything seem so . . . so tenuous. And then, a lot has happened these last few weeks. I've never . . . never been on the lam before."

I tried not to smile. "I know what you mean. Have you told Charlie?"

"No. I suppose we'll have to talk when he gets back."

With any luck, I thought, maybe never get back.

There didn't seem to be anything more to say. I scrunched over so Mom could lie down next to me. After a few minutes, her breathing became even. She fell asleep.

I lay there thinking about my last conversation with Sam, in the security room of the Asian Art Museum. We had just ascertained that Charlie and the Durbar were indeed gone.

"He probably just got it out of the way," Sam said, "don't you think? Before any questions could be asked? I would imagine he's returning it to its rightful owner now."

"Sure."

I closed my eyes again. Drifted off. The phone by the bed rang softly, and I grabbed it so it wouldn't waken Mom. It was Marcus. We talked a few minutes. "Don't worry," I said, before hanging up, "I'll get him, Marcus. I swear I will."

I glanced up to see the bedroom door open. Standing there, looking tired and older than his years, was Charlie Browne. I slid out of bed, went over, and stood in front of him. He didn't say a word. Instead, he walked purposefully around me and went to sit by Mom on the bed. She was curled up on her side, her face unlined and peaceful, like a little girl's. Charlie stroked her forehead tenderly.

I slipped out the door.

I was packing at around six A.M. to leave Mill Valley when Marcus called again. He beat around the bush a little, following up on our earlier conversation, but then he got down to it.

"I've been doing a lot of thinking," he said.

"About what?"

"My son. The things you said, about how Chris needs a father. I still think I'm right, that I can't let people know he's connected to me. It would put him in danger."

"I know. It's a tough one, Marcus."

"But you're right too. I should start seeing him. Maybe, when he's a little older, I could tell him who I am. A kid needs to know he has a dad."

"I'm glad. I'm so glad. You know what, Marcus?"

"What?"

"You are going to love that kid."

"I already do."

"Yeah, I guess you do."

"And Jess?"

"Uh-huh?"

"I'm thinking about changing some other things, too."

"Like what?"

"Like . . . some of the things I'm involved in. Maybe I need to take another look."

"I don't suppose that means you'll get out of the family."

"You know I can't do that."

"No."

"But maybe it's not as clean as I've been wanting to think. Business, I mean. Not all that different from the old days, in terms of people getting hurt."

"You don't say."

"I do."

I wondered if he'd been talking to Tark. It sounded like it.

"Sounds good," I said. "Everything."

"Just wanted to let you know. See you when you get home?"

"See you," I said.

CHAPTER 37

I tumbled into my apartment after seven hours in a cramped plane with rotten food, so I was mean, lean, and hungry. Thank God Bastard wasn't around. I'd have cooked him.

Mrs. Binty was away for a few days, a note from her on my door said. Visiting friends in Elmira. I dropped my carry-on and headed for the kitchen, flicking lights along the way. The fridge was well stocked, thanks to Mom's having been here a while. I reached into the freezer and pulled out some brown-and-serve rolls, a hunk of leftover pot roast, and a container of nonthickened gravy. Shoved them all together in the microwave. In less than five minutes I had a hearty French dip. I dipped standing over the counter, looking through the pile of *Herald*s I'd brought in with me. Mrs. Binty must have pulled them out of the rosebushes this time. They were all neatly stacked by my door.

That reminded me of Toni, who always used to arrive in the early mornings to bother the hell out of me, picking at the things I ate and the amount of coffee I drank. She'd bring the *Herald* with her and read through the sports section, keeping an eagle eye out to see I didn't take in too much Danish or bagels with cheese. I wondered if I'd driven her away, all that shit over Mom and stuff.

I picked up the phone and called next door. "Toni there?" I asked her mom.

"She's out with friends," Mary Langella said. "Jesse? I sure wish you'd talk to her. She hasn't been working out the way she used to. She's missing practice sessions, and her coach is livid."

"Hormones," I said with absolute certainty.

"You think so?"

"Sure. Kids get to a certain age, they start thinking about boys, not splits and backward bends."

203

"But she's wanted to go to the Olympics forever. It's been her life's dream, and she's close to making it. She can't afford to fall behind."

"Maybe she wants something else now," I said.

"Like what?"

"Like . . . something else. Maybe gymnastics doesn't make her happy anymore."

"Dear God, you think she'd give it up? Just like that?"

"Just like that. It happens."

We talked a few minutes more, but I guess I wasn't much help. Mary sounded more worried than ever when she put down the phone.

I took a piece of roll into the living room and nibbled at it, sitting sideways in the bay window and looking across the street to Mr. Garson's side yard. It was growing dark. Bleak, really, after the sunshine glow of California. I know daylight doesn't stick around any longer there than it does here; it just seems that way. Mr. Garson wasn't in his yard, but you could still smell the woody scent of his leaves burning. That flaunting of the law was, I supposed, Mr. Garson's Last Hurrah. A faint wisp of smoke rose from the blackened pile. Most of the trees in the neighborhood were bare now.

I felt bare, too. Like all my coverings had fallen away. Winter was nearly here, and that ordinarily made me depressed. But there wasn't time to be depressed now. I had things to do. I should do them.

I looked at the little travel clock on my desk. 7:27. I had an hour, maybe, to spare. I nibbled on the roll.

So Toni was reassessing things, was she? Not sure she wanted to be an Olympic gymnast anymore? Well, that'd be hard on Mary and Ralph, all those dreams they had for their daughter. But when did we ever fulfill—really fulfill—our parents' expectations? And whoever said we had to? Any more than they had to fulfill ours?

So far as I can see, we're all just bumbling our way through life. The most you can strive for is to not hurt anybody with the fallout every time you switch gears.

Speaking of Marcus—since it seemed like he, too, was switching gears—I wondered how that would all work out. I'd always thought it was only a matter of time before he started looking at where he was going. You can't be raised the way Marcus was—by loving, law-abiding parents, with truth and honesty your byword—and spend a life in organized crime.

Not and be comfortable with it—for long.

Tark had discovered that. It was why he'd made the break with Marcus. Whether it was permanent or not remained to be seen. The break itself was what counted: the announcement to oneself that something has to give, that one cannot go on as one has, that too many questions exist, and answers must be had.

And then there was all that Genius vs. Apostle stuff. Tark, inspired by Kierkegaard to make the move at forty-two to become his own man. Discovering that the genius exists in every man. Marcus could have told him that. *I* had told him that. But it's something, I guess, we all have to discover for ourselves.

Toni had been an apostle to her coach's ambitions and her parents' dreams since the age of five. Maybe she was getting an early glimpse of the possibilities: the world that might appear, provided she had the courage to take off the blinders and look from side to side.

Reassessment.

I felt my stomach flutter. I was beginning to get a glimmer of something exciting, something it was great to have in my head, to know. I wanted to hang on to it, sort it out, talk about it with someone wise.

Samved.

I hadn't talked to Samved in weeks. He was my guru, my shrink, my lifeline to sobriety—and I'd been drifting away. Maybe I'd wanted to drift for a while, but I felt it coming back again, more strong than ever—that urge to give up waffling and actually, finally, fully, live.

I dialed Samved's number at the Center for Natural Healing, prepared for his usual New Age message: "Good evening, dear ones. I am in my garden beneath the light of the moon, experiencing the fullness of earth's glory, communing with the planet and the guides . . ." Shit like that. Samved wasn't much use in a real emergency, off in the spheres and all, but he wasn't bad after the fact.

He startled me by coming on the line right away. A brisk tone, younger than the over-seventy I knew him to be. None of that usual wispy stuff.

"Christ Eternal!" he declared.

"Huh?"

"Christ Eternal! Do you know Jesus?" His voice was brimming with exhilaration. It was downright jaunty.

"Uh . . ."

"Jesus lives, my friend, and so do you!"

"Uh . . ."

"Tell me, how can I help you today? We're all one in the Blood of Christ, you know."

I sat there looking at the receiver, my mouth hanging slack. What I *did* know was that this was Samved. What I didn't know was what the shit was going on. He sounded like Oral Roberts. I almost threw up.

I put the phone to my ear. "Samved? What the *fuck*?"

"Ah, Jesse, I believe? Only you would greet a minister of God that way."

"A minister of God?"

"As of this very morning," Samved said.

"Samved—"

"My name is Henry now. Well, actually, it always was—"

"Henry?"

"Henry Dreeb." (Well, that's the way it sounded.)

"Uh-huh," I said slowly. I was having trouble making my tongue think.

"Uh, Henry—don't tell me. We're talking major reassessment here?"

"Definitely major," Samved-Henry replied.

"Hmm. You're turning in your flowing white robes?"

"And my prayer rug."

"You're giving up *Jeopardy*?" He had hidden his little color television behind a heavy curtain right in front of his prayer rug, but I'd discovered it one day.

"Well . . ."

I thought not.

"I've become a Fundamentalist," Samved-Henry said. "Television is allowed."

"A Fundamentalist. What does that mean?"

"Well, it's sort of old religion mixed with new. Evangelism, but born again."

Born again. "You wearing a collar, too?"

"Actually, a black suit. You do catch on quickly." He sounded pleased.

Oh, I catch on quickly, all right. "I suppose you have an 800 number for donations?"

"1-800-444—"

"Never mind."

First Tark, then The Three, Marcus, and now this. Christ, it must be something in the ozone.

"Why did you call?" Samved-Henry said.

"I don't remember. There was something—"

"Would you like me to pray for you?"

"If you must."

"You're not drinking again?"

"Not yet," I replied.

I checked the travel clock again. 7:55. Still time.

I sat, stretched, and put them all together—all the people in my life who were going through some kind of change. I should have felt cynical about their strivings; that was my usual M.O. Instead, I still had this funny little tickle in my stomach that I finally identified as tenderness. I actually wished them all well.

Shit. I must be losing it, I thought. If Bastard were here, I might even toss him a bone.

This would not do. I called Mom, just to feel irritated again.

"Jesse! What wonderful timing! I was just about to call you."

"You want to tell me how screwed I am?" I asked hopefully.

"What? You? Of course not, dear, I love the way you are, I always have. You know that."

"Right." Something was wrong.

"I wanted to tell you the good news," Mom said. "I've been reassessing things, dear."

I sighed. "Of course you have, Mom. That makes it unanimous." She was probably entering a convent, becoming a nun.

"I'm getting married!" Mom announced.

"Married? To *who*? Whom?"

"Well, Charlie, of course."

"Oh. Of course. Mom, didn't you just tell me you weren't sure you wanted quite so adventurous a life as Charlie leads?"

"That's what I reassessed, dear. I decided it's the perfect life for me, all that secret stuff—well, you know, I can't go on living with Edna, it's been too boring."

"Boring? Aunt Edna, boring?"

"Decidedly. All this Marin County, New Age, leftover seventies business. Not that I'm criticizing, dear, but you could use a little updating on that score yourself."

"Don't worry about it, Mom. If Samved has his way, I may be turning Baptist."

"What?"

"Nothing. When's this wedding, Mom?"

"Well, we're hoping for right after Christmas." Her voice trembled, but only a little. "That's if Iverson is caught and Charlie's cleared. If not . . ."

"He'll be cleared, Mom, don't worry." *You can bet my sweet ass he'll be cleared.*

"I'm not worried, not really, Jesse. For the first time in a long time, I do have faith that things will be all right. And we'll have the wedding out here, where the weather's warm —outside, you know—it'll be so wonderful, dear. Now don't you give me any excuses, you've got to come. I want you at my side."

"I'll be there, Mom. Wouldn't miss it for the world."

"About Everett Iverson, Jesse . . . he's left California, I hear."

"I know, Mom. I know." I squinted at the clock: 8:13. "Marcus told me. He's here."

"Iverson is there? In Rochester?"

"Came in on the 8:05 plane."

"Oh, Jesse! Stay away from him, dear. Let Charlie handle this."

"No, I don't want Charlie involved. It would only complicate things. It'll be all right, Mom, trust me. Look, I've got to go."

"Jesse—"

"I love you, Mom. Take care." I dropped the receiver in its place and stood there, looking out at the cold black autumn sky.

Feeling lonely in a way I never had before.

My mom—whom I'd just recently gotten to know—was getting married. And my best friend, (aside from Mrs. Binty, my landlady, and Marcus) was off in Italy somewhere, finding himself.

Tark. In all this world, he was the person I related to most. And yeah, sure, I wished him well—but I missed him so much my teeth ached.

Then there was Samved. I'll admit I'd put old Samved on a pedestal—thinking he at least believed in what he was doing, even if he was an old con. But the people I put on pedestals, for one dumb need of my own or another, are always having feet of clay.

What would Avery Carlisle tell me if I asked him about that? That not putting people on pedestals was the first great lesson?

There wasn't time to sort it out. I had work to do.

CHAPTER 38

I made my approach through Iverson's estate from behind the car barn, where Burton had been killed. The barn was dark, closed up, and the night was silent except for a cold wind that whistled through the trees. No moon. I inched along the drive. Closer to the house, Iverson's dark Lincoln stood, its nose pointed toward the street. Leaves clattered beneath my feet. Rustled. Blew against my ankles where my jeans didn't quite meet my shoes, making me think they were living things. I shivered, drawing my windbreaker close.

About fifty yards from the chateau I edged away from the drive, following a low stone wall to a spot beneath the trees about thirty feet behind the house. A bird flapped its wings and let out a throaty "whoo-oo-oo." I jumped a mile and stumbled over a dry, spiky rosebush. Scratched my hand on a thorn. Licked at it and swore softly.

Lights were on in the house, but not many. One or two, possibly, in a downstairs room that I remembered was a study. None up. I moved from tree to tree, stopping now and then to listen and look for unwelcome company. No security guards appeared. I reached the breezeway-styled living room where the party had been going on the night Mom, Charlie, and I had been here. A dim lamp cast light onto shrubbery outside, but the room seemed empty. I took out an assortment of lock-picking tools, all amateur and improvised, but they'd do. Marcus had run a computer check on likely security companies, not only in town but around the state, to see if Iverson had had a state-of-the-art system put in. He'd come up empty-handed, which didn't surprise me too much. It's often the way in places like Pittsford; people who grew up here, who have lived here since it was nothing more than a village, disdain alarms. They prefer to ignore the possibility that crime exists so close to home.

Iverson had locked up, but the French doors that had been open the night of the party gave way to my ministrations. A soft snick, and I was in.

I stepped onto the wood floor, then soft rose carpeting. The windows on both sides gave back my reflection. So did the mirror over the mantel. Flowers on a round table threw off a fresh scent, so I guessed Iverson's housekeeper had been on duty while he was away.

I stood motionless several moments, and heard a sound from an adjacent area like papers rustling. I moved quietly through the room to the hall. Across the way, sliding wooden doors from the study were open. A soft yellow glow came from a brass lamp on an end table in there. It shadowed the hall, the wide staircase, and the study. There was another light at the foot of the hallway stairs on a reception table, the kind where calling cards used to be left in the days before telephones, when neighbors dropped by. There was an arrangement of country flowers on that table too. I noticed again the mellow patina of the woods in this house, the rough ivory plaster— the beams and authentic French country feel. A beautiful home for a beautiful woman—and yet Iverson, presumably, had never lived with a woman here.

I guess we tend to think in stereotypes about male/female tastes, no matter how enlightened we propose that we are.

I didn't see Iverson at first. He was half-hidden by one of the double doors of a massive armoire in the study, twenty feet or so away. I inched slowly into the room and along its edge.

The armoire contained drawers and wooden file cabinets. Papers spilled over, some having fallen to the floor. A soft breeze from an open window scattered the papers; they drifted like brittle leaves across the wooden floor.

Iverson, whose back was to me now, was dressed in an elegant gray suit, every hair in place, and he was obviously packing for a trip. The briefcase he held was bulging. His movements were hurried.

"Like some help?" I said.

His head jerked my way in surprise, which he covered almost immediately. His left hand snaked into a long vertical space and came out holding a rifle so big, so much of an overkill, it could only be an elephant gun.

Shit. I hadn't much planned on being the next trophy on Iverson's San Francisco wall.

But he held the gun down limply, as if he hadn't much heart for the kill. "I wish you hadn't come here, Jesse. I truly did not want to hurt you."

"Or my mother?"

He shook his head. "A good woman. She deserves only the best."

"And this? Where are you going, Iverson?"

"Out of the country. A place to hide until all this blows over."

"It's not blowing over. Charlie will find you, if not the cops."

"Perhaps. But I've learned a lot over the past forty years. How to dissemble, how to hide." He spoke with bravado, but his slumped shoulders, and the loosely held rifle, said he was weary of it all.

"Why don't you tell me about it?" I said, moving casually to a deep armchair. I sat, and slouched. "Beginning with Anna."

Iverson glanced at his watch, a twinkle of silver in the dim light. He sighed. "Why not? We have a few moments." He closed the armoire doors with one hand, and crossed to a highly polished desk. Opening the desk's single drawer, he pulled out a passport, which he slipped into the inside pocket of his suit coat. Then he came back around the desk to sit gracefully on a straight-back chair a few feet from me. The rifle was positioned properly across his lap—a gentleman's accoutrement. It might have been an umbrella, or, if Iverson were a woman, a fan.

The brass lamp on the end table next to me cast its yellow light over the two of us—me in my jeans, legs and arms crossed boorishly, Iverson with back straight and knees together, as if at a boardroom meeting. He began to tell me about Anna . . . tiredly, but as if he had needed to talk about it for a long time. Perhaps this was his way of tying up ends.

"I met Anna through Robert," he said, "at one of her parties.

He was crazy for her, as were all the young men she gathered around her. Anna was a flame, a spark to their creativity. Just being near her was a joy."

"What was Anna to you?"

"A player, nothing more."

"Player?"

"Well, we do tend to have roles in life, don't we? Anna played hers to the hilt, although I don't think she realized it, for the most part. For Anna, the edges were blurred between drama and real life. They almost had to be. Anna was a woman alone in a city where anything goes, or did, in those days. And she hadn't very much money, you see. The man who fathered her son—"

"Charlie."

"Yes, Charlie. His father never returned from Germany after the second world war. Anna was left to fend for herself. I learned from Robert that she loved giving parties; one might even say she was made for it."

"So you supplied her with the wherewithal for those salons. In return, she invited all the right people. The connections to move your stolen paintings around the world."

He nodded. "I don't know how you figured that out—although, of course, you were behind that farce at the Asian Museum. I knew, from that moment, it was only a matter of time . . ."

"How did it start?"

"Anna?" He smiled, his gray eyes lighting with the memory. "It was a glorious time. Before Anna, I was a student at Brenthurst Art Academy—perhaps you know it? Near Cornell? There were many of us there who were young and starving. But not for long. It was easy to recruit students who wanted more than anything to ply their art rather than work for the equivalent in those days of a fast-food chain. The income from stolen art gave us time to do that."

"But you no longer paint."

His refined chuckle held a note of self-mockery. He shifted, crossing his legs, one hand on the rifle to hold it in place. "No . . . I suppose the money was simply too tempting. Or perhaps I realized I was just a third-rate artist, while at business . . ."

"At business, you excelled. This ring was nationwide? And

you did meet people at Anna's parties, later, who helped to move the paintings?"

"Oh, yes. And prospects too. San Francisco was the perfect city for that, with all its sophistication, its visitors from foreign countries . . . channels to Europe and the Far East, you know. Anna wasn't active in the thefts, of course. She merely provided the connections, brought us together in her home."

"She must have known what you were doing."

"I really don't think so. We never talked about it openly. I would ask her to invite someone and Anna would be happy to comply. She wasn't given to analyzing these things—a woman completely without guile. Simply talking to Anna, however, I was able to glean information. Such as who had, or wanted, which painting—and, if it was something I wanted, where it was kept, whether in a home gallery or a vault, summer house or winter. What kind of security existed. These things dropped quite naturally from Anna's conversation as simple gossip."

Anna couldn't have been that stupid, I thought. Men like to believe the airhead image a beautiful woman like Anna puts forth. It gives them a sense of power. But Anna Biernej-Browne, mother to Charlie, would more likely have used that weakness in Iverson to her advantage—I'd bet on it.

Not that I was judging. I've done a lot of things for cash, including prostituting my skills to sell stories to the worst of the yellow rags. I've always called it "work." Perception is everything, as Samved is wont to say.

Was wont to say. Ah, well.

The wind had picked up. It blew through the open window, rustling the papers on the floor again. The curtains billowed. Iverson glanced that way apprehensively, saw that the sound came from only the papers, and gave a tiny, embarrassed cough as he met my eyes. "Sometimes, here, at night . . ." He shrugged.

I remembered how nervous he had seemed in the upstairs gallery that night, and how he had lived here all these years alone since Robert had committed suicide—Anna's portrait a constant shrine and reminder. I thought of his secret life in San Francisco, the dead animals, the tokens to ward off evil spirits . . . a life he could never be open about and still maintain his conservative reputation here. It couldn't have been an easy existence, despite all the wealth.

"Were you and Anna ever more than business partners?" I said gently.

"Never! Anna wasn't interested, nor was I. I doubt that she slept with any of the men who loved her, for that matter. No . . . Anna needed the money to raise her son." He sighed. "Well, people do what they have to do."

"And what about the *Hare*? How did you come by it?"

Iverson looked tired again. Gray. "Robert . . . Robert found it. After he found Anna, dead."

"Robert *found* Anna? He didn't kill her?"

"Absolutely not!" Iverson seemed to pull himself together with the effort to defend his brother's name. "Anna was already dead. A terrible tragedy. She was planning to leave San Francisco, take Charlie to Seattle and raise him there with the help of her family. She was . . . breaking away."

"An interesting choice of words. By taking away her connections, she was breaking up your happy little arrangement."

A faint oily scent drifted through the room, and I jumped as the lights flickered momentarily. Iverson looked unnerved too—jittery. His pale fingers gripped the barrel of the rifle, knuckles white.

"Tell me about Robert and the *Hare*."

Iverson hesitated, then glanced at his watch again. His hand shook a little, and the watch glinted steel, like his hair.

"Waiting for someone?"

"My driver"—he made a dry, clearing-of-the-throat sound—"is coming in from the city. Before he arrives . . ."

"Before he arrives, you have to kill me. Distasteful as that obviously will be."

"I wish there were some other way."

"Killing *is* inelegant," I agreed. "Someday man will figure out a way to do it without fuss, muss, or even thought. In the meantime, why don't you humor me? Tell me about Robert."

Iverson's cold gray eyes became distant as they moved back in time. He probably wasn't aware that the nails of one hand scraped agitatedly on the back of the other. "Robert . . . Robert took the *Hare* to remember Anna by. A move made out of shock, of course. The hold that woman had on men . . . the absurd emotional pull—I realized the moment Robert brought the painting home that it would have to be hidden forever. If Robert were discovered to have it, he'd be questioned by the police. My connection to Anna would surface."

He looked down then at his hand, saw that he had scratched it raw, and stopped. He began to age before me, the way people sometimes do when they drink—the facial muscles droop and they take on twenty years.

It must have worked on his mind in recent years—the way Robert hadn't even had the comfort of Anna's painting after her death. Or had he gone to the cellar every day to view it? Had he been alone down there in the semidark, with cobwebs and dust and grief all around?

"Robert killed himself three months after Anna was murdered," I said softly. "How did he die?"

"He . . . my brother hanged himself. Up there." Iverson looked upward, to the ceiling. "In the gallery." His eyes were wet with tears.

Christ. "Where his paintings are hung?"

"It was his studio. I found him in the morning, just before dawn. I thought I heard something in the night, but you know how it is when you're only half-awake. You think you imagine it. Then you waken again, and you start thinking, and finally you have to go and look . . ." He wiped distractedly at the moisture on his cheeks. "I found him there. I ran to the kitchen for a knife, and tried to cut him down. He had used wire, though, a strong wire for hanging heavy paintings, and the knife wouldn't cut through. I couldn't find his wire cutters. I've always wondered if he hid them on purpose, before—"

I had to stop the picture from playing in my own mind. "Robert didn't kill himself only out of grief, did he? He found out that you had murdered Anna."

Iverson's eyes flew up to mine. He seemed to take a moment to process what I'd said. Then his head moved from side to side. "No."

"You killed her out of anger at her leaving."

"No."

The oil scent drifted through the room again. I sniffed. "What is that?" It was cold suddenly. I rubbed my arms.

"A . . . draft. It's an old house."

"A strange draft. God, it's bone-chilling."

Iverson's nose lifted. He wiped his palms on his trousers. "That odor—" His voice shook.

Then it was gone.

I sat straighter, eyeing the seemingly forgotten rifle on Iverson's lap. "As I was saying, you killed Anna because you were angry she was leaving—"

"I tell you I did not—"

"But you never told Robert that you killed her. And then you had to live with it. You had to live every day with his grief, and your guilt, knowing what you'd done to his life—"

Iverson jumped to his feet, grabbing up the rifle, his slender white hands gripping the hardwood stock. But his slack face told the story: He was a hunter without the passion, now, to kill. He didn't point the rifle. When he realized what he was doing he stumbled backward, staring at the gun as if it had come to life and joined ranks with his past to accuse him. He hit the desk with the backs of his legs, and a photograph toppled, slamming down. Iverson whirled to look, just for a second, but it was enough. I unfolded myself rapidly and lunged for him, grabbing for the arm with the rifle and pushing it up, knocking Iverson even farther back so that we were both across the desk, he on his back, me on top of him. I slammed the edge of my hand down on his wrist and he dropped the rifle. It went clattering to the floor.

But Iverson was stronger than he looked. With both hands free now, he grabbed my wrists and heaved, pushing us both upright. I aimed with a knee, missed the groin, but got the stomach. It broke his hold just enough. I got free, turned, and ran into the hall, with Iverson close on my heels. At the foot of the stairs, he caught me. We grappled, but I broke away and made it up two of the stairs before his arm went around my neck. I grabbed it—but suddenly it slackened, and dropped. I turned slowly, facing Iverson in time to see a look of absolute horror cross his face. His arm fell from my neck, a dead weight. I followed his awful, terror-filled gaze to the top of the stairs.

The lamp from below lit the area only dimly. But I saw it. I felt my mouth go dry and my limbs turn to ice. *"My God."*

Iverson whispered, "No . . ."

A figure stood at the head of the stairs. Rather it floated . . . drifted . . . shifting. The figure had long black hair. . . . It was a gauzy white cloud, ebbing and flowing . . . the hair like strands of dark silk blowing softly, lifting in tendrils away from a too-pale face.

The face in the painting upstairs, in the shrine-room.

Iverson stumbled backward and moaned. "*Anna.*"

The apparition touched the bannister with one waxen hand. The other reached out to Iverson.

"*No,*" he cried out. "*Oh God, no!*"

I was rooted to the spot, watching it all with a dreadful, primitive fear. I thought of the ghost stories I'd heard as a child and then as a reporter. Psychic investigators I'd at first pooh-poohed and then believed, or at least accepted that *they* believed. Pictures of "ghosts," proven not to be technically faked as I'd first assumed. We know things now that confirm the ancient myths. We know about auras, about Kirlian photography that shows energy lingering around the body after death. A soul? A spirit? Who can say?

The lamps flickered again, then went out. The vision of Anna was the only light left. She was incandescent, a shimmery veil, and there was that scent of paints and oils wafting down the stairs, that scent that clings to an artist no matter how many times he or she scrubs—

"*Murderer,*" Anna whispered. It was a breath, no more than a release of air from dead, dry lungs.

Iverson's mouth worked. No sound came out. Anna moved forward, floating weightlessly down another step. Then another. Iverson backed up farther. My eyes moved from him to the ghostly figure. My hands rubbed at my arms as I hugged myself, pressing my back against the wall. I couldn't think which was more frightening, Iverson or the specter of Anna. His face was melting clay, the muscles flaccid. In the pale, reflected light from Anna, he looked like something that had been dead for years, a mummy, a skeleton unearthed in a graveyard by a storm. In his eyes was the kind of fear that comes from years of expectation that a nightmare will someday come true. The ultimate horror—that someone you've harmed will return from the grave for revenge.

"I swear, I didn't mean . . ." Iverson was talking to the apparition, his voice broken and afraid. "You were leaving, everything coming apart. There—there was so much money to be made, and you—"

"Murderer!" Anna repeated, more forcefully.

"No!" He looked around wildly. His eyes settled on me. "It's a trick—you—"

I shook my head, my movements jerky.

Anna moved forward. Iverson backed up, his shoulders ramming the front door. His hands flew out to ward her off. "I told Rune not to harm you, he was only supposed to persuade you to stay! I wouldn't have hurt you, Anna. Robert—he'd never have forgiven me if I'd hurt you."

"Robert," Anna moaned softly. A soft crying began. "Robert . . ." The sobs rose to a wail. The wail became a crescendo of sorrow. I felt tears in my eyes and horror in my throat.

Another light appeared behind Anna. An impression, nothing so firm as a figure. A slight man, light-haired. Anna turned and touched the man's cheek. "Robert." A breath of love.

"I-Iverson," I stuttered, "make this stop."

He was sobbing, one hand covering his face while the other warded the visions off. "Bobby . . . God, Bobby, I told him just to frighten her! He swore that was all he did! I just wanted Anna to stay—we were about to get the Hamilton, worth millions of dollars, we'd be set for life, all of us—and we did get it, anyway, there was no *reason* for her to die!"

It spilled out in a torrent then, the grief and guilt. All about the paintings he and his ring of thieves had stolen in those early days. About how he'd cleaned his life up, legally, since then, except for personal acquisitions, like those in his San Francisco house—and except for Burton. About Burton, and how he, Iverson, had killed the assistant to keep him from telling Charlie where he'd found the *Hare*—to keep everything from crashing down.

When it was over, Anna was gone and the lights had come on, revealing a broken man with a ravaged face, a frail-boned shell of a man filled with remorse, who couldn't stop talking even now. The lights revealed, too, several video cameras being removed from their hiding places in the ceiling beams, lengths of hidden cable, four or five technicians . . . and a whole mess of cops, both at the top of the stairs and below.

I don't know if Iverson even saw the lights come back on, or Grady North and the several Pittsford cops standing in the doorway and at the top of the stairs. One of them was taking notes. If Iverson got a smart lawyer, the police might at some point have to deal with questions about the legalities of what we'd just done—but Iverson had told it all, right down to an admission about one of the major art thefts this country or any other had ever seen. He had given facts and figures that could now be checked. Legally, one way or another, we had him.

More importantly, Charlie was free.

Well, the human need for confession isn't without precedent. You can take it all the way back to the Greek tragedies. To the Bible. To Shakespeare.

I jammed my hands, which were still shaking, into the pockets of my jeans. I watched a technician leave with tape recorders and mikes. Someone else dismantled the special-effects lighting that had been concealed above the stairs, while Iverson was still in California.

I watched the local actor who had played Robert Iverson walk by. A small, light-haired man, he kidded around with a technician. It was all in a day's work for him.

"You scared the shit out of me," I said to Sam Crewe, who stood before me now in a business suit and heels. The drifting white silk that was "Anna" was no longer in evidence. Sam's long dark hair was pinned into a neat twist. Traces of theatrical makeup clung to her face. "For a few minutes there, I almost believed—"

"You were perfect," she said. "I couldn't have done it without your reaction. That was the icing on the cake."

"Christ, I wasn't acting, Sam! I was frightened out of my mind!"

"Even when you know," Sam agreed, "it's easy to be fooled. My dad says he scares himself sometimes."

"Where is he?"

"Downstairs, removing the oil-paint cartridges from the air conditioner. Disconnecting mikes." They'd had to cover all possibilities, wiring most of the house for sound in case my big scene with Iverson wandered from the study area. It had been my job, though, to eventually get him to the stairs.

"Your father did good," I said. "So did you." I rubbed my wrists, but still I couldn't get warm.

"A good shoot, Dad says, is when even the crew wonders —and they've seen it put together with their own eyes. I think sometimes—" She broke off and shrugged.

"What?"

"Well, it's silly, I suppose. But some of the best actors believe that the soul of whoever they're portraying enters them when they're on stage. Like Bobby Morse, for instance, doing Truman Capote. Or Anna, entering me." She laughed—a light, musical sound. "I don't believe in that sort of thing, of course."

"Of course." I did—now—but I sure wasn't about to say so.

"I'll take care of the paperwork," Sam went on, "as soon as I get back to California. I'll put all of this into a full report for you. Right now, I'm off to the police department to finish up here."

"Thanks. Send your bill to Charlie . . . and make it a big one. He and Mom will be grateful."

"I told you I always do my best to give a client what she wants."

"You told me you never promise it, though."

She grinned. "I couldn't let down a fellow movie buff, could I? Besides, this is the most fun I've had in years."

Then she was brisk and businesslike. We shook hands and I watched her leave the room, briefcase swinging, heels clicking on the slick wooden floor. Her assistant, Marta, followed with the white silk that Sam had worn on the stairs. It still had a life of its own, lifting and floating in the breeze of Marta's wake. I shivered, not at all sure I hadn't actually seen Anna Biernej-Browne on those stairs.

"Didn't we see some movie like that at your house one night?" Grady North asked, beside me. "That ghost bit?" He was in jeans, looking strong, in-charge, and cute, like Parker's Spenser—shoulder holster, T-shirt, dimples and all.

"*The Uninvited*," I confirmed. "Ray Milland, circa 1940s."

"Right. '*Stella by Starlight*,' wasn't it? The song?"

I nodded. We watch old movies together almost weekly, Grady and me.

"Damned spooky."

I cocked an eyebrow and lowered my voice to husky, standing on tiptoe to push a sandy curl from his forehead. "Afraid to go home alone? Want company tonight?"

Grady squared his shoulders and put on his tough-cop face. "I'm fine," he mumbled.

I grinned. Grady North, straight arrow, wouldn't know an opening line if it hit him in the face.

I'd known that, of course, when I delivered it. Nothing like playing it safe.

EPILOGUE

Mom and Charlie were married in a little chapel on a hill overlooking the Pacific. It was made almost entirely of glass, and throughout the ceremony the gulls soared in the sky above the altar—just like in the old *Mrs. Miniver* movie, where they're all in the church praying, the ceiling's bombed out, and people are crying, and . . . well, you know.

Mom looked like Mrs. Miniver, too . . . or Greer Garson, however you want to call it. Her hair was curly and glinted with auburn highlights . . . Roux Fanci-full Lucky Copper mousse, she said. She wore a huge ivory picture hat with pink roses that matched the five dozen pink roses Marcus had sent. He had wanted to come to the wedding, but was afraid his presence would attract unwanted elements and spoil things. That's the problem with Marcus's world. It lacks privacy as much as Sean Penn's.

As for the Genesee Three—they were back on Genesee Street, in the groove. Vacation was over, but they sent their best.

After the ceremony there was a reception right there on the church lawn, which stretched out over the cliffs. Mom and Charlie took care of all that silly mooshing of the wedding cake in each other's faces, then they danced. Ben Jericho, who was there with Melissa, asked me to dance, but I wasn't in the mood. I saw him deep in animated conversation with Sam Crewe after that, she in a coral designer outfit, and Melissa looking happy as a clam. Sam, it seemed, was her idol. She leaned over and fixed the bow in Melissa's hair, and wiped a smudge off her dress. Helping her primp.

That was something I'd probably never have the knack to do.

Charlie joined me later, over near the cliff where I'd gone

to stare out at the sea. A warm breeze whipped at the legs of my white silk pants and gauzy flowered top. (Aunt Edna to the rescue. She'd found the top in an old box. I seem to remember wearing something like it to high school graduation.)

Well, she saved me from having to go shopping—and if Mom only got married once, I'd never have to dress up like this again.

God, I hate froufrou.

"You okay, Jess?" Charlie came to stand beside me. He pushed my hair away from my eyes where the wind had blown it, then put his arm around my shoulders and gave me a squeeze. We stood looking out at the ruffled aquamarine sea together.

"Sure, great," I said. "God's in his heaven, all's right with the world. What's not to be okay?"

"Uh-huh. You want to talk about it?"

I shrugged away his arm and faced him. "Oh, I don't know, Charlie. I keep thinking about loose ends. Or maybe they're not loose ends. Maybe I'm just looking for trouble. Marcus says I do that almost by rote."

He leaned back to perch on a giant rock. He looked like Pan again, the way he had that first day, in the gallery gardens in Pittsford. His silver hair glinted in the sun; the Paul Newman blue eyes pierced mine in an almost professional way to unravel any secrets I might still have.

"What kind of trouble, Jess?"

"Oh, you know. I mean, we got Iverson, just like we set out to do. The police have charged him, and you're free. He's confessed to killing Burton . . . and to the art thefts over the years. Plus, he pinned Anna's murder on Rune Jenners. But I keep wondering—"

Charlie nodded. "Robert," he said.

I was silent.

"Robert," Charlie went on, "was the one who took the *Hare*. And Iverson's sticking to his story that he told Rune just to threaten Anna, not to harm her. So, what if that's all Rune actually did? What if it was Robert who killed my mother, after all, and Iverson is still covering for him by slanting the blame toward Rune? Or maybe Iverson never even knew, maybe

Robert didn't tell him what he'd done. And it was guilt, not grief, that made Robert take his own life that summer."

"You honestly think Iverson wouldn't have known?"

"Well, there's such a thing as denial. When we don't want to see things—"

"Yes." It's insidious, the way we close our eyes to things we don't want to see. The way we concoct just about any kind of fantasy in our heads sometimes, rather than have to deal with the truth.

"I guess the truth," Charlie said, "is that we'll never really know."

"Does that bother you?"

He shrugged. "My fath—"

He broke off, but I'd caught it. "What about your father, Charlie? He wanted Anna's killer as much as you?"

He looked away.

"I thought so. You know your father, don't you, Charlie? He's still alive."

He shook his head. I didn't buy it.

"I'd bet my soul you met up with him in West Germany when you were there in the sixties. You and he—you're in some kind of undercover work together, aren't you? For the Army, still? Or some other government's asshole agency?"

The blue eyes did a number right through my head. Assessing. "What makes you think that, Jess?"

"It all makes sense. The pieces fit. I can't imagine any man leaving Anna for long, not coming back to somebody like her, without good reason. And your father's name—Justin Phillips Browne—is on your birth certificate. But there's no record of him since the war years. Anywhere. Any more than there is for you."

"How do you know this, Jess?"

I didn't answer.

"Ah, yes. Marcus." And after a moment: "What are you going to do with these suspicions, Jess?"

I sat beside him on the rock. Put an arm around his shoulders and cozied up to him, thigh to thigh, eye to eye. "Well, Charlie, the way I figure it, Mom is happy. For the first time maybe in her life, she's happy. And she deserves that. I want her to have it."

His jaw firmed. A nerve pulsed. God, he was handsome. More like Paul Newman—and more like *The Hustler*—than ever. "Bottom line, Jess."

"Bottom line is that if I should ever find out Mom *isn't* happy—if she ever even has bad dreams—"

"You'll split me up one side and down the other."

"That would be too kind," I breathed.

He grinned, and before I knew it he'd planted a kiss on my nose. "I like you, Jess. I really do."

We sat like that a while, side by side. Companionably.

I liked Charlie Browne, too. But I didn't trust him an inch. There were things I'd never tell him, just as I was sure there were things he'd never tell me. After all, there was still the matter of the missing Durbar—how he'd come up with it so readily, and where it had disappeared to now.

And there were those goddamned shoes.

Mom called out then. We looked up and saw her coming across the grass, hips swinging in her silken ivory dress. Clutching her picture hat to her head so it wouldn't blow away. She was radiant, like a young girl in a perfume ad. Young at heart, in love—all those things I'd probably never be.

"So here you are," she cried. "The heroes of the day!"

Aunt Edna tottered along behind in high heels that didn't look any more natural on her than they would on me. "Humph," was all she said.

That's about right, I thought. *Humph. Me and Charlie. Heroes of the day.*

I stuck around a while longer, taking as much of the mushy stuff as I could stand. Everybody was pairing off, it seemed. Aunt Edna had found a cute young Adonis somewhere, all broad shoulders and deep tan. Mom and Charlie were nuzzling beneath a shimmering willow tree. Ben and Samantha Crewe—

Well, I wasn't sure about them. Sam wasn't the type to nuzzle. Too shrewd, too sensible. Traits I admired. But I kept seeing them around each other, with Melissa firmly in tow.

I slipped out when no one was looking and swiped Aunt Edna's car to drive to the City. Having finished my business with Charlie, there was one more thing I wanted to do.

At the Carlisle Foundation, I waited for Avery Carlisle in Anna's room, the solarium with her paintings. Bird sounds drifted down the corridor from the courtyard. Palms whispered softly against the windowpanes, and a brown rabbit eye, courtesy of Anna, winked at me from beneath a top hat. I stood looking out on the broad expanse of green lawn and trees, the exotic flowers, and breathed in peace.

Avery Carlisle spoke and I turned.

"I was almost certain you'd come back," he said gently.

"Yes."

"Would you like to sit down?"

I shook my head. "It's funny . . . I was just talking to Charlie about how we deny things that we don't want to see. I've been denying for a long time that I needed to grow. Then I met you. I don't even know you, but you've taught me things about peace, and letting go. About taking time to be quiet, to find a center somewhere inside myself. I learned that just from sitting down with you a couple of times. How do you do that?"

He shook his head, and there was a hint of sadness in the blue eyes. Filtered sunlight glinted on Avery Carlisle's balding pink skin. The eyes were so gentle you could fall into them and feel like you had fallen into bliss somehow.

"I just provided the tools," Carlisle said. "You made use of them out of your own need. You musn't give me any special powers that way."

He sounded like Samved. But Samved was gone now. And would I always need a guru, someone to follow? Or would I learn to be my own person, to think for myself one day?

Was I learning that already? Perhaps. It was why I was here.

"You killed Anna, didn't you?" I said.

His sadness was like the movement of an ocean, a terrible tide that moved across his face and churned through his slight body. "Yes," he whispered. "I am very much ashamed to say I did."

For what seemed a long time there was only the sound of the fountain's splash from way outside, and the quiet voices of students in the courtyard.

"Did you know this when you were here before?" he finally asked.

"No. I didn't have a clue. I . . . got quiet, as you suggested.

Sat around thinking in the silence. Funny thing. I found out you can do that anywhere." I'd done it in Rochester, before going to Everett Iverson's. The only thing I hadn't figured out at the time was what to do about it.

"That's the great lesson," Carlisle said. "And you've learned it early. Well, I've known since you arrived that first day that you'd sort everything out, that eventually I'd have to turn myself in. I've been putting it off, I guess, waiting for the cereus to bloom." He gave me a shy smile. "Foolish and self-indulgent. But it became a symbol—a noble act to follow."

He stood with shoulders back, fragile except for his spirit, which blazed in the steady blue eyes. As he moved, I saw the cereus on the table behind him. It was blooming. Tomorrow, I remembered, it would die.

Carlisle touched its lily-white petals gently. He sighed. "Shall we go?"

I nodded, and we walked down the arched passage along the courtyard, toward the front gardens. "Will you tell me how it happened?" I said.

He gave a slight shudder. "It was an appalling, senseless thing. I was hurt that Anna was leaving. I'd come to think Anna cared for me, but that, of course, was only a young man's ego talking. Anna loved no man after Charlie's father left. But we all loved her."

He stopped to shut the courtyard door behind us. We were in the gardens in front, on the walk lined with palm trees. Birds chattered in the aviary by the gazebo. The sky was a clear blue, the air almost balmy. It was a beautiful day . . . much too beautiful to lose.

"Let's sit over there a moment," I said.

Carlisle looked surprised. For the first time, he glanced around. "I thought . . . I guess I thought you would have brought the police."

"No police."

He hesitated, then nodded, leading the way to the white gazebo beneath the trees.

We sat opposite each other at the table, where we'd talked before. I noted again how Carlisle's feet barely touched the floor.

"I went to see Anna that night," he said, his shoulders bowed with the weight of the memory. "To plead with her not to leave town. I was so young, so naive. It took me forever to even work up my courage to speak to her. I had nothing to offer Anna—my inheritance was held in trust, I lived on only a small allowance, and as I've told you, I was insecure about my looks."

He sighed. "Anna wasn't cruel, or I'd never known her to be—yet when I told her how I felt, she laughed. She caught herself right away, but she did laugh. I was angry. My young man's pride was hurt. I turned to leave, and she grabbed my arm, trying to apologize. 'I didn't mean it, Avery,' she said. 'I was surprised, that's all.' I wrenched away. Anna was on her stool, leaning toward me . . . she lost her balance and fell against a metal sculpture. I didn't actually see it happen, I was turned away, but she must have struck her head. There was blood."

"You checked her, then? She was dead?"

"Yes. I couldn't believe it. I couldn't believe, or face, what I'd done. I was terrified. I ran."

I listened to student laughter somewhere across the lawn—picturing the scene, and the horror Avery Carlisle must have felt at his deed.

"After you left," I said, "Robert Iverson must have came to the studio. He found Anna's body, and in his grief, without thinking, he took the painting of the *Hare* to remember her by. A theft, of course—and that's why he never called the police."

"Actually . . ." Carlisle hesitated. "It was more than that. Robert saw what happened. He saw Anna die."

"He *saw*—?"

And then I remembered it. The drawing Anna had left behind, the one Charlie had me take from his hotel room in Rochester. A sketch of a man, presumably, with no ears—but a finger pointing to his eye. This was the man Charlie had always thought had killed Anna.

"The message from Anna," I said. "The sketch. It was Robert! Robert who couldn't hear, but saw—"

"Precisely. Charlie showed me that sketch years ago. I denied knowing what it meant. But Robert had come to me later that night. He told me he'd seen what happened. He was agitated, tense, afraid . . . but he wanted me to know that he understood. He loved Anna, as we all did, but he knew how she could be—not so much thoughtless, as careless." He spoke the next words tenderly, without blame. "Anna hurt a lot of young men, you see."

"Yet Robert did take the *Hare*, to remember her by."

"Yes. And poor Charlie found his mother, lying there, in the morning. An eight-year-old boy—to have walked in on that—I will always regret that, more than any of it, the wrong I did to Charlie."

"What about the police? The finding was death by person or persons unknown, but there aren't any records of the investigation."

"Things were hushed up," Carlisle said. "My father . . . It wasn't a matter of payoffs, but there were people, friends in high positions . . ."

The Old Boys' Network, as observed in San Francisco in the 1950s. And that was why some of the older cops who had been around back then, had refused to talk to Ben about the case. It would be an embarrassment to the Department now.

"And Charlie . . ." I said. "You helped Charlie through school, didn't you?"

Carlisle nodded. "I paid for his schooling, secretly of course, and afterward, I saw to it that people suggested he contact me so I could give him work. Over the years, I've tried to make up in some small way for what I did—but of course, no one can make up for the loss of a mother. I've lived with this knowledge every moment of every day."

Carlisle and Everett Iverson, living with their secrets. Trying to live out their lives as if nothing had ever happened. Yet Carlisle . . . Was it only my liking for him that made it seem he'd done so much better?

Part of my own reassessment in the past few weeks included admitting I don't know all the answers. Not that I ever believed I did—but I might have thought I knew right from wrong, and been a little cocky about "justice" being done.

"We should go," Carlisle said. "This is only putting off the inevitable." He began to rise. I rested a hand on his arm.

"Sit down," I said. "You aren't going anywhere."

He sat slowly, a hesitant expression crossing his eyes. "I don't understand."

"Well, I've been giving it a lot of thought, and it's like this. The prison system is pretty screwed. In some states, they're knocking time off sentences to get people out on the streets faster, because there's no room. And I hear there are even elderly people breaking *in* to prisons now—committing crimes so they'll have a place they can be taken care of a while. It's the old story of the bum throwing a rock through a store window so he can spend the night in jail, catch a few peaceful winks. Only now it's a few lousy months of shelter they're looking for. A few months, before they die."

"I still don't—"

"Think. You wouldn't want to take up space that could be theirs, would you?"

"I . . . I don't know."

"Then look at it this way. From what I've seen—and from what I've learned these past weeks through reports on you— the last forty years of your life have been spent in rehabilitation. The good you've done here for young people, helping Joseph and Sara and others like them to make a new life . . . Personally, I figure justice has been served as well as it ever is. So do the world a favor. Whatever remaining guilt you've got, work it out right here."

"But—"

I stood. "Hey, wasn't it Ingrid Bergman who said 'Happiness is good health and a bad memory'?"

I leaned over and kissed his bald head. "Be happy," I said.

When I left him, I wasn't sure what he would decide to do. But it's not often I give good advice. I hoped he'd play it smart and follow it.

I stood outside the gates of the Carlisle Foundation, looking about me at the expensive houses piled high on steep hills. The sidewalks were white and bright, the water and sky a crisp autumn blue. I turned down the street, deciding to walk a while and come back for Aunt Edna's car later. Ahead was San Francisco Bay, and the islands in it. Across the way, Marin and the Golden Gate Bridge. The air was brisk out there, roiling in from the sea. Windsurfers sped along the ripples like skaters on ice.

Well, one thing, I thought as I walked. Tark's on his way

back from Italy. Marcus told me that when he called this morning to wish Mom well. I have to admit I've felt a lightening around my heart ever since. I wonder if he's bringing Bernadette with him. I wonder if they ever got married. I wonder why that matters so much to me.

My pace picked up. I hummed a little tune. Whistled it, in fact. A well-dressed elderly couple passed by and smiled. I smiled back. It was a perfect day, I thought. A day to do something grand. Maybe I'd take the Dashiell Hammett tour . . . check out Fisherman's Wharf . . . go on to a show.

Or maybe I'd just go back to Aunt Edna's and watch the broccoli grow.

ANTONIA FRASER'S JEMIMA SHORE

Jemima Shore didn't plan on living a life steeped in detection and mystery. But at the age of fifteen, while staying at a Catholic boarding school, she found herself plunged into a bizarre situation involving a suspicious miracle and a flamboyant, manipulative Italian princess.

Now Britain's most popular newswoman, Jemima lives day in and day out with mysteries and danger from every walk of life. That first story, "Jemima Shore's First Case" and all her adventures are now available from Bantam Crime Line Books:

- ☐ JEMIMA SHORE'S FIRST CASE
       AND OTHER STORIES 28073-2 $3.95
- ☐ OXFORD BLOOD   28070-8 $3.95
- ☐ YOUR ROYAL HOSTAGE 28019-8 $3.95
- ☐ A SPLASH OF RED   28071-6 $3.95
- ☐ QUIET AS A NUN   28311-1 $4.50
- ☐ THE CAVALIER CASE   07126-2 $17.95

Enjoy any of Antonia Fraser's Jemima Shore mysteries, available wherever Bantam Crime Line Books are sold or use this page for ordering:

A crackling deep-water suspense novel of violence, passion, and betrayal.

THE COOL BLUE TOMB
by Paul Kemprecos

A 50-million dollar salvage operation. An expert diver dead at the bottom of the sea. An elegant mermaid in a black Porsche -- and an open invitation to dip into the troubled waters of her marriage. Cape Cod's Aristotle "Soc" Socarides, part-time fisherman, part-time private eye, is swimming with the sharks. Only problem is, he's the bait...and blood is beginning to boil to the surface.

Soc didn't think he could get in much deeper, but he'd better think again. A family debt of honor comes due -- a debt only he can settle -- plunging him into the middle of a lethal search for buried treasure. Now Soc's about to discover how deadly the Cape's currents can be. Snarled in a net of smuggling, treachery, and revenge, he's finding out that no matter how far down you go, nothing's harder to salvage than the truth.

The Cool Blue Tomb by Paul Kemprecos. On sale now wherever Bantam Crime Line Books are sold.